A
CREATURE
OF
MOONLIGHT

A Creature of Moonlight

rebecca hahn

HOUGHTON MIFFLIN HARCOURT
Boston   New York

Harcourt is an imprint of Houghton Mifflin Harcourt
Publishing Company.

www.hmhco.com

Text set in 12 pt. Centaur MT Std
Design by Christine Kettner

Library of Congress Cataloging-in-Publication Data
Hahn, Rebecca.
A creature of moonlight / Rebecca Hahn.
pages cm
Summary: Marni, a young flower seller who has been living in exile,
must choose between claiming her birthright as princess of a realm
whose king wants her dead, and a life with the father she has never
known—a wild dragon.
ISBN 978-0-544-10935-3
[1. Fantasy. 2. Identity—Fiction. 3. Dragons—Fiction.
4. Princesses—Fiction. 5. Forests and forestry—Fiction.
6. Flowers—Fiction. 7. Magic—Fiction.] I. Title.
PZ7.H12563Cre 2014
[Fic]—dc23   2013020188

Manufactured in the United States of America
DOC 10 9 8 7 6 5 4 3 2 1
4500465078

For my parents

PART ONE

ALL SUMMER LONG the villagers have been talking of the woods. Even those living many hills away can see it: their crops are disappearing; their land is shrinking by the day. We hear story after story. One evening a well will be standing untouched, a good twenty feet from the shade, and when the farmer's daughter goes to draw water in the morning, there will be nothing left but a pile of stones and a new tree or three growing out of the rubble. And all along beside it, the woods stretch on and on, where no woods were the night before.

In years gone past, this happened now and again: a goatherd would complain of his flock's favorite hill being eaten by shadows and trunks, or a shed alongside the trees would rust overnight and be crawling with vines in the morning. But just as often, an old fence was uncovered by the woods as they retreated, or a long-lost watering hole suddenly appeared again, where it hadn't been for near fifty years. The woods come and they go, like the sun, like the wind, like the seasons. It isn't something to fret about, not in a fearful way. The farmers have always complained of it, but they've never talked of it as they are talking now of this advance.

This year, the trees do not go; they only come, on and on, and rumors from all over our land say the same. They are folding in around us.

It terrifies the villagers something fierce. When they come to bring our supplies or to buy some flowers, they mutter about it with my Gramps. I see them shaking their heads, twisting their caps in their hands. Gramps tells them it's nothing to worry about, that the trees will take themselves back again, just as they always do.

They listen to him. When he talks, it's as if they forget the state of his legs and see only the calm on his face, hear only the slow, measured way he has with words. They leave more peaceful than they were when they came. They leave less worried about the creeping trees.

When they've gone, though, I see my Gramps sigh. I see him look sideways at me where I'm leaning against the porch rail, as if I won't notice that way. As if I don't already know he frets more than he'd ever let on. There's no one like my Gramps for fretting. Any sickness going around, any rumor of bandits—I see those eyebrows drawing in tight. He'll not talk about it, maybe, but he worries, more and more the less he can do.

Well, and this time, could be there's something to it. Since I was small, since we lived here and made ourselves the flower people to keep from getting our heads chopped off, Gramps has warned me not to wander into the trees that push up right against our place — out back, beyond the flowers and paths and bushes, over the low stone wall that rings around our garden. But out here, living so close, it would be near impossible not to follow my curiosity over that wall, and I've had years to be curious. My Gramps doesn't realize — I only go when he's not looking — how well I've always known our woods.

There's not much Gramps could do to stop me, stuck as he is in his chair, needing me for every little thing. Oh, he could yell, and if I didn't come running, he could get himself up with his cane and wobble out the back, and if I wasn't there, he could tear me down something wretched when he saw me returning. But I don't go so far that I can't hear my Gramps's voice. Not just because I'm avoiding trouble. Not just because I don't want to scare him, neither, though those are both good reasons. What if something were to happen to Gramps and I wasn't there to pick him off the floor or run for help? Or what if the king decided that today was the day he'd stop tolerating those flower people, and he sent some men and horses down, and I wasn't there to scream and scratch until they killed me for my Gramps?

So Gramps doesn't know how often I go to the woods.

There are all the things you would think of living there:

rabbits and squirrels and hedgehogs and, late in the evening, bats. The trees are spaced out like they must want to be. Nobody comes to chop them down. Nobody stops them from spreading apart or smothering each other or dropping their needles just as they please, in patterns and swirls and such. I wouldn't half mind being one of those trees. I reckon it's a peaceful life, with nothing but the birds, the wind, and the sun for your company.

It's peaceful visiting them, wandering this way and that through their silent trunks, humming and thinking my own thoughts.

There are other things there too, things you wouldn't expect.

There's a laugh behind a tree when nobody's around to make it. A flash of red from branch to branch, like a spark from a fire, but nothing's burning. A woman dressed in green, sitting alone on a log and knitting something out of nothing, out of leaves and grass and berries, out of sunshine. She looks up, and she has no eyes. Where her eyes should be there are lights like tiny suns, and she's smiling, but I don't know how, because she doesn't have a mouth like anyone else's, not that I can see. There's just a mist all around her head, and those burning eyes looking right at me.

I don't stop to talk to things like that. I used to, once, before I knew any better. Back then I used to play with the little people hidden under the bushes and make my own crafts next to the lady on the log as she knit and sang to me, and I'd fly away sometimes, though never very far, with great winged things that held me in their arms. I was always wary of straying too far from Gramps, even when I was small.

It was only gradually that I grew frightened of the woods folk. The laugh turned, bit by bit, from cheerful to menacing; the spark changed from beautiful to dangerous. I'd see the little ones eyeing me with something other than playfulness. I'd see the lady's clever fingers tensing as we knit, and I'd wonder just when she'd decide to grab my wrist, to take me away with her.

So I stopped listening, and I stopped looking. It's been many years now since I followed whenever the voices called from the woods. I no longer talk back to birds with people's faces, or watch as misty creatures dart through the brooks.

But when I slip out into the trees this summer, I hear the voices singing more, and I see the lights flickering here and there, yellow and blue and green, always just at the corners of my eyes, tempting me away.

I dare not go out when the sun is low in the sky. Then I'm like to forget, almost, who I am, and that I ever had a Gramps, and that the little people tugging at my skirt hem are not *my* people, and are not to be trusted, even though they bear the sweetest, most innocent faces in the world.

Yet I don't stop going completely, neither. When Gramps is sleeping the sun away, or when I've worked so hard at digging out weeds and pruning back bushes and hauling water to and from the well that I can't stand one minute more, or when I get to thinking on things just so, I hop over our garden wall and go walking out there, breathing in the pine and the damp, dark places of the forest.

It's a dangerous pastime, I know, but I can't help myself. There's a thing that draws me to the woods, even more than the peacefulness I find there. It's a humming deep at the bottom of my mind. It's a thrill that tingles, even when I'm only taking one step and then another, even when the woods folk are nowhere to be seen.

The villagers will tell you it's not just the creatures of the woods that require wariness. It's not just the obvious: the lights and the voices and the speaking owls, the faces in the branches.

It's the trees themselves.

There's something there, they'll say, whispering through the leaves, sleeping in the trunks. There's something that seeps through the spongy ground but never shows itself in any way you would recognize. If you walk enough in these woods, they say, you'll start to understand its language. The wind through the trees will murmur secret things to you, and you'll be pulled by them, step by step by step, out of the human realm. You'll be drawn to the shadows, toward the soft flashes of moonlight through the branches, into the hidden holes and tricky marshes.

The villagers won't let their children go into the woods, not even to the very closest edge, not even when the wind is silent and the sun shines full through the trees. It's an insidious thing, they say, the soul of these woods. It will rock you and soothe you until you've nothing left but trust and belief and naivety. It will fold itself into you, and you will never know it's there, not until you're ten nights out and there's not a thing that can bring you back again.

It's the girls that the woods take most often. Girls about my age, in fact, near grown but not yet settling themselves down to a husband and a family. There were one or two from round about our place when I was growing who walked from their homes one day and never came back.

The latest was a girl with dark curls, just old enough to be catching the eyes of the boys, and she was the closest thing to a friend I ever had.

That was just this spring, when she disappeared. She was my age, and she wasn't shy none. She'd talk up my Gramps; he used to smile more when she was about the place. She'd talk up the village boys, too, the ones she used to play chase with but now were chasing her, and eyeing her as if she wasn't the same girl they'd spent their summers playing pranks with, as if she wasn't as close to them as their own sisters.

It's not the easiest thing to keep friends when you live a good thirty-minute walk from the nearest village—nor when you're as close as we are to the woods. But Annel didn't care none about those things. The other village girls stayed close to home, but even young as a sprout, Annel would run across the fields and come stamping up to our front door, bursting in as we ate our breakfast maybe, or swinging right around to the garden, where I'd be at work. She didn't look like a farmer's daughter— she looked like a lady from the court, with that figure and that face — but she wore her skirts hitched up as often as not, and she threw herself down in the dirt alongside me as I pruned and planted.

Not that her parents approved, quite, but Annel had five brothers also running wild, and for one stray daughter to be off visiting the flower girl and her grandfather — who still spoke soft and sweet like the castle folk — there were worse things in the world.

When Annel came by our place, it was as if the sun had come down to visit. She'd go running with me out in the meadows, picking wildflowers, imagining shapes in the clouds in the sky. We'd talk things over, too: what it'd be like to fly up high with the birds; where we'd like to go when we grew up — across the mountains to the northern sea, or so far south, the winter would never come. Annel was always full of places she'd like to go. I think that was why she so loved our place — it was the closest she could get to another country, my Gramps and my world. Well, and I reckon I listened better than most of the village girls. How could I not? She'd paint such pictures with her words, of endless hills of sand, of bitter plains of snow.

Annel was good at that — making you see things with her words. Often as not, she'd stay clear through dinner, until the dark was creeping into the corners of the hut, and she'd curl up on our old wool rug next to me, her face all shining in the firelight. We'd have taken in a chair from the porch for Gramps. He'd sit straight as always, but with a softness in his face, as if he'd forgotten for the moment the pain in his legs, his fretful thoughts. And Annel would tell us stories, Gramps and me, and he would listen quietly, scarce moving, and I would eat them up like a river eats stones, rushing, gobbling every passing word, slipping on from tale to tale to tale.

Sometimes the stories she'd tell would get to be too much for my Gramps. A woman who got herself lost and never came back. A child without a mother, wandering far and wide, screaming so insistently that the earth opened up and swallowed it whole just to give it some rest. Then we would hear the chair scraping and the cane jolting against the floor, and Annel would stop talking until he'd gone out to the porch and sat down on the steps. She'd continue softer after that and stop her story soon as she could.

But she always kept on until the end. She knew, as I knew, that you don't stop a story half done. You keep on going, through heartbreak and pain and fear, and times there is a happy ending, and times there isn't. Don't matter. You don't cut a flower half through and then wait and watch as it slowly shrivels to death. And you don't stop a story before you reach the end.

Came a time as Annel got older that her parents stopped forgetting her. Came a time she only visited us once a week, and then once a month, and then not for months and months, and then we heard she'd gotten herself engaged to a wheelwright and would be married the next spring.

She visited me once that fall, just last year, and she watched as I turned the dirt over in our garden, readying the ground for the winter. I was listening to the flower bulbs settling into the earth, tucking themselves in for a long sleep. I was humming them a tune of warm dreams, dark waterfalls, green, hidden things. I've always been good with the flowers, just as I've always been good at listening to the trees and seeing the creatures that lurk in the secret spaces between their trunks.

For a bit, I let Annel stand there silent, unmoving as I worked. If she wanted to speak to me, she would. Could be I was angry with her some without realizing it. Even knowing it was not her fault, could be I blamed her for the lonely taste of those months.

"Funny," she said finally, when I'd reached the end of a row and she was still back in the middle of the garden, watching my shovel with a twisted puzzle on her face. "Funny, isn't it, how things can go and change all about you, and you can grow up tall and fill out your dress, and still there's something won't ever change inside unless you take it up by the roots and hurl it away as hard as you can? I imagine it's not this way for everyone. Is it, Marni?"

The crickets had silenced themselves for the summer; the frogs were sleeping deep in their lakes. A whippoorwill whistled close by in the woods, the only one speaking, the only one still awake. "No, I don't reckon it is that way for everyone," I said. I didn't know completely what she meant, but nothing was for Annel as it was for everyone.

"No," she said softly, but the breeze flipped it round and brought it my way. "No, some don't care about the tearing. Some replant whatever's going to work in the new soil. You do that with your flowers, don't you? Whatever works, whatever's going to survive, that's what you plant."

"I guess that's true," I said. "Whatever's suited for the amount of sun and shade we get back here."

"Not everything's suited, though."

"No."

"What if — what if, Marni, you're so in love with a flower you can't bear to rip it up? What if you couldn't smile if you didn't see it growing in your garden?"

"There's no such flower," I said. "Or there's only the dragon flower, which won't go no matter how many times I try to chase it out. And that's the one I hate, the one I wish would disappear."

"The dragon flower," said Annel, "which won't go no matter how you try to kill it."

"Can't make my garden without that flower."

She nodded. The dusk was growing now. "Was a time," she said, "I didn't think of nothing but running down from home to here, and back again when I felt the urge."

"When you're married," I said, "you come get a flower for your table every day."

"Can I, Marni?" She laughed a bit. "Can I have a dragon flower?"

"Every day," I promised her.

Then she moved, finally, coming down the row, and she hugged me, dirt and sweat and all. The whippoorwill had stopped. Only the wind through the woods rushed out toward us, flicked leaf bits in our hair. "Thanks, Marni," she said. "I'll remember." She pulled back, still holding my arms. "My mother sent me down to tell you about the wedding, but I guess you know all there is by this point. I'm to invite you—you and your Gramps."

"We'll come," I said.

"Well, then." She smiled at me, though it wasn't much more than a flash of gray in the draining light. "Well, then, I'll see you again for the wedding in the spring."

Only there was no wedding. As soon as the pale green tips of the dragon flower stems were poking out of the rich brown earth, even before the springtime thunderstorms had rolled off to the south, my friend took herself to the woods. They searched for her round about the villages, thinking she might have run off with this or that farmer boy. They came to our hut, even, stood with their caps in their hands, but you could feel the suspicion dripping from them, those men. You could see them remembering how often their Annel had come running down the path to us, and it wasn't any other girl who felt the need to do that, and it wasn't any other girl—well, not for a few years past anyway—but it was hardly anyone else who disappeared like this. And there I was, as clear as could be, my mother's daughter, telling them I hadn't seen Annel since winter fell, but still, they all knew, you could see. They knew that those visits with me had something to do with this.

They didn't say it straight out, though, or dare to threaten me or any such, not with Gramps sitting right next to me. They glared, and asked their questions, and went away after I'd answered them. I stayed clear of the woods for weeks after that, as my Gramps never left me out of his sight. After a time they stopped looking, and Annel became just another story, another girl who had grown up to be swallowed by the woods. And just like all those other girls, she hasn't ever come back.

There's a reason we plant our flowers at the back of the hut, away from the road, as close to the woods as we can get without actually growing them in the shade of the trees. Something in the flowers likes something in the woods; or something in the woods, could be, some growing, magic thing, likes the flowers, and those nearest the trees are the happiest.

We've the best there are. You won't find purple lilies like ours for sale in the city center. There aren't nasturtiums as vibrant and long-lasting as ours clinging to the windowsills in the villages. There's something here, I think, and maybe something too in the way I care for them, that makes them grow brighter and stronger than anywhere else.

Well, and no one else has dragon flowers, do they?

In the middle of our garden, there's a patch of them. You can't reach them on the paths. You have to edge through rose thorns or tiptoe betwixt lupine stalks until you reach their bed. We never planted them. But there they grow, no matter what I do — and used to be I tried, and Gramps tried, to rid ourselves of them. They always came back, and nothing else would grow where they had.

We gave it up, but Gramps still mutters about them now and again because dragon flowers are just the sort of thing he'd rather not have near.

There are stories about dragon flowers. Stories that tie them to the woods and to the thing that mothers frighten their children with, that gives the flowers their name — the dragon, of course.

The story Annel told most often about the dragon flowers took place in the time before the farms and villages and cities. It was in the time when the woods were everywhere, before we even had a kingdom, when people ran and hid and never dared come out at night for fear of getting snatched away.

In those days, the dragon flew free above the trees. He went where he pleased. He took the people he wanted; in this story they're girls, always pretty girls who don't know what's upon them until he steals them out of a clearing, or from a branch where they're perched picking nuts, or out of a cold, clear pond where they're fishing or cooling their feet.

What he does with the girls we don't know; something awful.

But one girl he took to more than the others, who knows why. He grabbed her as she was picking these pale blue flowers, tiny fragile things, not good for eating, not good for medicine. He asked her what they were for, and she said they were not for anything but holding in her hand and putting round her hair and placing in the window of her parents' hut.

She was a dimwitted thing, most like. If I were living in the woods, I'd not have time for picking flowers. I'd be running and hiding like the rest, and tearing my teeth on squirrels and gathering food for the winters.

But the dragon must have seen something in this girl because he snatched her away, as he was wont to do with girls he liked. And he must have liked this one even more, because one year later she came wandering home with a baby on her hip, a well-fed belly, and roses in her cheeks. She never married any man of the forest, but stayed with her parents until they died, and round their hut there grew the flowers, the thin, blue, pointless flowers that never did any good. While the girl's parents lived, she did just fine. The father hunted and the mother cooked meals. But when they were gone, try as she would, this girl couldn't make ends meet. Her boy was a dreamer, as she'd been, and with even less wits, if that were possible.

Well, and in this story, one way or another, they starve to death, and the dragon never cares enough to take them away again.

That's why the flowers are called dragon flowers, and that's why when a girl gets pregnant and won't name a father, they call the baby a dragon baby.

And that's why Gramps doesn't want the thin blue flowers in our garden, one reason anyway. We need no more reminding, not of woods nor of dead girls nor of a baby nobody wants.

They sell, though, those dragon flowers, and not just to the ladies, who wear them in their hair and twist them for bracelets. The village women buy them too, when they've saved money enough.

That's the thing about magic, and the thing about the woods — as much as we want to, or are told, or think we should forget them, there's nothing we can do to stay away. As sure as we dream, as sure as between one breath and the next we look up into the sky as if hoping, really hoping, to see that beat of wings and to feel the claws grasping us, lifting us away from it all — as sure as that, the woods keeps drawing us in.

It's something to do with freedom, isn't it? It's something akin to the way Annel dreamed so hard about all those many places her life could go.

"Marni," she used to say to me, "don't you settle down until you've no other choice in the matter. Once you do, there's nothing left: no running through fields, no laughing with boys, no dancing."

"Married women dance," I'd say, squinting up at her through the garden's sun, or pouring a glass of water from the well bucket, or as we lay on our backs in the meadows near the hut.

"Not the way you do before you're tied down," she'd say. "Not when you've got children and a house and a thousand things to do. Not like you do when you could go any way you want, and no one would stop you, because the whole of your life was still there, still fresh and new."

Well, and that was what took her, wasn't it? I think that's

what takes all the girls who disappear. In the stories, they don't have any choice — they're snatched away whether they like it or not. But I know my Annel, and she wouldn't have run if she hadn't wanted to. I know what it's like to want anything but what the world has planned for you.

I don't even have that future to run from, the one every village girl has, and every lady. I don't dream of a husband. I don't dream of children.

I dream of my mother walking out of the woods, alive.

I dream of doing what Annel used to plan — taking the king's road north through the mountains to the other side, to lands untouched by our woods, where no one knows my name. They have human witches and sorcerers in other lands. I could seek one out, a magic user, and ask for a poison so pure, our king would never know it was there until it was too late.

Maybe that's what I will do when my Gramps is gone, when I'm alone in truth. It makes me feel like a real dragon's daughter to think such things. It makes me wonder what I might become that day when I've nothing to hold me back, when I've only the flame in my gut and the beat of my wings to take me through the dark.

TWO

T WAS LAST year, about the time
that Annel was inviting us to her wed-
ding, when a boy from a village not far
away stopped by to talk and sit with
Gramps. Jack, his name was, or something like. He was a man
grown, I guess, though only three or four years beyond me.

I brought him milk from our cow, Dewdrop, and I gave him
a smile as I handed it to him. I'll smile for the villagers, and I'll
give up some of our bread and milk for them. We can afford
to share. We pay them well for what they bring our way, too:
flour, honey, vegetables. We've got Dewdrop and the chickens,
but we've not time for growing all our own food if we're to get
the garden ready every spring. The king and his court like it to
look nice here. That's why we tend our paths so carefully and

plant the flowers in neat rows, with the yellow next to blue, and the blue next to red, and so on around the garden, so that to step from our hut to our backyard is like stepping from a hovel to a castle yard.

Not that the nobles go through the hut when they come to walk in our garden. They take the path around it. They don't put their shiny boots on the floor of our kitchen. They don't throw their eyes on our beds and our one small dresser with our winter changes of clothes. They don't touch a finger to the mantel I wipe down every night with my own two hands so it gleams like theirs do up in their castle without them ever doing anything about it. I'm not sure what I would do if they tried to slip themselves through our front door.

They come too often for my taste as it is, those lords and ladies from the king's court. They come on horses, some of them, and some in fancy carriages, and some come walking on their own two feet, laughing and strolling along without a care in the world. Gramps calls out to them as they canter or roll or amble on up to our front porch, where we've set out our roses and marigolds and the rest, laid in rows all along our wide railing.

I don't talk to them.

They laugh with my Gramps. They sit across the porch table from him, in the chair I use when no one's around. They gossip about the doings at court and how the crops are coming in on their acres and acres of fields — not that they're the ones who tend their own crops, but they talk as if they were, as if they sweated over the planting and burst their fingers with the harvest.

They don't talk about the way the woods keep moving in, not even this summer, when their estates must be having as many problems as the smaller farms.

I hover at the back of the porch, a wisp, a shadow. When they've done with the talking and get on with deciding what they want, I step up and pull the flowers together for them. I pick out the greens and the ribbon. I tie them all in a bunch, and I hand them to my Gramps.

And then some of them remember me and give me a smile.

"How's our Tulip?" they ask. They've always called me that, as long as I can remember. My tulips come in so many colors, they near make a rainbow, and in my garden they bloom all summer long.

I don't answer. I step back against the wall; I duck my head away. I owe them nothing.

They know it, too, and they always laugh a bit forcedly — the ladies high and bright, the lords a deep chuckle — and never push it. They take their flowers from Gramps, and then they get back on their horses or step into their fancy carriages or link their pretty arms and saunter up our path over the hill toward the city.

Gramps never answers for me, neither. He could. He could tell them what I've been up to, how long it's been since I had a sickness. He doesn't, though. He grows still, just like me, and waits until they're done with asking, done with paying me any mind, before he turns back into the helpful, talkative flower man.

There are some things Gramps understands about me. There are some things even he won't do, some things even he won't say to make them happy.

But I welcome the villagers when they come. I invite them inside when they've a mind to visit before the fire, and I feed and water them too, and happily.

That afternoon last year, after I handed Jack his cup of milk, I leaned back against the wall, my hands behind me, my bare feet scratching each other, tapping on the porch floor, my braid hanging over my chest. Jack sipped and talked away with Gramps about the harvest and the new babies in the village and the weddings that would be coming in the spring. Gramps smiled and laughed with him, just as he does with the ladies and lords. Not one for any false sense of importance, my Gramps.

The time wore on, and still Jack sat there, clutching an empty cup now, and running out of things to say. My legs were falling asleep, but if Gramps could wait him out, so could I, and there wasn't another chair in the house to fall into, and I wasn't going to sit myself down on the porch. The village girls, they might have done that. They might have smiled and nod-ded at Jack as he talked on — he sure was smiling and nodding at me. But I wasn't a village girl, was I? So I stayed standing there, and I let my mind drift off into the woods, where the sun would be dappling through the trees about now and the squirrels would be chittering, racing one another from branch to branch.

Into the silence of the porch and the silence of the woods in my mind, Jack said, "Well now, sir, and your wee Marni's grown right up."

It wasn't something no one had said before. The women who bring our vegetables and such are always talking on about how I've shot up since they've seen me last, even if it was just two weeks ago. Them I give two or three smiles, if I feel like it. They make Gramps laugh, not just a politeness laugh, but a laugh deep from his belly, and there aren't many who can do that. Them I like, and I don't mind when they talk about me, so long as they don't expect me to talk all that much back.

But the way Jack said it, as if he meant more than what he said—that I didn't like at all. I pushed myself out of my slump, up straight against the wall, still keeping my head down but ready to run or fight or I didn't know what.

Gramps had gone still, too. "She's older than she was," he said, "though I don't know if I would say she's completely grown."

Jack shook his head at once, taking it back. "No. No, sir, not completely grown, that's true. But grown right up, she has, into something beautiful. What do the noble folk call her when they come to buy your flowers? Daisy? Violet?"

I could see my Gramps not wanting to answer, but a name like that—a daisy, a violet, only the commonest of flowers he could have chosen—that I couldn't stand, not even through my unease. "Tulip," I offered, a bit put out.

Then I wished I hadn't spoken, because Jack looked around

at me as if the clouds had parted and the sun itself had started to speak. "Aye, that's it," he said, real soft. "A veritable Tulip you are, and you don't mind me saying so, miss."

"She might not," my Gramps put in, "but I'll have a word or two to say about it, you may be sure."

"Yes, sir, yes, sir." Jack turned around again so fast I thought he'd lose his cap. "But I mean nothing wrong by it, you know that, sir. I mean to pay my respects, that's all."

"And now you've paid them," said Gramps, still calm, but with something in his voice that said that Jack would get up and go if he knew what was good for him.

No one could say that Jack didn't know what was good for him. He stepped up and off the porch as quick as could be, tipped his cap to Gramps, and nodded toward me, almost a bow, if an awkward one. I didn't nod or smile back, but only stood there as he walked away and watched until he disappeared over the hill.

So I'm growing up, that's all that is.

Jack was the first, but he's not anywhere close to the last. It started last fall before the deep snows, and it picks up again this summer. They come on sunny afternoons and rainy evenings, these village lads, to share news with Gramps and sip their cups of milk, watching me all the while from the corners of their eyes. I pretend I don't know what's happening, and Gramps turns them out soon as he's able, soon as he can without seeming rude.

I sometimes wonder why they're interested. Not that I don't

understand that I'm growing into a woman, and they are men. I mean, I'm not a horror, but I'm nothing special, neither. I work outdoors with the flowers all day long. I take no pains to wash my face or hands. I wear a dress as patched as any you'll find on a beggar in the city, I wager. My hair would be something pretty if I took care to brush it every night. But most times it's tangled and dulled by the dirt and the weeds and from getting torn by rose brambles and by branches in the woods.

I figure it's not me they're watching, though, or anyway not the girl I look like. It's the thing I'm not anymore. It's how I'm not one thing or another, but something else, something unlike anyone they know.

Gramps did ask me once, last winter, if there was any lad I fancied. I was putting a loaf over the fire to bake; I turned round, still bent over, and stared at him.

"It would be a way, Marni, to be forgotten once and for all. It would give you more protection than you'd ever have living here with me."

I straightened, feeling the flush of the flames on my cheeks. "There's life, Gramps," I said, "and then there's life. I wouldn't marry one of them if it were my last chance before the axe. What, and wear a village skirt and drink from the village well? Wouldn't be just the king and his court who'd forget me. I'd forget myself."

Gramps looked over my dress pointedly, and he sighed and shook his head, but he didn't say nothing more. Yes, some of the village women wear better dresses than me. But then, they have the time to sew, or a wagon for traveling to the city for better cloth. And my dress doesn't say I'm one thing or another. It's just a piece of fabric, taking the place of what I should by rights be wearing. Now I wear the dress of — what? A flower girl? A made-up thing, a nobody. If I started dressing like a villager, I would become one. I'd give up what I'm not anymore.

Gramps didn't say, *You could marry a villager to make me safe.* He didn't say, *This is no life, Marni. Become someone else and start again. Who you were is gone, as good as dead.* Gramps understands things sometimes.

Still, he watched me close all the rest of the evening, and I went to bed uneasy that night, with an itching in my feet.

It may be irritating, to be courted with sideways glances and half-formed flatteries, but at least these village lads are harmless. The real danger, I know, is from the lords.

Jack and the others might get frustrated. They might raise their voices, pushing for a word from me, an answer to some fool question — but a snap of Gramps's dark eyebrows, and they hush again.

They're in awe of him. They're in awe of how he speaks, the way I never learned to, with the short vowels and the clipped consonants. Every word out of Gramps's mouth sounds like he means it, like he knows just what he's saying and why. Out of my mouth, out of the villagers' mouths, the words all mash together, as if we can't be bothered to keep them one from the next, as if we haven't any time but must rush headlong from one thought to another. Times are I've tried to speak like Gramps, but it never seems natural. I've always latched onto the villagers' way of speaking — it's how my mouth wants to work, I reckon.

He sits so still, too, my Gramps, so tall and straight. He holds his cane across his lap, and he rests both hands along its shaft lightly. His shoulders roll back. His neck stretches up. Not even the lords or ladies sit like that. They loll lazily in their chair, bending forward when they laugh, leaning an elbow on the table. I imagine it isn't easy for Gramps to sit just so. His legs are half dead, so the other half of him has to work twice as hard to get across the floor or to reach for a cup or to rise up out of his chair. But he sits so easy you'd think he doesn't strain at all, that it's nothing.

When the villagers come, I see them sitting as straight as they can too, imitating him. The lords and the ladies don't even try. Could be they don't care what he thinks. Or could be that to give in on this, Gramps's standard of posture, would be to acknowledge something they can't bear: that Gramps is better than they are, and that they knew it once. Once, they hung on his every word; once, they fought for the honor of sitting at his side.

Maybe it's this refusal to remember that makes the lords glance my way with eyes the villagers would never dare make at me. That's a newer thing than the visits from the village lads; it's been a month or two, now, that it's been happening. There I'll be, leaning in my usual place against the wall, watching our morning glories curling around the wooden porch columns, and I'll sense a pair of them, dark and hungry eyes. It'll be someone not sitting on our visitors' chair, but the escort for a lady or a tagger-on to a large carriage group, someone not talking with the rest, someone whose mind has been able to stray.

And Gramps can't do a thing about it. He notices, sure, and I see the tightness in his face. At first I'd get all tight myself when it started to happen. They shouldn't be able to do that, I knew, and I worried what would come of it, who'd finally make some move toward me or come back late at night when Gramps was snoring and I was lying awake in my bed by the window. I used to stare up from my pillow at the moon, waiting for the shape of one of them to darken it, to reach in toward me, to cover my mouth before I could scream.

Now I stare back, as often as not. If they want to make something of it, they should go right ahead. Nothing has been stopping them all these years from coming round in the middle of the night to smother us as we sleep. Nothing stops them now from coming round to do other things. Nothing but the king, I guess — assuming he'd do anything about it. And their own small honor. And their fear of something else, of how close we are to the woods, of how strong Gramps always looks despite his legs, of how my mother was the only one who ever came back alive.

There's a story Annel used to tell about this girl, near grown, who was out in a meadow or somewhere, picking flowers. She was singing to herself, happy I guess, and as she reached down to pluck this red tulip, up comes a big brown horse with a man on its back.

Except it wasn't just a man, it was a sorcerer, and he didn't just happen to ride up right then. He had been watching the girl with his magic, and there was something about the way she picked the flowers, something about the way she leaned over with her hair all long and flowing and her lips spread wide in song, that made him love her. Or at least that's what he told the girl when he had gotten off his big brown horse and was standing there in front of her, and her mouth was wide with surprise now, and the tulip was still in her hand.

He wanted to take her with him back to his big old sorcerer's house, and he said she'd have jewels and dresses and anything she could want. Only thing was, if she came with him, she wouldn't ever go back home.

Well, the girl cried for a bit, thinking on the choice she had to make, but it turned out she already had a sweetheart back in her village. So she said no to the sorcerer, and he got angry and threatened her with his magic, and she stuck out her tongue at him — either brave or real stupid — and she ran back home and didn't tell anyone about it.

Except it didn't matter whether she told them or not, because two days later the sorcerer came around and killed them all. Killed her whole village: her parents, her brothers, the old teacher at the schoolhouse — everyone the girl had ever known. He left only her alive, and when she was sitting by the grave of her sweetheart, crying herself a lake, he came by on his big brown horse again and got off and stood by her.

He said he was sorry, that he didn't want to hurt her, but she could see, couldn't she, that there really was nothing to do but come with him. There was no reason anymore not to come.

But that girl didn't stand up and get on the horse and ride away with him. She sat there crying and crying, and while he watched, she stopped being a girl at all. She bent down toward her sweetheart's grave, and she trickled out of herself until she went and sprouted roots. And then there was nothing left of the girl the sorcerer said he loved, and all that was there was a red tulip, wet with dew, bending in the breeze.

The sorcerer could have plucked her up and carried her away with him, I guess, but he didn't. He let her be. He climbed back onto his horse and went home to his big old house. The girl stayed there like she wanted, though I suppose she hadn't planned on being a flower, and when the winter came, she shriveled up and died.

When I see those lords staring with their dark and hungry eyes, when I see the village lads shooting their looks at me, I think about this story, and I imagine a sorcerer riding up to our front porch or around to the back of the hut while I'm out picking flowers. I imagine him reaching out a hand to me, telling me I can come with him or I can stay at home, and I look up at him, and I don't cry or stick out my tongue.

I leap from the porch or get up out of the dirt. I jump on

his horse before he has the chance to change his mind. I leave with him at once, and I don't ever turn myself around to look behind.

That's what I imagine, anyway. And then I look across the porch and see Gramps there with his legs all twisted, and I know if it came down to it, I couldn't really leave. Not for a sorcerer, not for anyone.

Not if the dragon himself came down from his mountain and told me he would kill everyone who'd put us here, and all I had to do was leave my Gramps behind.

See, Gramps never left me behind. Not when his own son wanted me dead, not when the world thought I was nothing, no one, as wicked as anything. He picked me up and carried me here, even when he couldn't walk. He spent his life becoming no one too, so he could live with me, so they would let me live.

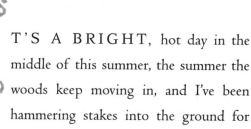

T'S A BRIGHT, hot day in the middle of this summer, the summer the woods keep moving in, and I've been hammering stakes into the ground for the tall plants, the hollyhocks and the delphiniums, to brace themselves against, to reach up toward the sun. Gramps was helping earlier this afternoon, hoeing the tough ground where the stakes didn't want to go in. But as the day got hotter, I could see the sweat growing on his forehead, and he was pausing to breathe more often than he was hoeing. I sent him to cool off in the porch's shade with a glass of water from the well.

I'm eyeing the shade of the trees myself. If I get a few more of these stakes done, I'll be good for the day. And Gramps won't miss me for a time. I can almost smell the deep pine there'll be if I get in a ways. I can almost hear the soft crunch of leaves under my feet, the crunch that never quite goes away, not even in the height of summer, with the grasses trying their best to carpet the woods.

I'm so caught up in my thoughts, I don't notice our visitor at first. He's come slipping his way around the hut — though I reckon if this one took a mind to go through, even I might not dare tell him no.

When I do see him, pacing round and round the geraniums on the far side of the garden, I stop and stare. Oh, he comes down now and again, like the rest of his court. But usually it's to have a quick word with Gramps; I've never seen him walking alone like this.

I get back to my hammering, but I keep an eye on him. He looks a bit like Gramps, around his serious eyes and in the shape of his nose. His hair is darker, but Gramps hasn't lost all his color yet neither, and their hair flops the same way about their ears, little bits of it sticking out no matter what I do to smooth Gramps's down with my fingers; no matter what, I guess, his servants do to smooth his down with their dabs of scented water and their soft hands.

He's shorter, though, than Gramps would be standing up out of his chair straight and tall; and he's stockier; and he walks with determined, quick steps, unlike Gramps's careful stroll. I think Gramps would walk real careful even without a stick, taking each step just as he does everything: picks up his cup, places it down, turns from folk to folk, lifts his head to smile at me. This one is in some sort of hurry, to be always stamping about so.

He goes all along our paths, through and under our fences and bushes, to the edge of the woods and back. He never looks my way, and he never comes up close to me until he's walked the whole garden back and forth at least three times. Then he stops and does look, all the way to where I'm putting the spade and hammer back into our shed. He looks at me as I've never seen him look before, straight and steady, not turning away the next moment, not pretending he never saw me.

I let him. I don't stop or smile or . . . or wave, or whatever it is that people do to people they want to see.

But today I can't figure him out at all. Not only does he keep on looking, but he makes his way across the garden toward me, not stepping quick now, but almost as slow as Gramps, and after I've closed the shed door, I just stand there watching until he's right up close.

I've never seen him quite this close.

Whenever he comes and talks to Gramps, I don't stand listening on the porch. I go out back and don't return until they've finished. I've always stayed out of his way, just as I was staying out of his way a minute ago when he was still ignoring me, as he did for the first sixteen years of my life.

But now he's not three steps from me, and I can see the colors in his eyes, and then I don't want to. I know now who shares my green and brown swirls; they're staring right back at me. And I can see his teeth, how he's missing an upper left one, so his smile's off a bit — or it would be were he to smile. When he scowls, as he's doing now, you barely notice that empty space until he opens his mouth to speak.

He opens his mouth to speak.

"You've grown tall, Marni."

Am I supposed to answer that? It's the first time I've heard my name pass those lips.

But he is the king, so I say, "Yes, I suppose I have."

Then there's this silence, as if he's about to say another piece at any moment, but he can't pull out the words, and he's glowering at me, and I'm looking back at him, as cool as I can manage.

And then he's gone again, back across the garden, over the path around the hut, and I'm left there, thinking things through in my head. I've *grown tall?* If that was all he was after, he could have said it at any moment of my life; I've been *growing tall* since before I could even talk, I reckon.

When I fetch another cup of water from the well for Gramps, the king is with him on the porch, talking in a low-down voice. I stop before the open front door, sliding back so they won't see me.

"No one's noticed her but a few of the village lads, and they only see that she's a girl growing up into a pretty woman." That's Gramps.

"It's only village lads so far," the king says. "It won't be long, though, before others take notice — if they haven't already."

"You can control the men of your court, I'm assuming," Gramps says in a bone-dry voice, his ironic voice.

The king snaps, "Of course." There's a pause, and then he continues. "That's not what I mean, anyway. You know it. There are other sorts of attention, from other sorts of people . . . and things."

"Things . . ."

I can hear the head shake in that; Gramps will be rolling his eyes, sighing a bit.

"Don't give me that look. Just last night, the woods at the northern border moved in ten whole feet, and the villagers there are hearing birds cry from the woods, birds they haven't heard in years; and they've seen—" A pause. "They've seen a phoenix flying across the mountains."

"I don't see what that has to do with us."

The king, impatient: "You know as well as I, what with the woods moving in like this, what with all the things her mother was mixed up in—"

"And you know better than to talk about your sister to me, Roderick." There's no irony there. Only silence, a long silence that stretches and stretches until I almost want to burst from the length of it, and the water is growing warmer in my hand.

And then Gramps says, "You should be getting on, then," and he sounds almost like me, his words running together, as if he's changed in the length of that silence from a man who could reprimand the king back to the flower man, a nobody living on the edge of the kingdom.

When I can't hear the king's footsteps — even holding my breath, closing my eyes, and opening my ears real wide — I step through the door to hand my Gramps the water.

He smiles at me as though nothing just happened, as though the world is as it always has been. He takes a drink, but he doesn't seem about to say a word, so I ask, "What is it the king wanted?"

He takes another drink, then twists the glass on the table. He's fidgeting — my steady Gramps. "Nothing much," he says. "Court matters."

"In truth?"

"In truth, Marni." Now he does look up. I know the stubbornness in his eyes. He'll not be telling me another thing. So I swallow my questions, and I pat the top of his head with my hand, the way he used to do to me before I *grew tall,* and I go out to walk and think my thoughts in the woods.

The woods at this time of day are long and spread out, the silence patient. If you hum as you walk, you might forget how many eyes are watching you.

I don't think, as I step over fallen logs, around bramble thickets, about the scowl on the king's face.

I don't think about what he and my Gramps were talking about, neither. Not at the top of my mind. Underneath, there's a voice that whispers to me, words I can't make out, but they slide in anyway, and I know from the feel of them they're about my mother.

These half-formed thoughts blend with the rustle of the leaves, the scurry of the creatures through the undergrowth. They swirl and sift through me until I'm whispering to myself, the story that pulses in my blood, the thing that tells me who I am. My Gramps doesn't like to talk of it much, but I know it inside and out, all he's told me.

My Gramps, he was the king then, and my mother was a princess. There was a prince, too, Gramps's son, her brother. My uncle, who's now the king.

You will remember what I said about the girls who vanish into the woods not ever finding their way back home. It's true. It was true for Annel, and it's true for almost all the girls who skip off into the trees.

Almost all, but not quite.

One got lost, just as the hundred girls before her did. One ran away, following a laugh on the wind, believing in a wild dream, and her family fell into pain, just as the families of all those girls do.

But this one, ten months later, as the snows were melting, this one came back. She stumbled, shivering, out of the trees and ran all the way home, and her father near didn't recognize her, and her brother cried and cried with joy to see that she yet lived. Then it was with joy.

Later the tears turned to fear, and then the fear to rage.

See, this one girl didn't come back alone. She was carrying me within her—the child of the woods, the child of the dragon.

It would have been better, maybe, if I'd been fathered by a

village lad. At least then he would have been from our kingdom. At least then he would have been human. As it was, it struck the prince as something quite like treason.

My Gramps tried to calm his son down, keep him reasonable. But the prince wouldn't listen. Wouldn't be turned from his path, wouldn't stop telling everyone what she had done to them, to him.

Soon enough, half the king's army was after her, and the king's son as angry as a hornet. I've asked Gramps, and he says there was nothing he could do, not without risking his own men turning on him. So the princess was on her own, just one young girl not that much older than I am now, and she was running from a whole big country.

And she escaped. For many long months she kept hidden — I reckon she must have been clever to keep away from them for so long. I was almost one by the time they found us, and they'd been looking since before I was born.

They killed her, then, my uncle and his men, and my Gramps couldn't stop them. He did try — he got in the way of the sword before it found her, and that's the one that took the strength in his legs, that made it so he'd never walk straight again.

If it weren't for my Gramps, I reckon my uncle would have killed me, too. But the shock of seeing him cut down his own sister, and near to lame his own father — and the sight of me looking on at it all wide-eyed, a baby girl scarce able to toddle about — I think they wondered, then, the king's soldiers, whether they'd done right after all to follow this prince. It's one thing to think on doing something, one thing to plan, to dream of it. It's another to see it in front of you. It's another to have the world change all about you and be unable to put it back the way it was. I reckon even my uncle may have had a shock when he saw his sister's blood draining away.

So when my Gramps pleaded to be allowed to take me away, when he offered his son the kingdom, even, if he'd just let me live — my uncle gave in. My Gramps pulled me up onto his horse, and we rode and rode until the pain in his legs near made him fall, and we stopped then at the very next village. The villagers there took care of us until Gramps's legs had healed as much as they ever would. And then he built us a hut — far enough away from anyone else not to bring the new king's wrath down on them, if he came for us again, and within a few years I was growing my flowers out back, so we'd no need to depend on the villagers' generosity for food, neither. And he's left us alone all these years, though he still comes down to ask my Gramps's advice now and again. And my Gramps has never said a word about wishing he was still king.

I think on it sometimes, how it must have been to be my mother, waiting in her hiding place, dreading the moment she'd hear the soldiers coming, and hoping every morning it wouldn't be that day, that she'd have one more day to see the sun and feel the grass and watch me grow. I like to think she wanted that, to watch me grow. My Gramps says she loved me, but how would he know? He never saw me until that day, until he rode up with his army to her door and tried to save her, and fell, and never quite got up again. He wouldn't know if she used to kiss my hair. He wouldn't know if she sang me to sleep or if she sat there staring out her window, wishing for her monster to come and get her, wishing anything but that she had a baby girl who was like to kill her just by living.

He wouldn't know, and she's not here to say.

It's as I'm thinking these things that the green-clad lady on her log looks up with her bright, shining eyes and tells me I ought to come with her.

I don't know how I got here. I haven't come this far out since I was a child. I haven't heard the voice of this lady in at least ten years, but there she is now, talking to me, holding out her hand as if we sat together only yesterday.

She's glowing in the dim forest light. The tips of her fingers set off sparks in the air.

"Child," she says in a sweet, airy lilt.

"I'm not a child anymore," I say, firm. I should be stepping away at once, but I'd forgotten how beautiful this lady is, in the way that nightshade is beautiful. I can't bring myself to turn away.

Her misty head tilts. "You are our child, still," she says. "Won't you come and walk with me?"

In all my years of avoiding her, she's never come this close before. I'd see her looking up from her log, a ways into the woods, and I'd turn and walk fast in the other direction. Or I'd hear her knitting needles going click-click-clack just around the next batch of trees or over a rise in the ground, and I'd hum to myself and back away until she had faded out again.

She was never in the same place twice.

I reach out — I can't help it — to touch her fingers, to see what they might feel like. The woods' shadows fold down upon us, and it is only our fingertips, inching closer and closer and then, just barely, brushing at the seams. We stop like that. It's like the moment between now and then. It's like the last note of a sunset before it drains away. It's like the almost-there tip of a new flower stem, or the instant before a petal falls to the earth.

She looks, too, at our fingers there together. If she had breath, it would be as caught as mine.

I pull back. She lowers her hand.

Before she can say another thing, I turn and walk away, all the way back to our hut.

That night, I can't get myself to sleep, and I know my Gramps is just as wakeful, though he lies still in the moonlight. He thinks he has it figured out, how to act so I think he's fast asleep and not mulling over his own thoughts, as I am over mine.

But I know the sound of my Gramps's waking breaths. Times are, in the dark of night, I've heard him crying softly. My eyes will be turned toward the wall, to where I can see the moonlight slipping in under the shutters. He lies still, too, not moving a bit, but I can hear his sobs, dry, muffled by his pillow.

I don't think he cries just for me, all cut off from the world, not one thing or another. I don't think he cries just for my

mother, neither. I think he cries too for what he used to be—
a king, a someone, power in his smallest gesture, his slightest
smile. And now he can't even walk right, and his smiles do no
good, or at best hold off the king's wrath from me, one almost-
grown girl, and him, one crippled old man.

He'd never let me hear him talk of it. He'd never say what
it was like—life—before I came. Doesn't matter, though. You
don't live with one person that long and not understand the
things he never says. Comes a time when not saying them speaks
more than if he did. Comes a time I can read the sadness in his
eyes better than the smile on his lips.

I don't think he wishes me dead and gone. I don't think he
wishes that he'd never saved me, that he'd never tried to save her,
that he hadn't given them a reason to break his legs and take his
throne from him.

Life's not as simple as all that. More like, you'll be wishing
for things that couldn't be. That the cold of winter be turned all
of a sudden to springtime joy. That a baby was born even without the mother's carrying it and giving birth. That you could
go far away and stay forever, all at the same time. Those are the
things we're like to wish. Things not possible. Things not even
those in the woods could make true, no matter what they might
promise.

Midnight has come and gone before I slip into a dream at
last, and as far as I know, my Gramps stays wakeful long after
that.

 RAMPS NEVER does say what the king wanted that day, and I never tell him about the lady in the woods, neither. But in the weeks that follow, as we're getting a new rumor every day about the woods moving in, or about another phoenix appearing in the sky, terrifying our livestock, giving our children new, monstrous dreams—all through those days I never stop going to the woods.

I know I ought to keep out. But if Gramps can have his secrets, so can I, and anyway I don't face the lady like that again. I do begin to let her walk behind me on my rambles. I let her sing her melodies, and at times I hum along as well. But that's all. I don't talk to her. I don't turn to see her face. She's a hidden thought, scarce brushing against my mind.

It's normal, almost, those last weeks of summer. Out in our hut, we're not touched by the movement of the woods. It's funny, when I think on it, how our trees never budge. A row of sunflowers lines the garden beds just before the wall, and outside the wall of our garden a dirt path runs all around, and beyond that are the trees. We don't lose one sunflower or one stone off the wall or one inch off that path.

It makes it easy to dismiss the rumors. For a time, we can pretend that everything's as it always has been. For a time, nothing bothers us but the everlasting parade of village lads and the unwelcome looks from the lords.

It's not until the leaves are beginning to drop that a lord I don't recognize walks down to our hut late in the day, and he doesn't buy a flower, and he doesn't look at me where I'm standing against the hut; he just sits and chats with Gramps until I'm about to scream from the boredom of it.

After a while, he isn't even talking anymore or making a show of it. We're all silent together on the porch, Gramps sitting straight in his chair, eyeing this lord calmly; the lord looking out up the path over the hill, toward the darkening sky; me twisting my hands in my skirt and counting to a million. I figure if I get that far, I'll forget all my Gramps ever taught me about being polite, and I'll turn and leave this lord to sit to his heart's content. And Gramps can do what he wants to me, because really, enough is enough.

But as I reach one thousand three hundred and twenty-one,

and as the darkness is thickening, spreading through the porch like fog or like cold, the lord speaks.

He's young, a black-haired, handsome man. Tall, and sure of himself. He's been deferential to my Gramps to this point, and he speaks with an ease, a camaraderie the lords rarely manage.

"Things will change soon," he says. He waits a moment, letting us settle into this unannounced conversation. He's talked about the impending harvest and crop prices. He's talked of the woods approaching and of the road through the northern mountains closing down in parts, overrun by trees. There's something different in the way he starts this new topic, and when he continues, it's different too, as though before he was only mouthing the lines of a character in a play and now he's stepped offstage and has begun to speak as himself. "The king grows older every day, without an heir. There are some who think he never will have one. There are some who wonder what will happen when the king is no longer here."

"My son is young," Gramps says. He speaks hesitantly; he rarely refers to his relationship to the king. "It will be a long time before he is no longer here."

"That could be true." The lord leans forward over the table toward Gramps. "Still, there will be changes soon. Already there is talk of things no one would have mentioned just months ago, hidden-away things, forgotten things." His voice slides through total darkness now. The stars are concealed by a bank of low clouds, and this lord isn't even a shadow, but a blank spot in the night.

"Does the king speak of such things?" my Gramps says.

"No." Quietly. "Not yet. But he hears it, and it shows in his face that he knows what they are saying. What we are saying."

"Talk does not mean action."

"Maybe not. And yet . . ." His chair creaks as he settles back again. "As we were discussing, the woods are on the move, and the king has no real solution. Some blame the hidden-away things for this — attack — on our fields. Some blame the ones who forced those things into hiding, and feel an uncovering is well overdue. I will say it again: there will be changes soon."

All is quiet again. I wrap my arms about myself as a breeze whips by with the first scent of autumn. *Changes.* There've been no changes since Gramps and I ran off to this hut. Only year after year, and lord after lady, and short visits from the king, and trading with the villagers. Only recently attention from those village lads, and looks from the nobles come to buy flowers and turned gawkers at the flower girl. Those aren't the changes this lord means.

"My lord," the man says — the lord! — speaking to my Gramps, the flower man. If it was quiet before, it's as dead as dead now. His words take up all the space and all the sound on our porch. "My lord, there will be dangerous times ahead. It would be wise to take alliances with those who offer them."

"And are you offering?" It's almost sharp, my Gramps's voice.

"I am. I am offering, my lord, for your granddaughter's hand in marriage."

It has always amazed me how the village boys could stop by and pay me court without once talking to me. But even they glanced in my direction. Even they showed in a thousand ways that they knew I stood only three feet away, listening to their every word. I could tell by the red that crept up their necks. I could tell by the stammer in their voices.

This man's voice is as smooth and as pale as cream. If he's blushing, I wouldn't know it in the dark, but I haven't seen his eyes on me the whole of the evening, and the sound of his words just now wasn't directed toward me. He's shown in no way that he knows I exist.

"Have you the blessing of your family's head in this?" That's my Gramps, sharper still.

"I am my house's head, the last of the House of Ontrei. And I am not without friends at court. There are those who know what it is I came to ask tonight."

Now I start to wonder, as I didn't think to wonder before, whether Gramps might actually jump at this offer. It's seemed so like a dream, the nameless man in the dark, his cryptic words. But now he's given us his name, and he has friends, and others know of this conversation. I could be riding back with this lord this very night to stand before a court official and sign a document and leave my Gramps behind.

And I don't want it to happen.

When I shut my eyes, I can see the glowing hand of the

lady in the woods once more, reaching, beckoning, telling me to follow far and away to where possibilities never disappear. And I see my friend, my Annel, running after that hand and laughing, and letting her hair free from her braid, and never looking back.

This wouldn't be like that.

This would be putting one foot in front of the other, slow and steady, day after day, wherever this lord might care to lead.

I know every inch of this porch, just as I know every flower in our garden. I move along the wall until I'm behind the table where the lord and my Gramps sit, and I place my hands on it.

The men grow still at my presence; I can hear their breathing. "My Lord of Ontrei," I say, trying to speak somewhat like the ladies I hear day after day, "you honor us with your proposal, and we are appreciating your warning of the changes of things."

I take a breath to figure my way from here, and my Gramps says, "Marni, let me deal with this."

"It's all right, Gramps," I say. "I've got the words." And I do. I go on. "We're appreciating the proposal and the warning, my lord, but we find ourselves unable to accept your offer, generous though it is. We'll be staying as we are, as we've always been."

There's a pause. "Our thanks, though," I say, to show I'm finished.

"My lord, this is your reply as well?" the Lord of Ontrei asks. There's something—disbelief—that I don't like in that tone.

"Marni is young," says my Gramps. "But if she's unwilling, I'm afraid that's the end of it."

"I see."

Another silence. "It's getting dark," Gramps says, maybe a bit late in the evening to be commenting on that, but that's not what he's saying, really.

After a moment more, the Lord of Ontrei shifts his chair back and gets to his feet. He has to pass Gramps to reach the steps, and he pauses there, no doubt figuring his way around. Then he's across the porch, down the steps. At the bottom, he stops. He says, "I meant no disrespect to you, my lord, nor to you, lady."

We neither of us answer.

"When the changes come," he says, "remember that I have a more open mind than some. I can point you to others like me. There are plenty who would make the same offers of friendship I have — and maybe in time my alliance will prove more welcome to you both." The night swallows him then, sound, shape, and presence, and it's only Gramps and me on the porch again.

Gramps sighs. "You won't take a villager; you won't take a lord. Who will you take, Marni?"

"No one," I answer at once. "I've no need for anyone. Just you and me, Gramps, and the flowers."

"It used to be that simple," he says. "But nothing lasts forever."

"Well," I say, taking his arm to help him up, "we've no need to worry about forever. Just today, and tomorrow, and the next."

He's quiet as we get him to his feet, and I leave him leaning against the door frame while I light a candle from the embers of our fire. As I'm standing, cupping the flame with my hand, he says, "That's what I thought about her."

I catch his eyes. He's all still in the candlelight. "What did you think?" I say, soft, so as not to scare him from the topic.

"I thought worrying about one day and the next would be enough. I thought when it came down to it, something would change — your uncle's heart, my soldiers' loyalty. I thought I'd never have to worry about forever."

I go over to him and take his arm again. Close to him, fierce, I say, "They'll never take me from you, Gramps."

He switches his cane to his other hand and puts his free one over mine where it rests on his arm. "You're a good girl, Marni. None of this is your fault, you remember that."

I laugh a bit; I can't help it. "Oh, Gramps," I say. "It's all of it my fault. Now come along, it's high time you were in bed."

But he holds me back a moment more. I say, "What is it?"

He doesn't say a thing, just looks long at me, as though he's readying himself to draw my portrait or some such. Then he shakes his head and turns away. "Nothing," he says. He squeezes my hand again and switches his cane. The firelight glints on his cheeks.

He lets me lead him away at last, and this night I'm asleep as soon as I've pulled the covers up.

I wake up early the next day and go out while Gramps is still abed. I stand on the back step, breathing in the crisp air, pushing last night's lord out of my mind.

The birds are singing in the lilac bushes in our garden and all through the woods. The flowers are turning brown; some have already dropped. Soon I'll be picking the last crop, hanging it to dry in the rafters of our hut, and our job will be done for the year. I've bought vegetables and stored them in the space underneath the floorboards in the kitchen. I've dried meat and put it out in the shed, where we can tear ourselves a hunk whenever we're craving some soup or a fried piece in the morning. I've packed the chicken house with dead leaves and stems. I've packed our cow in too, singing to her as she chewed her grass with mournful eyes. I never have met a cow with joyful eyes. Could be they don't appreciate being crammed into wooden stalls. Could be there's a great cow knowledge of what it is we do to them when they've outlived their usefulness and we're hankering for that hunk of meat to go with our eggs.

We're ready for the cold and the snow and the winds. We're ready for another winter inside our hut, sitting by the fireplace, me sewing and Gramps sketching pictures with the bits of paper and charcoal we get from traveling sales folk. Gramps has a gift for drawing; if you didn't know better, you'd think he'd lived his whole life as an artist. A few strokes of his charcoal and the flowers draping the porch are transferred, alive and elegant, to the paper. Or he'll do a portrait of a child from a nearby farm, and the quirk of the boy's mouth and the glint in his eyes and the pixie ears will all be there in the drawing, just as they are in life. Come the winter, he'll be sketching away, tucking drawings into every corner and shelf in our hut, handing them out to everyone who stops by. Our visitors will dwindle to almost no one in the darkest, coldest weeks. It'll be as though the world out there doesn't exist anymore. It'll be as though we've found a place to disappear in truth. As the food runs low, we'll find ourselves wishing for the spring, but in the beginning, and for a stretch in the middle, we'll be perfectly happy to bundle up and forget it all.

Today, though, the cold and the snow are still holding off. Animals run, hurry-scurry, through the flower beds and under the cracks in the wall, piling up their hoard before the winter. Won't be many more days like this one. Won't be many more chances to slip out through the garden while Gramps is sleeping in the soft dawn light and to hop over the wall and into the trees.

At once, the scent of crumbling leaves fills my nose. I breathe in deep. It twitches my fingers. It lifts my lips in a smile without me quite knowing why. It makes me laugh. My hair flips back in the breeze. I walk on, and for once, I don't blink away the spirits dancing round. They're as much a part of the season as the wind is, as the nuts ripe on the branches and the early setting of the sun. I see it in their dances: the way the world is turning out of summer, out of languid, heavy heat into quick motions and shivering flights through frozen hills. There will be months of staying indoors, yes, but also urgent strikings of flint and keen-eyed hunters stringing their bows for rabbits the color of the snow.

The spirits dance like that now, quick, nothing excessive, with joy in the danger and the running.

I don't want to look away from them. I'm as caught up in

the world today as they are, maybe more so. Despite what I said to my Gramps, I know that lord was right about the coming changes; I know that tomorrow or the next day we could lose the meager safety we've hoarded so long. My uncle might ride down this instant, demanding that I come with him, that I pay the price my mother did for her dallying with the woods, the price I've avoided for sixteen years only by his grace and by the foolish love of an old king.

I know it's coming, but I scarce can think of it just now, not when the woods are sparkling and dancing like this. The world has always moved from one extreme to the other, year after year, from scorching, dripping heat to blazing, breathtaking cold. The movements of a court, the fear of an uncle — what do they count compared with this?

And besides, something has been happening here in the last few weeks. I've sensed it growing, the little magics gathering, the voices multiplying in a way they shouldn't be at this time of the year. The floating lights should be dwindling, the speaking owls should be gathering fluff for their winter nests. But the creatures of the woods have only been running more, flitting here and there more, talking to each other incessantly as the air has cooled.

It makes me want to run forever, this thing the forest is doing. It makes me want to jump up high, to scream out loud, to become something I've never been, a beast, a voice — *magic.* I let this feeling run over me. I glory in it and don't think on all my fretting about forever.

I know it when she walks up from behind and joins me. We continue side by side, up over needle-laden hills, on into the woods. She sings, eerie and thin, a lullaby from long ago. She has a pair of needles in one hand, like the needles on the ground beneath our feet but fifty times bigger, and a skein of light trails from her arm.

She wouldn't have come at all if I hadn't been paying more attention than is sensible out here these past few weeks. If I'd been ignoring the creatures of the woods, if I'd been ignoring her as has been my wont for ten years now, she wouldn't have come up to me like this, all smooth and pleasing. There are things beings like her can do, and there are things they can't think of without your giving them leave. It's something to do with the difference between us. It's something to do with us being human and them being something not quite, yet not quite not, either, if you see what I am saying.

But I'm not feeling quite human now either, am I? So I let her walk beside me, and when I stop at last, when the forest is all about me so there's nothing else in any direction, only the mossy dirt and rough bark and silvery, whispering leaves, I turn to her, and she turns to me.

I know better than to talk to her, but though the changes seem far off in this place, they're never so far that I can forget them completely, and this might be the last chance I have for speaking. So I say to her, "What would happen, then? If we just kept walking and I never did go back?"

"Anything might," she says, and keeps on with her humming.

"No," I say. "I won't take that for my answer. I'm not seven anymore. I'm a girl of near seventeen, and I'm just the sort you want to spirit away. Maybe I'd think on it, but first I'd want to know what would happen next. What do you give those girls in truth? Quick death? Slow torture? What?"

"Anything," she says again. "We give them anything they want."

I shake my head. "Not *anything*. Not a true love. Not a pile of money to spend back home."

She takes a step closer to me, and I steel myself not to back away. Though I've no wish to brush against her, I'm not about to let her see my fear, neither. "We don't promise things we cannot give," she says. "Come with us, little Tulip, and you'll get exactly what you want."

It's not only the lords and ladies who call me that. I don't know who started it first, in fact — the people who don't want to remember who I am or the creatures who don't care. I haven't heard that name from this lady, though, in many years. "Not so little anymore," I mutter.

"No, and not so free."

"I never was free."

She breathes in and out through that mouth I can't ever see, and she's reaching out her hand again and saying, "Then leave it all. Come with me, follow me." And she's promising me, she's promising more than I can bear with that hand, that voice; the whole woods shudders with this, the possibility of what I might find if I give in. "You think you're just another one," she says now, excited, urging me. "You think you're another of those girls, that we don't see any difference."

I frown. "You say that to everyone?"

"No, Tulip. Only to you. For the others, it is an exit, an exodus." She's inches from me, but she's still not touching me. She could, with one swoop of her hand, one brush of her misty hair toward mine. "For you, it will be an entrance. Come with me, my flower, and you will be coming home."

There's something flashing behind my eyes, some dark laughter, some impossible thing. I'm not backing away from her now, because I can't. I can't stop looking at her. I can't stop seeing the way her dress falls like needles and her hair floats like fog. She is so familiar. She's a dream I used to have.

"*Remember*," she says, and she's so close it's as though her voice is in my head. "Remember what you are, Tulip. Remember what you could be."

And it's then, with her dress all lit in her hand's light and her hair drifting about and her face as hidden as the dark spaces between tree roots, and I'm not feared of her, I'm not thinking on how strange she looks, because I'm somehow as used to her as I am to my own Gramps, my own flowers—it's then that I remember the things I had forgotten about these woods, and what they were to me as a child.

I have said, haven't I, that long ago I would near lose myself in the woods, wandering, singing, forgetting. I wasn't the king's unwanted niece, and I wasn't the flower girl; I was someone else.

I was anyone I wanted to be, maybe, but it was different from that, too.

Remember how I said I used to knit with the lady on the log when I was a little girl? Well, I didn't knit plain old human things. I didn't bring out my wool and horse-bone needles and sit there next to her knitting my Gramps's socks.

I knit what she knit.

I knit with pine needles I'd picked from the ground and held in my hand as they drew out long and strong. I spun my thread from the beams of light slicing through the trees, dappling the forest floor. I sang the song the lady on the log sang, the one with words I never could remember the moment I went home again, and we knit warm nests for the birds and secret crannies for the squirrels to hide their nuts in, and when we had been wronged by some inhabitant of the woods, we knit a revenge and sent it soaring away on its glowing wings to take our price.

And when I ran with the little ones, I shrank myself down to their size, and I grew myself a pair of wings as delicate and pale as theirs, and I screeched in their language as we went marauding against the other tribes of the forest or danced the afternoons away or sat in council, determining laws and punishments.

And when I met up with the bigger of the woods' peoples, when a phoenix or a griffin came down south near my Gramps's hut, I spoke to them in song, and when I was lucky, they took me up on their backs and flew me so high that I could see over almost the whole of the country: the king's castle gleaming by the river, the many-colored fields to the east, the mountains to the north, and the trees rolling on and on forever to the south. No one saw us, the great beautiful birds and me. Now there's a new sighting of a phoenix every week, but then it was as though we were hidden from the human realm.

Seems like all those memories had gone clean out of my head somehow. Oh, I knew I had talked with the creatures in the woods, the ones that weren't human, the ones that breathed magic for air and were as like to sing you to your death as to your sleep.

But I had forgotten how close I was to becoming one of them before I stopped letting myself see them, before I cut myself off from their dangerous voices. I thought the song these woods sang for me was no different from the one that tempts so many girls. I thought that's why they wanted me, because I'm a girl, not — not because I'm the dragon's daughter.

I can't help it; I stumble away from the lady. I reach out a hand and hold myself up by a tree. "I had forgotten," I say.

"It has been a long time," says the lady. "And you weren't ready to come with us yet."

"And now you think I am."

"Yes."

"What do you want me for?"

"Tulip," she says, "we want you to come home."

Home. There's that word again, and this time it rings all

through me, and I've an urge, like a hunger, to do those things I'm only just remembering. To sprout some wings. To run on all fours. To dance through the trees alongside the spirits.

When I can, I look up at the lady again, and she's standing still where I left her, waiting for me to speak.

"I can't," I say.

"Why not?" She sounds so unbearably bereft, as if it breaks her heart to hear me tell her no.

But I shake my head. "He never left me."

She doesn't ask who I mean. "That's enough to stop you from being what you're meant to be?"

I say, "It's enough for anything. It's enough to tell me what I *should* be."

He'll be awake now back at the hut, and I know it. I imagine him peering out our back door, looking here and there for me. I'm not sure, this far away, if I would hear it when he called. If I went with this lady, I would never know how long he searched for me. I would never know how many weeks it was before he grew sick with fretting and lay down in his bed. I wouldn't know if the king would take pity on him, the flower man without a flower, and would take him back to the castle finally, or if he would let him lie, stay silent, and with his turning away do what he hadn't dared to do all those years with an axe or a knife or a drop of poison.

The lady's looking at me now with her head half turned, a wary look, her eyes sharp pricks of light. Her arms are at her sides. "You used to sit with me happily," she says, still in that eerie voice, whining now. "You know you did. You were perfection, my dark flower. No questions, just laughter, just dance."

"I grew up."

She shakes her head at me. The knitting hanging from her left hand is a comet flash through the woods. "You don't have to," she says, quiet and quieter. She's sidling away, slipping back through the trunks. "You can have what the others have, what the others want, and more, because you are more. You can have your freedom."

And then, between one thought and the next, she's gone. She's taken the spirits and the other magic folk with her. Only an ordinary wren tilts her head at me from a nearby branch before taking wing out into the depths, into that place where anything might happen. She's gone, leaving me behind, and the gray is filling in the corners of the woods like the shading in a drawing, and I go back from the farthest I have ever been, and when I get home, the sun is setting behind me, and I know as soon as I set foot in our garden that something is horribly wrong.

THE FLOWERS are restless. I sense them, swiveling their heads toward me, quivering all along their stems. Only the faintest light still brushes the garden. I thought my Gramps would be at the door, frantic, calling my name. I thought he'd have gathered a search party, and all the meadows round about would be speckled with torches.

But it's dark, and it's silent, and there's a dread growing in me as I climb the back step into the hut. The flowers turn to watch me go. I've never felt them so upset. I've never felt them so uneasy with the world. Something has happened.

My Gramps isn't in his bed. He isn't sitting before the fire, and when I pass through to the front porch, he's not at his table there, neither.

Someone else is.

The Lord of Ontrei's eyes flash at me through the dusk. He stands. He's holding something in his hand, a piece of paper, looks like. I don't say nothing. I can't think. My Gramps's cane is lying on the porch, just before the steps, as though he threw it down there and never came back to pick it up. But he wouldn't do that, would he? There's no way my Gramps could go traipsing over the countryside without his cane. He couldn't go ten feet without it.

"Lady," the lord says. "I've some terrible news."

"Was it the king?" I can scarce hear my own voice, there's such a ringing in my ears. How could I leave him for this long? How could I go so far away that I don't even know now if he screamed? "Did he take my Gramps?"

But the lord is shaking his head. "No, lady. No one took him away."

"What, then? Where did he go?"

"Please," says the lord, "take a seat."

I do, without thinking, without realizing that I'm crossing the porch, pulling out the chair, sitting in it. The lord sits across from me.

He says, "I came to see if you'd change your mind."

It takes me a bit to think on what he means. "If I'd marry you after all," I say.

"Yes. You've no idea, lady, what the king's been saying, what he's been talking of doing."

"I reckon he'd like to kill us both."

There, that's surprised him. "Not in so many words," he says. "But that's the general idea. It's the woods. It's that they're moving in, and he thinks that you have something to do with it."

There's a rustle of leaves in the bushes lining our path, and I shiver, not with cold, though. It's a tingle, a rushing in my blood as the memories of running with the woods folk flash through me again. For a moment I scarce can blame my uncle for being afraid. For a moment I think I'm the sort of thing that could kill him with my gnashing teeth or take his kingdom with only a whispered word.

But I shake my head. "They'll take themselves back again. They always do." It's what my Gramps says, and I recall the strangeness in the flowers, the cane abandoned at my feet. "Where is he?" I say. "If he's not been taken, where did he go?"

The Lord of Ontrei takes a deep breath, and the dread comes back a thousandfold, and I know before he says it, the worst words in the world: "He's dead."

"No." We talked of this only last night, of time running out, of not escaping from forever. Just one night ago. It can't have happened already. The world can't—mustn't work that way. We ought to have today, still, and tomorrow, and the next. Today, tomorrow, and the next day—and then the day after that.

"I came by this morning to see if you'd changed your mind. He was here, where I'm sitting now. He was already gone."

"No."

"I think it must have been his heart giving out. There was no sign of a struggle. He sat with his head upon the table, with this paper under his arm." He pushes it toward me.

I don't look at it. "What did you do with him, if he was gone?"

"I buried him out back."

And there, those words. Those are the ones that make it real, that make him not just *not here*, but somewhere horrible, buried, like a crocus bulb that never comes up in the spring. I say, "Without me?"

"I waited hours, lady." His voice is soft. "I didn't know when you'd be back. I didn't want to leave him here, to risk someone from the castle finding him. They'd have told the king, and I didn't think he would want that. I didn't think you would."

And I wouldn't, I guess. The king would take the body. He'd bury it himself, where kings are buried, I suppose. He might talk over it, make some big fuss. I wouldn't want the king touching my Gramps.

The lord pushes the paper another inch toward me. "He left this for you," he says.

It's dark now, so dark the words are near impossible to make out. I take it into the hut, where our fire still simmers, and I stir the embers with a stick, make them flame up into life. I tilt the paper so it catches the glow.

There's a drawing at the top, with squiggled, faint lines, as if the charcoal were shaking as it drew. But still I know the face, the hair, the smile I feel may never come again. It's me, and it's my Gramps's hand. He's drawn me so many times before, I'd know it anywhere.

Under the drawing is a line. Just one, and in my Gramps's writing, too. The village girls can scarce read, most of them, but he made sure to teach me my letters, to make me practice at my writing day after day. I'm grateful, now, not to have to ask the lord beside me what it says.

My Marni, I'll love you always. Be safe.

It's like Gramps, isn't it, to be warning me to the last. That was all he lived for, so many years. Keeping me safe. And when it came to it, I couldn't even repay the favor. When it came to it, he died alone.

"He must have known." The lord's still here, still slipping in where he has no right. "He must have had a few minutes when he realized what was happening, that he wasn't long for the world."

"Where did you bury him?" I say.

"Out back."

"Out back where?"

He hesitates. "By the lilacs to the north."

Then I'm out the door, running to my Gramps's grave. I know what the flowers have been trying to tell me. They're trembling all through them to have seen my Gramps put down into the earth. They know him, sure enough, as much as they know me. They know he ought to be out in the air, walking about,

not rooted down deep under mounds of dirt. They know something's wrong, and that's what I hear as I pass them by: *Something's
wrong, something's wrong.*

I know! I cry back to them. *Everything's wrong!*

And there it is, under the northern lilacs, the place where
the dirt has been turned up, where he is. I kneel down next to
him, and my tears are coming quick now at the wrongness of it
all. He shouldn't be dead. I should have been here to hold his
hand. He should have had the greatest doctors, the strongest
medicines, the softest sheets. All the kingdom should be crying
now to know that he is gone.

My mother should be living to cry that he is gone.

The lord is back at the hut still; he didn't follow when I left.
I don't want to think on him. I don't want to think of sleeping
alone in our hut tonight or living one more day out here without
my Gramps. This was our place. This was where he came to keep
me safe. This was where I stayed to be with him. It needed both
of us to work. It's not home now, and I can't stay here, and if I
go back inside, the lord will be telling me the same, that it's not
a safe place anymore.

The woods are calling my name.

I fold the paper and slip it into the waist of my dress. I kiss
the dirt mounded up at my Gramps's grave. The flowers' song is
heart-rending as I stand, brush down my skirt, and walk through
them over to the wall. As I pass the dragon flowers, they cry out
to me, so powerful I near hear it with my ears as well as my mind:
Tulip, come home!

The lady is waiting near the wall, but I don't cross over. She's back a bit in the woods. It seems an age since I last saw her, though it can't have been more than an hour. She's watching me. She's expecting me to come to her.

I call out softly, "I need a vengeance."

She blinks; her eyes go dark for a moment. "What sort of vengeance, little flower?" she says, and her words twist this way and that through the air, lighting quietly in my ear.

"To kill the king."

I hear her soft sigh. "I cannot make you such a thing."

"Why not?"

"He's not here. He's out, beyond." She lifts a hand toward the edge of the woods. "My magic only works in here."

I take a breath. "Then I can't come with you."

She moves; she's close to me in an instant, facing me across the wall. "There's nothing for you there now," she says. "Forget it, little one. Nothing matters but your freedom, but the life you can have with us in the woods."

But she's wrong. My Gramps lies dead in our garden. My mother never saw me grow. And the man who ruined both their lives walks free, unpunished, as happy as he ever was. And I know of things this lady may not, with all her mysteries, with all her secrets. I've heard tales of sorcerers and witches, away in far-off lands. I'm half dragon, yes, and that half is pushing me on, across the wall, into the woods. But I'm half human, too, and could be I can do things this lady would never dream.

I'm tall enough these days to reach across the wall, all the way to the forest floor, with one toe still in my garden. I snatch two pine needles, and before I bring them back over the wall, I lay them flat in my hands and I whisper the words I'm only just remembering, the words the lady taught me all those years ago.

The needles shimmer; my hands sting, sharp, under them. Between one blink and the next, the needles draw out long and strong, the same as the ones the lady keeps tucked into her dress. She doesn't say a thing, not as I call them into being, not as I pull them across into the garden, and they don't shrink, they don't disappear into nothing. They dim in the twilight so that they could be taken for any old knitting needles. But I can feel it still, the humming power spiraling down their lengths.

"Tulip," says the lady, "don't do this. There's only more danger for you there, only more heartbreak. Come with me, back where you belong."

I slip the needles into my waistband, next to my Gramps's note. "Maybe when I'm finished, I'll follow you," I say. "First I've a vengeance to take."

"We will be coming for you," says the lady.

"You can try," I say. "You've not had much success just yet."

"No," says the lady. "I mean that every one of us will be coming after you."

There's a coldness in her voice, a low note I don't remember hearing before. I'm almost frightened, hearing it. I back up from the wall. "There's not a thing you can do," I say, "without me letting you."

"You are not like the others," the lady says. "We will do everything we can to bring you home."

She's looking at something behind me, something in the garden, and she's backing away into the woods. I hear, before she disappears, as though she's speaking straight into my head, *You can run, little Tulip, but not forever. Someday you will be ours.*

"Lady?" It's the Lord of Ontrei, coming toward me through the garden, calling out.

"My lord," I say, going to meet him. He stands tall on the garden path. I look up at him, calm, certain. I see again how handsome this one is, with his dark hair, with his sharp eyes. He's looking all mournful at me too, no doubt hoping I'll believe he sympathizes. I say, as straightforward as I can, "You'll be wondering what my plan is now, what I'm thinking of doing without my Gramps."

His voice is measured. "There's only one thing you can do, considering the king's current state of mind."

"That will be marrying you and coming to court."

I wait through his surprise. "Yes," he says at last. "Though I understand the idea is distasteful to you."

I don't answer that. Instead I say, "You mentioned something of an alliance."

"An alliance is always strengthened by family ties."

"Any alliance is better than none at all, I'd think. Especially when your ally is the king's only heir."

There's a silence again, and I can feel the flowers shuddering still, but I can feel my needles thrumming, too, and it eases me, sets my mind to its purpose.

The lord says, "What would you expect out of such an alliance?"

"That you'd have my back while I'm at court. That you'd support me in front of the other lords if the king took an idea to move against me."

"And what would you offer in exchange?"

"When the king is gone," I say, "there'll be many lords thinking on what they did while he was still around, regretting things, no doubt. I guess there'll be time enough then for offering rewards to those loyal to me."

"I see."

I reckon he does. It's a dangerous game we're playing, him and me. We'll both be hoping for things we've no way of guaranteeing. Could be he'll step away right now, leave me to figure my own way out. Could be it's not worth the risk for him.

But the next minute he says, "It's growing late. Don't you think it's time the king was told you'll be coming to court?"

And he's offering me his arm—me, with my old ragged dress and my dirt. I take it, holding my needles in place with my other hand. We walk through the garden, around the hut. I've nothing I wish to take with me. Just my Gramps's drawing, and the needles, and the memories of the woods burning a fire through me, telling me things that make me think I've a power greater even than the king, goading me on to use it, to finally bring him down.

Out front, the lord unties his horse from the porch railing and he lifts me up across the saddle before hopping on behind. And then we are stepping away from the hut, past the bushes, up the hill. The stars are coming out, and I imagine my garden glowing, our windowpanes sparkling in their light. But before long we've come out onto the road toward the city and are cantering north through the meadows, and I'm looking only straight ahead, never turning round to see what I'm leaving behind.

PART TWO

 HERE ARE a thousand stories about how the first dragon died, leaving the woods to shrink in on itself, leaving the humans, us, to blink in the open sunlight for the first time, and to plant crops, and to build cities, and to feel safe from all manner of luring voices.

There are a thousand stories.

Some ways it's told, a brave young knight searches out the dragon in his lair and chops off his head, chip-chop, just like that, and it's done.

Too simple, that one, I think.

Some ways, a brave young maiden lets the dragon carry her away, and just when he's fallen asleep, she slips a poison twixt his jaws, and he shrivels up and dies there while she watches, and it's done.

Too unlikely, that one. Where'd she have gotten the poison after the dragon took her away? And what chance of a human poison working on a dragon anyway?

Dragons, they're not killed by swords or poisons.

Takes something else entirely to worm its way in past a dragon's tough skin into a dragon's heart. Takes something else to burn it until it screams from agony. Takes something stronger, something truer, something much more terrible.

Something like a wish. Something like a dream that comes back again and again, every night, every morning before you wake, one that flits at the edge of your great dragon eyelashes all through the day, something that consumes you, scale by scale and tooth by fang, until you're nothing but it, nothing but the pain, the unflinching, unyielding reality of this yearning, this dream.

Some say the dragon took one girl too many from the woods to his cave, and one day he fell for his latest catch, not with a momentary passion, a passing infatuation with her beauty. No, this was deeper than the dragon cared to admit; this was something different. When this girl laughed, the dragon's mouth turned up. When she cried for her parents, his own eyes welled up and his tail quivered with her pain. When she spoke, begging for his mercy, he scarce could keep his lungs breathing for the sound of it, and when she sang herself lullabies to drown out her rising fear, his blood near froze and all the fire in his belly fell to ash from his yearning to be nothing but a pair of ears, nothing but her song.

Could be she realized, before the end, how the dragon loved her. Could be she told him she loved him, too, whether she did or not, thinking maybe he would let her go.

He didn't.

When she died, the dragon lost his mind, these stories say, and dreamed only of her, night and day. And before another week had passed, the dream had killed him, and his woods and all their magics retreated silently before human axes and human tears.

TWO

"MY GRAMPS is dead." That's what I say when the guard at the gate leads me all the way into the castle, through corridor after corridor lined with carpets and tapestries and great flaming lamps, to where the king is sitting up with his wife and a dog in a plush firelit room. It is the first time I've seen such a place. The chairs have velvet covers. The fire is as big as the great round table, which is so polished it reflects the flames. Even the dog shines bright, lifting one droopy eyelid my way, already nodding back off to sleep moments after the guard shows me in.

I've come alone. Once we reached the city, the Lord of On-trei left me in a silent square, its fountain gleaming in the moonlight, and I made my own way from there to the castle gate. We've no need to let the king know of our alliance just yet.

"He died all alone," I say, "and I buried him in our garden, beneath the lilacs."

The king is frowning. His wife, the queen, is sewing something colorful in her lap, and she looks up at me now and again, quick little flashes of eyelashes and the whites of her eyes. She didn't greet me when I came in. Well, but then I didn't give her a chance to, neither. The king started to rise, but before he could say a word, I cut him off with the news of my Gramps's death.

"I am sorry, Marni," he says now. He even looks it, with that frown. He looks near as fretful as my Gramps. "You should have told us first. He *was* a king, and the father of a king. We would have given him a fitting funeral." He's forgetting not to meet my eyes again. He's forgetting he's only ever said four words to me.

"Thank you, sir," I say, as though I've no inkling how his heart must be singing to hear this. I grasp the needles hidden in my skirts, let their power run up my arm. I say, "But I've not come just to tell you the news."

"No?" says the king.

"No. I've come to ask you, sir, if I might find a place at your court, now I'm all alone."

The queen stops sewing and peers at me with her head half tilted. The king's face goes blank. "Ah," he says, and nothing more.

"Yes," I say. "I don't expect to keep a noble's position, but—I can sew and I can cook. I'll earn my place. I can't very well go back to our hut now my Gramps is gone. I know we've had our differences, sir, but it's one thing when I had someone to watch out for me. Who would keep me from harm there now?"

The king's blank look is growing dangerous. It'd be a stretch to say my Gramps could have fought off a squirrel.

I wait. I'm sure he's near to turning me out, calling the guards, but then the queen clears her throat with a little cough and looks up for real, folding her hands carefully on her knees. She gives me a pretty smile, all sparkling and bright. Despite everything, I blink at her. I don't think I've ever seen a smile quite that pretty. "Don't be ridiculous, dear," she says, and the air thins a bit. "Of course you'll stay with us, and you won't be working in the kitchens or any such nonsense."

The king says, "Now, hold on—"

"No, don't you say a thing, Roddy." She turns her smile on the king. "There's not much point in sending her back, is there? You were bound to bring her in someday. She's your niece, the only blood you have left. You couldn't leave her out there forever."

"No? And why not?"

She only keeps on looking at him, her hands still folded just so in her lap, as calm as anything—and after a few moments the king drops his eyes.

I'm astonished when he says, all quiet, "You say he died alone?"

Even hearing him say it, even from that voice I hate to bits — it makes my throat close up. I nod.

There's a long pause. I'm looking at the king, and the queen has her hand over his, and the king is just sitting there staring at his knees. He sighs. "I am sorry," he says again. "I wish it could have been different." He looks up at me, and I think for an instant that he means not only my Gramps's death, but a whole host of other things as well. There's something there, in the king's face. There's something dark and deep, a pain I'd hardly wish on anyone.

But this is the king, and I say, sweet but also sharp, "Don't trouble yourself, Uncle. You've always been so good at protecting us. Me and all my kin." That's all I say, but he knows what I mean. The pain dissolves into something harsher. It's hatred, pure, undiluted after sixteen years, and I reckon what's on the king's face is on mine as well. It hovers there between us, a near-tangible thing. I'm fingering the needles in my skirts again. I'm wondering how fast I could knit myself a vengeance, throw it at the king's throat.

But then he breaks the gaze and leans back in his chair. "I *am* sorry, Marni, for your Gramps's death. Whether you believe that or not, it is true. And you're welcome to stay in my castle. Your aunt is right. I had been thinking in any case of . . . keeping a closer eye on you." He reaches out for a glass of wine on a side table, swirls it as he says, "Where were you, anyway, that he could have died alone?"

My mind goes blank in an instant. There are a hundred

excuses I could make. Selling flowers in the villages. Paying a call to a farmer's family. My Gramps never came along with me farther than our garden. But I can't think, and I say, "Out back. I was out back when it happened."

"Out back," the king says slowly. He takes a sip, sets the glass down again. "Would that have been in the garden—or farther back still?"

I don't answer him. He already knows. He knows where I was; he knows what sort of thing I was talking to. I wait for him to say it.

But he doesn't. Instead, he turns to the queen. "I suppose you know where to put her."

"For the moment," she says. She makes a move as though she means to rise, then stops when the king raises a hand.

"Be advised, my girl. I won't tolerate anything that endangers my kingdom or my people. Not for a moment." He holds my gaze again, a long, hard time. Then he waves the hand my way. "Go on, both of you," he says.

And then, quite suddenly, the queen is standing, somehow sliding her sewing gracefully and easily into her seat as she does so. She comes over to me and takes my arm, leads me past the unmoving guard at the door and out into the hallway. I follow, unresisting, keeping my needles hidden from her with my free hand.

I am shaking. The king's last question has frozen my mind, it seems. The queen is pulling me down the hall, up a wide staircase. My feet are sinking into the carpets, and the lamps are casting an orange glow everywhere, over my very thoughts. I feel the brush of a breeze through darkened woods, and I shiver. For an instant, the lights from the lamps are the lady's glowing eyes, and the carpet is a soft, deep moss.

When I blink myself back, the queen is still tugging me along. She takes me to the left at the top of the stairs and down another hall, around a bend. A square block of light falls from an open doorway ahead. We stop when we reach it and look in at a wide fireplace — not as big as the king's, but nearly — and a small round table and a small carved chair and the largest bed I've ever seen, with a little dark-haired maid tucking in the sheets.

"Good," says the queen. "It's ready." The maid straightens at her voice, dropping a curtsy. "Sylvie, this is the king's niece, the princess Marni. She'll be needing a room; this is as good as any for the moment." The queen peers up at me. I have an inch or two on her. She has a round face and that dazzling smile that lights up sparks in her eyes. "We'll get you somewhere nicer soon," she says.

I shake my head at that. "This is nice."

"Yes, but somewhere *nicer*." She looks close at me, sighs. "Oh, my dear. I know this is all terribly new to you, and you've just lost the person you loved most in the world. But really, in some ways it's for the best. He wasn't going to live forever. And you're growing into a lady. You can't do that as a flower girl. It's time that you came home." She nods then, once, and takes off down the hall again. Home. Seems there are hordes of folks wanting to tell me where I might find that. This particular home comes complete with a bedroom twice the size of Gramps's and my hut, and an eager new aunt, and a maid who is curtsying again, calling me *lady*.

And the queen had called the king *Roddy*.

It is as much as I can handle for the moment, never mind the lady in the woods wanting me to run off with her, never mind the king with his sharp questions or his pretty wife. I can't keep my thoughts steady anymore, with all this soft light, with the little maid chirping round my heels. I only just manage to slide the needles and my Gramps's note beneath the mattress while the maid's not looking. And then she's gone, and I'm tucked into that enormous bed, without Gramps, without even the moon to watch over me.

I turn my head to muffle my tears just as he used to do, and I cry until it feels there's nothing left of me, and then I sleep.

That's how it begins, everyone pretending I'm a princess.

It starts that night after the queen leaves me, and my new little maid is calling me *lady* and waiting on me, and there's nothing I can do to stop her, because I can't think of what to say. And it continues the next day when that same maid, Sylvie, shows up moments after I've woken, carrying a tray heaped with food. There are eggs, steaming in a pile, and sugared toast, and spicy sausages, and a bunch of ripe raspberries, big, round tame ones, not like the little things I snitch out in the woods. I'm marveling at them, at how such a perfect taste could exist and I never knew it, and when she's taken away the dishes, I'm so full and dizzy with the strangeness that I let her brush my hair, for hours it seems, until it's a bright russet color it's never been. She buttons me into a deep green satin dress that sets off my hair. It holds my shoulders just so, and other parts of me as well, so that I'm twisting this way and that, trying to figure out a new way to breathe.

And then the queen comes round in a sparkling silver gown. She peeks in through the door, shooting that smile at me where I'm sitting on the small carved chair. Sylvie slips away through a door near the fireplace that must lead to her quarters or the kitchens. "You look marvelous, dear," the queen says.

I know I ought to thank her, but I'm still dizzy with it all, and I barely manage an answering smile. She bustles on into the room, patting down a crease on my bed, rearranging the little statues of animals lined up along my fire's mantel.

I push through my haze to frown. "There's no need to watch over me," I say. "I'm sure you've a thousand things to do, and the king will be wanting you for breakfast or some such."

"Oh, no," the queen says. She doesn't pause in her straightening, meddling, shifting, and her voice gets even brighter. "He left early this morning."

"For what?" I say.

"Ah," says the queen. "I'm not entirely sure. Something to do with the woods. Well!" She straightens up tall, as tall as she can, and quirks an eyebrow at me. "No doubt your uncle will be back before long, and meanwhile, I'll take you down to court!"

She sweeps out into the hallway as if certain that I am just behind, and after a brief, unsettling moment when I'm sure the world is about to roll up underneath me and spill me over, I take a deep breath and follow.

By *court*, it turns out she means the main hall of the castle. It's lined floor to ceiling with great glass windows, and there's a gigantic fireplace taking up one whole corner. There's not much to furnish it—no tables or couches or such. But it's not for lounging, is it? It's for grand events, and for the lords and ladies to meet and talk, to scheme and gossip.

When we walk in, there are a dozen of them there already, and they turn their heads at once to look our way. These are the same ladies who came down to buy our flowers, time after time. They are the same lords, some of them, who stared at me with hungry eyes as I grew. Then, they were a procession of colors and silks and bright false laughs—I knew their faces, but I never bothered with their names. Now the queen introduces them to me, and they bow and curtsy, calling me *lady*. There's the beautiful dark-haired Lady Elinor and the grumpy-looking Lady Flan, who grasp each other's arms as we turn away, already tittering over something. Lord Beau, who's not much younger than Gramps, is dripping in many-colored jewels, and he looks down his nose at me as he bows in a way Gramps never would have to anyone. Lord Lesting holds a handkerchief to his face as he greets me—the queen murmurs that he is perpetually sneezing, and means no offense by it. Lady Hettie is a round, bright-faced woman whose smile is like to split her face as she gives us her curtsy.

"Don't worry, dear," the queen says when we've greeted them all. "They'll be eager to introduce themselves again—and again and again—all day long. Their own princess—come home to them at last!" She squeezes my arm, her eyes shining at me. "Now, Marni, don't be shy! Make friends!" She reaches up to pat my cheek. "Yes?"

"Yes," I say at once, reflexively.

"Good," she says. "I'll check on you this afternoon." And then she's gone, and then they're all surrounding me, making more bows and curtsies, even kissing my hands, some of them, until I put an end to that by hiding my hands behind my back. I don't know what to say to them, but it turns out there's no need. They're happy enough to talk for me, the ladies fussing over my new dress, the lords going on about things I don't quite understand—rents and politics and such—all of them telling me over and again how sorry they are for my loss. Over and again, I can't think how to reply. It's not real, any of this. It's a dream, and tomorrow I'll wake in my old bed with my own tattered nightgown and my Gramps just across the room, breathing.

Four of the ladies soon enough pull me aside to one end of the hall. "You poor little thing," says one, a Lady Susanna. She's piled her hair in a mass atop her head—it looks ready to topple at any moment, and a few times I see her stabbing a pin through it. The others wear their hair down, in ringlets along their backs. The dresses of all these ladies are gleaming heaps of fabric, and their fingers glint with colorful jewels.

"Oh, yes?" I say. "And why would you say that?"

"Well," says another, the lovely Lady Elinor, "you've been holed up in that dreadful place for so many years, haven't you?"

"Oh, yes," says round Lady Hettie. "We all saw you there." The ladies nod at me; Lady Susanna's hair tilts dangerously to the left. "We wanted to do something, really we did."

"About what?" I say.

"About your *situation.*" The fourth, Lady Charlotte, says this in a hushed-up voice. She's holding my arm and looking this way and that, as if watching for eavesdroppers, though it's clear enough where the other lords and ladies are. "We were *just horrified* with how the king—with how you were stuck out there in that hut, digging in the dirt all day. When I think of your poor fingernails . . ." She's shaking her head mournfully, her mouth turned down and her eyes all worrisome.

"Yes," I say weakly, "my fingernails sure did suffer."

"Well," Lady Elinor chimes in, "and your hair, of course, and your hands from stitching all those rough clothes."

There is a murmur of agreement from Lady Hettie and Lady Susanna.

Lady Charlotte nods. "Yes, exactly," she says. "Now, the others will tell you that I myself wasn't yet at court when *all that* happened. You know what." She's making meaningful eyebrows at me. I nod, just as serious. "But I know what's right and what isn't. And a *princess,* in a hut like that, with only an old man for company . . ."

"He was the king," I say, maybe louder than I ought.

"Yes, yes, of course, dear," she says quickly, flicking glances around the hall. "Still, we know what's proper." The others all nod again, bobbing bright visions. "And you may believe us when we say that we did not approve. I mean that we did not approve *at all.*"

They're looking at me, staring, more like. They seem to expect something, and I've no porch wall to hide against and no Gramps to send them on their way. "I see," I say, and I try to make it all dripping with extra meaning, the way they do. "I appreciate that."

Thankfully, that settles them down. They fall back away from me again, smiling pleasantly.

"Well," says Lady Hettie, "who's up for a game of pins?" There's a general murmur of agreement, and the next thing I know, I'm sitting with a number of ladies on the wide castle lawns overlooking the river, watching the lords play.

"Do you ever play?" I ask Lady Susanna after a bit. She's managed to seat herself next to me simply by refusing to ever let go of my arm.

She laughs. It's sparkling, a bit like the queen's, but thinner. "Oh, no," she says. "I wouldn't want to get all hot and sweaty."

I peer over at the men. Seems to me they're scarce moving at all. Still, with these dresses and Susanna's hair, could be it's more taxing than it looks.

We have a luncheon there on the castle grounds. I feel all uneasy being waited on by the castle servants. I keep trying to help myself, though that draws sideways looks from the lords and ladies, and I stop after a bit.

And then when we're done, the queen comes by to take me into town to shop for dresses. We spend all afternoon poking through the city markets, looking for the finest cloth for new day dresses and evening gowns, summer skirts and ball gowns. Or the queen pokes, and asks questions of the storekeepers, and hands them piles of coins — and I trip along behind, watching, getting dizzier by the minute.

"But, Aunt . . ." I say when the sun is nearly set. She's asked me to call her "Aunt," and I don't see a way to object.

"Yes, Marni?" She's rubbing a piece of flowered cream muslin between her fingers, frowning at it.

"I'm not going to need all these dresses. Truly, Aunt — four ball gowns?"

"Better too much than not enough!" she declares. "Sir," she says to the storekeeper behind the counter, "are you *sure* this is the highest quality you carry?"

So I give up on that. It's her money, isn't it? Anyway, soon afterward we're marching back to the castle. The castle servants will bring up our purchases to us; we've only one bundle, a red satin dinner dress the queen says I'm to change into the moment we get back.

And then, at last, when Sylvie has buttoned me tight in that new shiny thing and gone away again, I get the chance to slip my needles out from beneath the mattress and look at them in the last of the light from the window.

They seem like any other knitting needles in the faint sunshine, though when I peer close, I can't quite say what they're made of. As I touch them again, it's as if another sense gets turned on, and my skin fizzles and my hair flies out at the ends. I think hard on what I want these for. I think hard on who I'm aiming to strike with every turn and every twist these beauties take.

There's the scent of him on the air. I tuck my needles into my skirts, into a clever pocket on the left side. I brush one finger along the bedspread, across the posts that hold the velvet canopy, and I look out the window, across the meadows to where the western woods shine dark beneath a red sun.

Then I slip through the door and go down to dinner.

All the courtiers are there — for the first time that day I see the Lord of Ontrei, a few tables away, though he doesn't look in my direction. The queen waves me over to her table, to the seat on her left side, and just as I sit down, the king comes in to join us.

Then the last of the rather pleasant dizzy fog, which has been following me about all day long, disappears in a sudden flash of cold. I watch the king come up close; I see the moment he sees me sitting at the head table, at his family's table. I see the jolt of something deep inside him, and how it takes that much more effort to walk to his chair and kiss the queen's cheek.

He's holding himself steady, smiling all about at his court, eating his mutton chops, but it's there, clear as day: the pain it gives him to keep on going when all the while I'm only two seats down and he has but to lift his head to see my face, the face of his sister, the straight back and stillness of his crippled father.

There'll be no joyful welcoming from this man. He avoids

meeting my eyes again all through that dinner, and as soon as he's finished eating, he pushes back his chair and returns to wherever he came from.

That night, alone in my room, when I bring out my needles and try to knit myself a vengeance, I find I scarce know how to hold them. The smooth cotton of my nightgown slips across my skin, alien. My window is shut against the breeze, and I can't even feel my legs, tucked under the soft quilts. The needles fit awkwardly in my hands, and they fit awkwardly in this room, and I can't remember the first stitch I'm to make, or think on what manner of thread I should be pulling from the fire or the air or — or maybe from the curtains draped around my bed.

I fall back at last and let them go for the night. I'm sunk into my mattress, near to swallowed up by my blankets and pillows, and there is such silence here, even more than there must be now in our old, lonely hut. There at least you could hear insects through the night and the wind rushing by on all sides and animals burrowing under the floorboards. Here there is nothing, only stone and fabric and more stone.

I hold my Gramps's note, tracing each letter until my finger knows their every curve and line, until when I close my eyes, I think I hear them, leaping from the paper to whisper in my ear in that voice I'll never know again: *My Marni, I'll love you always. Be safe.*

I'll learn the knitting. I've been sewing Gramps's and my

clothes all my life, and I reckon I can figure the right stitches for a vengeance if I put my mind to it. No doubt the queen and her ladies do needlework. I'll practice with them until I've relearned all I've forgotten, until these needles know my will, until they're nothing but tools for getting my heart's first wish.

VER THE NEXT few weeks I discover what life is like at my uncle's court.

There are buildings enough here to house all the ladies and the lords, and their children and their servants and their servants' children, and still to have room for dancing floors and dining halls and kitchens and stables.

The lords and the ladies spend half the day getting dressed and the other half tittering to one another, going for walks along the river, sinking deep in bows and curtsies if my uncle ever saunters by. The gossip here flows as free as air. They talk of my uncle and his barren wife. They talk of the woods moving in, and whether or not that is the villagers' and farmers' fault—

though where they got a notion like that, I haven't the slightest idea.

My uncle's attitude does nothing to keep them from seeking me out. We socialize in the main hall. I take tea with them sometimes or join a whole group for games and a luncheon out by the river again. They seem to expect me to laugh at their jokes; they seem to expect me to smile.

It seems they've forgotten the flower girl, the one who stands against the side of the flower man's hut and never speaks, and hardly looks at them. They think now that I've come to the castle, I'll be different. I'll play their court games, abide by their rules. I'll forget those years, the guilt in their eyes, their awkward questions: *How's our Tulip?* I'll forget digging for bulbs and shivering in the cold, tucked beneath too few blankets, sipping broth with too much water, hoping, only hoping that when Gramps got sick, he would recover on his own, because no one would come to help us, not when a death like that would make the king happy.

They don't talk of it, who I was before, and none of them even hints at a mention of my mother. It's as though she never was. As though she never walked these halls. As though she never wore dresses just like mine, and had a maid, and slept in a feather bed, and watched the geese on the river arrowing in from the north. As though they never fell all over her as they're now falling all over me.

The queen, especially, seems well and determined to

befriend me. She finds me at least once every day and takes me into town to buy more material for dresses, or walks with me about the palace grounds. When I am lucky, we sit by a window in her rooms and practice our needlework. She, at least, is a pleasant enough companion. She tells me of the countries beyond the woods, especially the country she comes from. She tells me things I've never heard before, not even in Annel's stories.

"Are you sure?" I'm asking her one day, almost a week after I've arrived. "It's just — I can scarce imagine such a place."

"I'm sure, my dear." We're knitting woolen hats for the children of the castle. We're in her sitting room, the same room where I found her and the king that first night. Even the same dog is here, sleeping in his spot before the fire. "Magic isn't viewed there as it is here. In my country, old superstitions have been replaced by carefully controlled powers, and a person who uses magic for ill is held to account by the highest judge in the land."

"You do have woods, though."

"Yes, some, the hard sorts of trees that can grow in our rocky dirt."

"And they leave you alone? The voices, the creatures — they don't lure away your girls?"

She puts down her needles and yarn and sighs. "Oh, Marni, in my country there is no fear of — of little people or twinkling lights. We've moved beyond the old myths of forests filled with sorcery. The power in our lands lies with the people, as it should, as it always will if we've the courage and the intelligence enough to grasp it."

I lower my own half-finished hat as well. "You don't fear magic, then."

"Not at all, not when it is used correctly. It can be a greatly useful tool. There is nothing inherently wicked or tempting about it. No more than any power."

"Your sorcerers use it without any urgings to run to the woods."

"Marni," she says seriously, leaning forward with her little hands tucked fast in her lap, "you needn't believe anything they've said about your birth. The woods are only woods. Your mother was only a frightened girl who did something she oughtn't have. *You* are only the king's long-lost niece, restored at last to your rightful place by his side. All else is nothing, a fairy tale, a country's collective imagination run amok. Hmmm?" She nods at me, and somehow I nod back, though I imagine I look somewhat odd with my mouth hanging open. She picks up her work with a quick little motion, shifts it into place between her fingers. "Let's keep on with these; we have ten more to finish by tomorrow."

I obey, swallowing my sigh. The dog is snuffling in his sleep, maybe dreaming of something tasty. The sun is high in the sky, so there's no danger of being called to dinner for hours yet. There's nothing quite as tedious as knitting children's hats, but at least it's good practice. I'm using my own needles, the needles I made; the queen doesn't know the difference, and they slide themselves into whatever shape I need, swiftly, quietly, so that she never notices.

While we're knitting, I listen to them, to the murmurs they send up through my skin. All this past week I've been remembering, slow but sure, how the lady taught me thus, to let the needles guide me, to feel that they are extensions of my fingers, doing my bidding as my true hands do. I murmur a song to them as we work, and it is an eerie, lilting tune, just as the lady used to sing. The queen shivers as she listens to it, but she doesn't tell me to stop. I even catch her murmuring along with me, adding a harmony, weaving a descant into my melody.

I'm not telling the needles to add in curses, not yet. I'm telling them to wait, wait. And to practice. The designs we make in our children's hats aren't as elegant or well stitched as the queen's bright patterns, but they're the sorts of designs that could easily contain a spell. Looking at them sends my head spinning off into places I half remember, and when I close my eyes against their twists and turns, I hear the far-off echo of a cry, the sort of cry that makes my bones shudder and my shoulder blades twitch, as if hoping for wings.

It's not just with the queen and her pretty yarn that the needles and I practice.

Soon after I've arrived, the queen moves me to a tower room, a suite really, filled with inch-thick rugs and rare oaken desks and chairs. She says it's a room meant for princesses, and though she doesn't say it straight out, I think she means my mother lived here once. My bed could fit eight village lasses, and my fireplace seems as if it could warm the whole castle. From my window I can see all across the land: past fields and villages, all the way to the mountains, which are orange now, and red and gold and every shade of brown.

At night, when the lords and ladies start yawning and crawling up the stairs, I go to this room, and after Sylvie's changed me into my nightgown, I sit up before the fire and stare into it until I can see how it weaves together, the separate flaming strands.

I think as little as possible, and I reach out a hand to grasp these strands, pull them out straight and thin. I wrap them around my needles. I listen to them murmur, and they listen to me sing.

We knit a thing with wings and a beating heart and six sharp talons. It roars and leaps away from us, across my room, out through the window. It flies off, always north, and always I watch until I cannot see it shrinking against the mountains. It's not a vengeance yet, just a creature of flame, and I reckon it flaps itself into nothingness before it reaches the woods.

I am not sure who I am on these nights. Part of me is that creature, the one I've knit from fire and song. It's flying free, as I long to fly free. It's sweeping through the air, as bright as a dream, and it knows nothing of mothers or Gramps or any king.

It's my father in me, I guess, though *father* is such a people word, and that thing — that fire, that longing — is everything people aren't.

And the other side of me, the side that puts her hands on

the windowsill and feels the indents of other hands, from years ago, and hears another sigh from another girl who watched these same mountains — that side wants only to stay forever, to feel close to that other girl, to know her in a way I never will.

That part turns from the window when the thing has gone, searching through the trunk against the wall, reading the spines of the books above the fireplace, and lying in bed wondering about that girl. I never find anything in the trunk but my own clothes, and the books on the shelf are only the ones the lords and ladies hand to me as gifts, and all my wondering solves no mysteries.

Then, just before I fall asleep, the two parts come together in a fiery rage at the man who took that girl from me, and I'm certain again of who I am and what I'm doing here and how delicious it will be when the many-taloned thing looks up at me and sees the purpose in my eyes, and screams, and goes at last to take our lovely prize.

But the king is gone more often than not since I've moved in, and I would have little chance to send my magic his way even if I had figured out how to knit my vengeance. He rides around the kingdom, chopping down the advancing trees. He takes some lords with him, the ones who've learned to do more than gossip and scheme. Always he takes the Lord of Ontrei.

As one week turns to two, and two to three, I never once trade words with that lord. He comes with the king whenever he rides in, and he talks to the other nobles, sure enough. It's not as though I'm seeking him out, but I do wonder at the way his face never turns my way. I know now what it means that the Lord of Ontrei has offered me his hand. There are three great noble families: Cavarell, from which the disdainful Lord Beau has bought his way to the top; Handon, led by a tottering old man twice the age of my Gramps who scarce can hear a word these days but nonetheless kicks his many grandchildren from here to the woods and back; and Ontrei, the oldest, most powerful house, the house the king keeps at his right hand always, the house he trusts above all else.

I know the lord's name now, his own name: Edgar. And I know how the other lords and ladies speak of him: in hushed tones, not from fear, but from respect. Three years ago, a rare company of bandits found their way through the mountains, down the solitary road to our fields and villages, and laid waste upon the farmers and the townspeople. Edgar of Ontrei, whose holdings are in the north, led a host of soldiers against them, and him only nineteen. He slaughtered them to a man.

In a country like ours, where there's little risk of war with other nations, such an act carries everlasting honor.

I needn't explain, no doubt, how the single ladies dream of him, nor how the gossip turns his way more than his fair share.

When the king is in, the lord trains with his own men in the empty fields across the river, and the courtiers on the castle banks sit on blankets and wear their gloves and hats, braving the chilling wind to catch sight of him fencing or wrestling or riding in formation with his soldiers.

I don't join them. There's some would say I'm a foolish girl not to fall for him now that I know his status. He offered me help before anyone else; he talked in the dead of the night of protecting me, of seeing me through all these changes; and some would say I'm downright dumb not to seek him out, not to tell him I'm of a mind to marry now.

In truth, though, the thought of giving him his kingship, of spending my days fluttering like these ladies, of carrying my uncle's wife's glittering smile — it makes my throat close up, and I long to dash for the woods, and take the shining hand of the lady there, and run and run.

Still, as the weeks go by and the bushes around the castle turn brown and then bare to the wind, I'm settling more and more into my uncle's court. Every night I stitch away, trying to make a vengeance, but every night there's something still missing from my creature, some breath, some purpose. I keep on with it, but I'm giving it up earlier every night. With my uncle scarce around to remind me of my intention, and all the comforts of his court to turn me soft and slow, I've not the same will for it that I did when I arrived.

Well, and I've not the same misery, either, have I? My Gramps's absence is a jagged hole inside, deep and unhealing, but the lords and ladies are pleasant enough — and in truth, I look forward to seeing the queen each day. For all that she's my uncle's wife, I've come to like the small, bright woman.

I think sometimes that she was lonely before I arrived. She

doesn't speak at dinner, except when the king or a noble says something to her first. She flits around the court with the ladies, laughing and being witty, but she's not best of friends with any.

And one chilly day when we're out walking in the meadows on the far side of the river, she says, out of nowhere, "You know, Marni, you shouldn't expect that everything will become rose petals and rainbows when you are queen."

We're bundled up against a cold breeze. The last dregs of warmth have slipped away overnight, and we're left a bitter, hard day. I smile at the queen. "I don't expect nothing, Aunt."

"Anything."

"I don't expect anything. I don't expect even to become a queen."

She laughs, her usual tinkle. "Oh, it'll happen, Marni. It might seem centuries away, but one day you will wake up, and without you quite knowing how it happened, it will have slipped up on you. There it will be: all you've been dreaming of, everything you've worked for. Some of it will be marvelous. The dresses, for instance — not to sound coarse, my dear, but the dresses you will *love*." She looks down fondly at her own cloth-of-gold afternoon gown. Half the queen's wardrobe is cloth of gold. "Oh, and the pageantry, and the feasts, and the banter of the court." She waves her hand about, smiling knowingly.

"But you must prepare yourself to endure some disappointments. There will be long hours when you've almost nothing to do but sit and feel useless. There will be the gossip — there is always gossip; it doesn't matter who you are, but it stings more when it is your sworn subjects who are doing the gossiping. And there will be times, you know, when you will be at odds with your king, with whomever your uncle decides you are to marry." She's perfectly serious now, holding on to my arm and looking close into my face. "You will marry someone kind, Marni, I can make sure of that, but that doesn't always solve everything, does it? Your uncle is kind to me, but it doesn't solve everything."

I can think of nothing to say to this. She believes every word, I can see it by the way she looks at me so steady. But my uncle, kind? *He stood over the body of his sister*, I think of saying, *with her blood upon his sword.*

This is the woman who believes there is no dragon, no griffins, no magic of any sort in our woods. Even when her husband rides out to battle back the trees that creep overnight into the streets of a village, she laughs at them all and decides they have lost their minds and forgotten the shape of the world.

If she believes that my uncle is kind, who am I to tell her it's not so?

"You'll have a wonderful time," she assures me. She lifts her nose to sniff the air. She's like me in that way, wanting to get every last sensation out of the wind, the grasses, the dried-up wildflowers. "Only be warned that it won't *all* be butterflies and diamonds."

Because she has been kind to me in truth, I smile at her and say, "If you are what a queen is, Aunt, I'll count myself honored, and I won't complain none."

"Complain *at all.*"

"Yes, I won't complain at all."

"You're a good girl, Marni. Now," she says, cheerful again, "shall we finish our walk and go back in for tea? Roddy will be coming home for the winter festivals in only a few weeks, and wouldn't it be a nice surprise to have your first embroidered pillow ready to show as he walks in?"

Yes, I am thinking as I follow her away, *and won't it be a nice surprise to have my first knit vengeance to present him with, too?*

But for whatever reason, the thought doesn't give me the same sharp thrill that it usually does. There is a light snow beginning to fall, the first of the winter season, and far in the distance the mountains are gray and black, bare and stark, ready for the cold.

IT'S ONLY A FEW days after that walk with the queen when the lords begin to remember themselves, remember that I'm not just some waif the king brought home to raise, and I'm not just a princess, neither.

I'm a girl.

I'm a girl the right age for marriage, and there are plenty of single men at court wanting something more from life. Wanting a kingship, maybe.

Not that they say it like that. I'm taking my usual morning stroll along the river—there are several of us out today in the lukewarm sun—when the little Lord Bran makes the first attempt. He's only a year younger than me, so not that little, but he struts more than walks, and his skin is smooth-soft, and he's never seen the things I have seen in the woods or thought the things I have thought late at night, with the moon looking in on me and Gramps and all the future that was taken from us pulling the breath from my chest. So he's little in his way, and he comes over to me as I'm going along and starts out with some general chitchat about the king, who's off now to chop at the trees that have been creeping in from the east.

Then, as we reach the bridge over the river, all of a sudden he stops and grabs my hand. He's looking at me with eyes so round and pleading, and he puts my hand to his lips with fervor, near trembling. In my shock, I don't think to pull away; no man's ever kissed me before, except my Gramps. This lord's lips are cool and dry. "How lovely you are today, my lady," he says, low and intense.

I pull my hand back; he resists for a moment but then lets it go. "You scarce know me, my lord," I say.

"I know what I need to know. Your every movement, your every word speaks of your beauty." He makes a grab again for my hand, but I've stepped back and out of his reach. He moves toward me; I step back again. The other nobles out this morning have gathered in twos or threes, talking and watching us, every one of them.

"Does the king know you are speaking like this?" I doubt my uncle wants a boy like Bran for his son-in-law.

"Does he need to? I speak for you alone. The king does not hold the key to my heart." And then he is kneeling there on the cold, damp ground, even clasping his hands before his chest, his eyes cast up at me dramatically. "Tell me I may hope, my lady. Tell me I may dream of knowing you better."

I am sure there are rules for this sort of thing. I am sure if I'd been raised at court, I would know how to handle this, how to refuse him without offense, without making an enemy of his family or any such thing. They are all watching me still, waiting for me to — what? Jump into the arms of the first lord who offers for me? The first lord as far as they know, anyway. "It's kind of you to say those things," I say at last.

"No kindness, lady, when I speak but the truth."

"Yes. Well. I appreciate it, still. But you haven't the slightest hope, I'm afraid. You'll always know me as much as you do now, and that'll have to be enough for you. Good day." I turn and start off toward the castle, hiking up my skirts as much as the queen would approve of and stepping as quickly as I can in my slippers and stockings.

It isn't fast enough, though, because Lord Bran is up and in front of me before I go ten paces. "This isn't the end," he proclaims. "I will prove to you, lady, the sincerity of my affections. You will see what I can offer you; you will come to my way of thinking by and by." His eyes are flashing now, not with passion, but with anger. I suppose it's not pleasant to be rejected in front of the king's whole court.

"Good day, Lord Bran," I say again, firm. He stands there in my way for five seconds more, and then he bows out of my path. I lift my skirts, not caring now what the queen would say of how high, and I sweep up to the castle and spend the rest of the day until dinner in my rooms, away from them all.

After that, it seems the whole population of single lords reckons they'll try their chances with me. Most are less pushy than Lord Bran. They bring me flowers as I'm walking about, or they kiss my hand upon taking their leave of me, or they pull out chairs for me when I'm wanting to sit, those sorts of things. None of the others makes a declaration. None of the others goes down on his knees. But they want to, they're telling me with every look and gesture. I've never had so many people all wanting to talk to me at once, all laughing at my every joke, all so attentive.

It puts me off my ease.

The queen knows what's going on, sure enough. She tells me once, as we're walking together from the main hall to dinner, that I'd better go ahead and pick one before the king decides to pick one for me. I know that's how it works. I know she hadn't met my uncle before she married him, and she went right along with it anyway. Hers was a political marriage, mostly. Her country's the one we get our wood from, carted over the mountains on wagons. No one here would dare go into the woods to cut down a tree for lumber to build a house. And we send her people grain and seeds. Theirs is a dry, lowland country, not covered over every inch with rich black soil and fields of crops like ours, but sandy and rocky all the way down to the sea.

She's told me of the sea—as far-reaching as our woods, blue some moments, green or black the next, always moving, except on still days when it spreads out as flat as glass. Her people catch fish in the sea; they go out in big wooden boats, and times are they get themselves lost in a storm and don't come back. Very like our woods in that way, I tell her. Both the sea and the woods are like to swallow people up.

She doesn't say a thing when I say that, of course. Still blind to our magic, is the queen. But she does get a look on her face when she's talking of her country, of the way the waves roll in and in, of how you can see the clouds coming from miles away.

She loves it, sure as sure, in much the same way that I love the silence of the woods, their dangerous beauty. And still she doesn't complain that it's so far from her. When they told her to get on her horse, she rode away and never looked back.

I'm not as willing to put up with such nonsense, though, and more and more I find myself walking off on my own, over the meadows to the north or around the castle gardens.

There's a garden of flowers on the eastern side of the castle, past the vegetables and the chicken houses, right as the hill begins to rise toward the horse stables. I didn't stop to look the first time I saw it. Just a whiff of dying aster, just a glance at a larkspur stalk, and my eyes start burning, and I can't blink away the shape of my Gramps, standing in the flowers, digging holes for stakes, and looking up to smile at me.

One day, though, I pass the flower garden when a girl is in there working. The queen has let go of me for the day. I finished embroidering my first pillow this afternoon — it's sloppy enough, and I reckon my uncle wouldn't be all that proud even if he did care about such things, but the queen says it doesn't matter. I finished it, and that's the important thing.

I've the rest of the day to myself, and as soon as I can manage, I run from the lords' daft smiles and the stale air of the castle out to the shriveled grasses and the brisk wind.

I'm glancing over the flower garden on my way past, thinking on how ours must look now, with no one to care for it, and I notice the way the girl working in there is holding her pruning shears, and I stop. She's got such a look on her face, as if she's certain that the whole plant race has it in for her. I start to laugh despite myself, and after a moment I give in and make my way toward her.

It isn't anything like our garden down at the hut, this castle thing. Each flower has its own square block, and the roses go all together in one section, and the petunias in another, and they haven't been planted for color or scent or nothing. Just higgledy-piggledy, this castle garden. Well, and I guess if they wanted a better one, they came down to our hut to walk our paths. I wonder if this ugly cousin of a garden has wilted out of competition with ours or if it's always been this boring.

The girl looks up as I come by. She is trying her best to snip the old blooms off a thorny rosebush — not easy without good gloves and a sharp pair of shears and knowing the way of those thorns. "Lady," she says, sinking into her curtsy.

I hold out my hand for the shears. "Give those here," I say. "Have you done this before?"

"No, lady," she says, wary. "It's my job, though, and I don't mind doing it."

"Never said you did. Here." I gesture again, and she hands them over, frowning.

"It isn't right," she says as I test the blade with my finger and eye the rosebush. "It's not a job for a princess."

Crazily, I grin at her. There's something moving now through my blood, something that's been slowing through the last few months and had near stopped. The flowers are perking up all about, even as brown and dry as they are, to sense that something moving in me. "Only recently it was that I became a princess," I say. "And truth be told, I'm not sure what the job entails. Pruning flowers, though, that I can do."

Bit by bit I bend the thorns into shape, and bit by bit I show the girl what she is to do, and when I hand the shears back to her to finish up the job, she's talking and smiling almost as if I were one of her friends. Almost. Like the women from the village talked to me, kind and friendly, but with a reservation that never quite went away—all except Annel, of course.

Still, it is something better than the empty gossip of the court. I watch as she trims the last few stems, closes up the shears. It's late afternoon, and dinner will be served soon in the castle.

The girl is remembering, now, who they all have decided that I am. As she puts the shears into a pocket on her apron, she twitches her fingers this way and that, and her eyes dart for an escape. I ought to let her go. It isn't just the dinner waiting for me; girls who work in the castle aren't given time to dawdle, and she will be expected back soon.

It's so novel, though, to stand among flowers again and talk with a girl who wants nothing of me, and I say, "Won't you show me around the garden?" and what is she to do? Tell me no?

There isn't much to see this time of year, but she takes me past the drooping orchids and marigolds, the dried-up pansies and chrysanthemums. She's new to the whole gardening business, and sometimes she can't name a plant, but I know them all, and it doesn't matter. I trail a hand along their stems, speaking their names beneath my breath.

In the center of the garden, in among the tulips, of all things, there's a block of tiny, delicate blue flowers nestled in a bed of creeping vines. I stop dead when we come upon it, tasting something fresh, something wild on the wind.

"I didn't know they bloomed here," I mutter.

"They don't," the girl says, following my gaze. "Not usually. I remember all about *this*, at least. They never bloomed here before, not even this year until a few months ago. No one knows why, or anyway everyone has a guess: the woods coming in, the griffin they saw, and, of course, they appeared just when . . ." She trails off.

"Just when I arrived," I guess.

"Lady—"

"No, don't fret yourself." I'm not meaning to, but somehow I reach down to touch a petal anyway, to make sure it's real. The sweet scent of rain drifts out. I blink, and the lady's bright eyes flash, and half a note of her song brushes my ears. "What griffin did they see?" I say, turning from them.

"Lady?"

"You said they saw a griffin. Where? Who?"

"It was all through the castle," she says, "how the king's army went north and how the Lord of Ontrei, as he was standing guard one night with a soldier on the edge of the woods, looked out over the trees, and there, feathers glinting in the moonlight, a griffin flew."

All through the castle, she said — and yes, I'm sure everyone would have heard this news. Almost everyone, that is. It seems the lords and ladies are better at keeping things from me than I would have thought. After all, there are new stories every day of the woods, and the courtiers have never seemed reluctant to pass them on to me. I hear that the king himself has been rolling up his sleeves to work alongside his men, and that the villagers and the farmers and the country nobles, too, join in with the army. I hear that at the northern edges of our kingdom, there are only the sharp thunks of chopping, and the grunts of the men and women, and a deep silence from the just-born woods.

"A griffin," I say. "I'd only heard it was phoenixes before."

"Yes, and they say it will be the dragon next, that he'll come and bring his woods and he'll never go back again."

"And here are his flowers," I say, "right on the king's castle grounds."

When I look down toward the castle, I see lights in the

windows. They'll be readying themselves for dinner, putting up their hair, spraying bits of scent.

The girl is eyeing me, her hands twisting in her apron. I wait, and she says, "Do you know what it is, lady, that's bringing them, the phoenixes and griffins and such, and that's making the woods close in on us?"

I shake my head. "I don't know."

"It's just — it seems no one actually cares. Everyone talks of it, sure, but the next moment it's gone clean out of their heads, as if it doesn't exist. And if the dragon's really coming, well, we'll all be sorry for it, won't we?"

She looks so concerned, so sure that something ought to be done about this, and sure that I am the one who'll know what to do. "In my experience," I say, "there's nothing we're better at than pretending things don't exist. We think if we pretend long and hard enough, the things will disappear." I shrug. "Sometimes it works. Sometimes it doesn't."

"Which one is this?" she says. "Will it work with the dragon?"

"How many times did the gardeners try to dig up the dragon flowers?"

"Every day for a week," she says, "and every morning they'd regrown themselves overnight."

I look at them, so delicate, so fragile. "I think this is like that," I say. "We can push it out of our heads again and again, but it won't make no difference in the end. The woods will keep

on coming. The dragon will appear. We'll walk half blind, thinking we're safe, and one day we'll turn and he'll be there, right
beside us, waiting."

Now the lights are starting to flicker *off* in the castle, and
I'll have to run if I want to get to dinner on time. "Don't worry,"
I tell the girl, maybe a bit belatedly. "The king's best men are
on the job." I smile, the bright smile of a lady. "Don't forget to
ask them to get you new gloves," I say. "Your old ones won't last
through the spring."

When the king comes home for the winter, he doesn't stop to
say hello on his way in through the main hall, where I've been
talking with the nobles and the queen, but he rushes on by, only
shooting me a glare so full of malice, so full of contempt, I ac
tually take a step backwards from it. He's come for the festivals,
the ones the castle throws before the start of the real cold and
the burying snows. The country nobles will be coming in soon
from their estates, riding up in sleighs and light carriages, filling
up the rooms in the unused wings of the castle. They'll go home
again at the end of two weeks, but the king will stay with his
men. There'll be no escaping them when the weather shuts us all
indoors, not unless I keep myself to my room and never come
out. The king may be hoping I'll do exactly that.

"My lady Marni."

I turn from watching the king sweep out the back of the
hall toward the stairs to his rooms. It's the Lord of Ontrei, Edgar, and he's bowing over my hand before I know what's what.

"My lord." I give him my best curtsy. The queen has followed the king, and the others around us bunch into their own separate groups. We are alone, or near to it.

He lowers his voice so far that I need to bend in to hear him. "You must not think I have abandoned you, lady," he says. "I wanted only to avoid it seeming as if I have spoken to you before."

He's so conspiratorial, with his half-raised eyebrow and those twinkling eyes, that just like that I forgive him for all those weeks of ignoring me, and I nod at him. "Makes sense, my lord."

"Now that the king has returned for the winter, I can pay you the attention we will need to justify our engagement in the spring."

It takes me a moment to react to what he's said, even in my own head. It's not just the sheer brazenness of it. He speaks as though I have no say in the matter. He speaks as though I agreed to this proposal last summer, rather than all but spitting in his face and kicking him off our porch with the heel of my bare foot. I try to steady myself, but my voice comes out loud and shaky anyway. "You must not have heard me right the last time we went at this, my lord. I would have reckoned you'd remember a thing like that, but I guess with an arrogance your size you've no room left for memories."

Now we're getting looks, sure as sure, and my every word will be passed around the court by morning. When the country nobles start arriving next week, it will be the first thing they hear.

The Ontrei lord has grown right still. He keeps smiling in

that blasted confident way, but his face has frozen too. Next moment, though, he slides back into action, giving me a bow and saying, loud and clear, "Forgive me, lady, for my impertinence. I will take myself away and bid you good night."

And then he is gone, and I'm left with a whispering court. When we all converge for dinner, the king doesn't even glance my way the whole time, and somehow it's been arranged that I'll sit at a table many places down from the royal family, among a whole slew of round, spoiled nobles' children and their grim-faced nanny.

I speak to nobody and pick at my meat, thinking of all the reasons I'd rather have the Lord of Ontrei for a friend than a sworn enemy.

That night I can't knit a stitch. The needles clack together; they scrape. I cannot bend them to the shapes I need them to be. I give up at last and go to bed, but I lie there sleepless, staring into the dark corners of my canopy, and I imagine myself as my mother, just the age I am, growing up in my Gramps's court.

She would have had a father who loved her, sure, and a brother who adored her, before she ran off anyway. There would have been dozens of lords all trying to win her, as they're trying now to win me. I wonder if she loved any of them. If there was a boy, maybe, that she'd grown up with, who'd known her before either of them understood things like princesses and kings, someone she trusted.

Maybe it wasn't a lord, even. Maybe it was a servant boy or

a villager, and she'd ripped herself ragged trying to think of ways for him and for her to be happy.

I don't know. There's no way I can know.

There was some reason, though, for her running off to the woods. Girls don't do that on a whim. They don't wake up one day, free of all care, get themselves dressed, eat up their breakfast, give their hair fifty brushstrokes, and then say to themselves, *Wouldn't it be nice to run away to the woods and never come back?*

Not even princesses think like that.

Maybe she was worn down by all the things they wanted her to be. Maybe my Gramps was different then, before he'd lost her, before he had a baby nobody wanted, before he became a nothing himself. She wouldn't have had a queen giving her the tips my aunt's been giving me. Her mother was dead long before she had grown, as she was for me.

If I ever have a baby girl, I'm going to run us away, over the mountains to the land with the rocks and the sea, and I'll find us a home there, where no one will come knocking who knows our names, who might want to take us through with a sword. When my baby girl cries, I'll be there to hold her. When she stubs her toe or skins her knee, I'll take her mind off it with stories, and I'll sing her to sleep with songs. I'll teach her how to plant flowers, though we'll grow them only for ourselves, and we'll bake sweet bread together and go for long walks and catch toads just to set them free, and she'll never have to stare up into the darkness wondering why she's all alone.

THIS IS WHAT it's like to ride a horse: terrifying, thrilling, fun in a way that flows right through me, pushing back all the parts I've been devoting to fretting and lying awake at night, throwing them out into the clear, cold sky, so that I laugh as we ride along, as if all I needed to feel this way was to get my feet off the ground, to give up my safety to this hulking beast that huffs and rolls beneath me, near to pitching me off, but I hang on, grinning, my skirts sweeping back all around and my boots tucked tight into the stirrups, fingers twisted in reins and mane.

I could do this forever and never tire of it.

The Ontrei lord is riding just behind me; I think he's somewhat startled by my taking to this horse-riding thing so fast, especially because when he told me where we were going, I said I'd never ridden my own horse in my life.

"No time like the present," he said, pulling me away from the flower garden. I'd been telling the girl I met there, Emmy, where the daisies should be moved in the spring — they had planted them next to the *buttercups,* as though any daisy could shine as it ought to alongside that garish yellow. I've been coming out almost daily in the last week to teach her how to ready the garden for the snows. The gardeners, the real ones who planted all the flowers to begin with, don't bother us none. They leave us be as we squat in the dirt, mulching and trimming and making notes of what to plant. I reckon they don't mind me training their new girl for them. Emmy is like a new bud in spring: fresh and honest, somewhat unknowing of the ways of things. I never met a girl like her out by the woods, but it could be that living so close to the trees changes a person, fills you up with a sense of danger you don't get in here, where the whole world's wide and open.

My maid, Sylvie, tsks to herself at the state of my gowns, but she doesn't say nothing to me about it. Could be she senses the spark — the something that runs through my blood after I've spent a day out with the flowers — that isn't there when I deaden myself chatting with the nobles for hours on end. Could be, too, that she doesn't dare complain to the girl who might one day be queen.

"I'll teach you to ride in no time at all, don't worry, lady," the lord said as we left Emmy still taking her notes and made our way to the stables. "I've been training soldiers how to ride since I was half grown."

Still, after he'd handed me up onto a gray mare, I needed no more help. Well, it didn't take brains to figure this out, did it? The stirrups were for the feet; the reins were for the hands; kick the mare to get her to go; lean back to get her to stop — but why would you want her to stop when you could fly like this across the meadows and the whole world was only wind and pounding hooves and grasses rushing by, hill after hill after hill?

I've seen horses and riders all my life, stepping their way down the path to our hut or racing into the castle yards with this or that message for the queen or the king. I never once dreamed it would be like this, as if the horse and I were working together to conquer every yard.

It's only when we've come to the end of the meadows south of the city, when we've gone so far we've reached the fields and villages near Gramps and my old hut, that I pull up, and the mare and I sit there, panting and sweating. Lord Edgar and his roan canter up beside us. They slow to a halt. His mare puffs noses with mine and stamps her feet. We're up on a hill, and we look out over the checkered countryside, brown and black now that the harvest's through, scattered here and there with white clumps of snow. Villages and nobles' great houses dot the valleys, and off to the west the woods stretch south, curving to the east. I shiver, seeing them so close. It's been almost three months now since I stepped in through those branches, felt their needles under my feet.

"You're a natural," Ontrei says. Blast him, he's barely breathing hard.

"Not much to it," I say. "Get her going and hold on tight." I can feel the smile cross my face, though. I can't stop it from sitting there, lighting up my eyes no doubt, and making me look all friendly and such.

"Twice now," he says, "we've gotten off on the wrong foot. Shall we call the past the past and start fresh today?" He's holding out his hand, waiting for me to take it.

I don't move a finger, and I only barely keep from laughing at how easy he makes it sound. Just shake hands and we'll trust each other, never worry about any stabbing in the back. Seems he's never heard my history with stabbing. "Is that why you dragged me out today? You're making sure I'm still up for that alliance?"

He looks down ruefully at his poor rejected hand, then brings it back to pat his mare's flank. "Yes, if you like. You've made it clear you're not interested in my proposals, but there's no reason we can't be friends, still, and allies."

"Hmmm." I look him over. He's truthful and eager in the morning sun, not a bit like the shadowy stranger on my Gramps's porch, nor again like the arrogant nobleman in the great hall yesterday. What sort of man changes day to day like that, as if he were cousin to the shifting winds, the blowing clouds? "Race you to that village." I point it out to him, check to make sure he's looked, and then take off before he can say anything.

I don't push my mare as hard this time, and once we're back

on the road that runs down from the city, I slow her further, to a quick trot. Lord Edgar pulls up alongside with an irritated look.

This time I do let myself laugh, right in his face.

He smiles, looking startled again, and nudges his mare on ahead, grinning over his shoulder. "Better hurry, my lady," he calls.

I kick, and we're off again, the dirt hard under the horses' stamping feet.

He's ahead, but I'm gaining, and my mare has a determination in her huffing, a straining in her gallop that makes me think she's with me on this one. I lean forward over her neck, giving her the control. We're almost there, his mare's hindquarters a hair from my horse's nose, and then I see the path leading off down the hill to the west, I catch a flash of the hut through the bushes, and I'm sitting up, pulling back on the reins before I know what's what.

My mare tosses her head at me, clearly unhappy at our sudden exit from the race. Edgar's realizing I'm not behind him anymore; he's looking back, pulling up, stopping. Before he can call out, I've turned my mare around and we're on our way down the hill.

Lord Edgar catches me up as I'm dismounting in the yard before our porch.

He leaps to the ground as well and steps in front of me, his roan following his lead. "Marni, we shouldn't be here," he says, all serious.

"Shouldn't we?" I sidle around him to tie my mare to a bush; she's happy to munch on its leaves. "Seems to me this is the place they put me when they decided I shouldn't be any-where else. Seems they can't make up their minds if one day this is the only place I'm allowed, and the next it's the one place I can't go."

"I'm not disputing that," he says. "I know it's crazy. But you can't be seen here."

I climb the porch steps, not paying him any mind. Gramps's cane still lies there, getting soft with the damp. I rub its edge, and a layer of wood comes off on my finger. "Here's where we met, my lord," I say, as cheerful as I can manage. I don't mean to say it; I don't want to remember, but it's as though my Gramps's shape is there in that old chair, sitting at that selfsame table. He'd be scratching away at a sketch or sipping his cup of tea or looking out along the path up the hill and dreaming.

"Yes," Lord Edgar says. "I remember."

I pick up the cane, hefting it my hand. Great bits of it, rot-ten the lot of them, shed themselves and thunk onto the porch. I watch them fall, forcing my thoughts away. I look out at the lord. He's holding his horse, framed by our bushes, looking up at me all still, all worrisome, as if he knows my thoughts.

"We should go back, Marni," he says, and his voice is so gentle I near hate him for it.

"Funny thing," I say, "how there's times you call me lady, all respectful, and then there's times you think it's fine to call me by my first name. No explanation, neither, no apology, as though we've known each other all our lives — or as though you didn't think me a real lady. Do you think me a real lady?"

"If I've offended you —"

"I'm not," I say. I let the cane drop down the steps, thunk, thunk, rolling onto the grass and stopping a few feet out, another branch among the leaves. "I'm no lady, my lord. I'm no village or farmer's lass, neither. They called me a flower girl, times past, but they've got their own garden beside the king's castle, and it doesn't matter how little the gardeners know about flowers; there wasn't any need for another garden on the edge of nowhere. Wasn't any need for them to take themselves down here to spend their money when they had all they could want for free up there in their city."

"There weren't any flowers like yours."

I have to admit, he doesn't talk like the other courtiers. He talks straight and clear, as though he means the words. He stands tall and steady, too, looking at me all somber. He's seen battle, I remember that. He's not little inside, not like most of the lords up there.

"You wouldn't know." I laugh. "You never bought none."

I've surprised him again — third time today — and he gives me a smile. "You wouldn't remember, would you?"

I back up until I'm resting against the wall of the hut, just where I used to stay when Gramps had one of his visitors. "I remember," I say. "I never spoke, but I heard everything they said, saw every one of their faces, and the guilt they kept there, that drove them down to buy their flowers. I memorized them, you might say. You weren't one."

"Is that a strike for or against me?"

I shrug. "You got your strike when you sat right there"—I point to my chair, across from Gramps's —"and told my Gramps he better marry me off to you for his own good."

Well, and he doesn't say anything to that, does he? Not for all of a minute, almost, and I can see the thoughts flashing in his head, how he's going to keep me allied with him now. I wait until he stops looking at his boots and says, "Lady, I hope—"

"I'm going to see my flowers," I say, and I slip through the door into the hut.

I don't look at what's there. I don't want to think about how this place, where we told stories and laughed and ate, isn't ours anymore, how it's falling back into the earth. I haven't heard Dewdrop or the chickens since we came down; no doubt some villagers will have come and taken them for themselves. They're welcome to the animals — but I wouldn't expect they'd care enough to keep our old hut nice.

So I look straight ahead, and I go straight through our sitting room and the kitchen, out the back door and down the step, and then I'm there in the garden, back with the fading roses and the tangled heaps of thorns.

It's a few minutes before the Ontrei lord ties his horse up and makes his way around. I walk the rows, looking at it all. It doesn't bother me that this place has gone untouched. The flowers will fall to the ground; the ones that can will push themselves up again next year, and the ones that can't will go back to the worms and make food for the rest. Nothing sad about this. They're happy enough, the sleeping bulbs and dwindling stalks. They whisper greetings to me as I walk through, soft murmurs. It jumps me a little when I pass by the dragon flowers in the center and see that they've shriveled up, petals, leaves, and all. I spent so many hours hacking away at them, and now they've left on their own.

As the lord's picking his way around the hut—he doesn't go through like I did, which I appreciate—I go up past the well and the sunflowers, and then to the wall at the edge of the garden, and I look hard into the woods.

There's a voice that's been calling me since the moment we passed the turnoff to this place. It's grown stronger the longer we've been down here, and now, at the start of the trees, it's near shouting into my head.

"Marni, we should go back." The lord's hand barely touches my shoulder, and his voice is as soft as a breeze, careful. My fingers are tight against the wall's stone. I tell myself to relax, but it takes some will to lay them flat.

"What did I say about my name?" I say, as light as I can, but my voice is shaking; there's not a thing I can do about that.

"You didn't," he says, still soft, still careful. "You didn't say whether you liked it or not."

"I like it."

The voice wants me to follow it. It wants me to jump across the wall and run into the dappled places of the woods, where it will find me, where it will lead me on to things I can scarce imagine.

"They haven't moved here, have they?" I say.

"What hasn't moved?" But he knows what I mean. He's been following the king around for months, probably all year, for as long as it's been happening, at least.

I don't want to say it, so close. I turn my head, as if they won't be able to hear if I'm not looking at them. "The trees. They're moving in all across the kingdom, yes?"

He nods slightly. Maybe he can feel it too. Maybe he can hear it.

No. It wouldn't be calling someone like him. "But not here. They haven't moved an inch since I left for the castle."

"No," he breathes, agreeing.

"Doesn't that *bother* you?"

"Marni," he says, and now he's looking away from me, at something there, something under the branches. "I really think we should go now."

It's her. I know it's her. I've known it was her voice since I heard it, since I stopped my gray mare in our race for the village, since I recognized the tune, the words, the song we used to sing as we knit our gifts.

"You can see her?" I ask him.

He doesn't answer, but he doesn't need to. His eyes are as wide as coins; the hand on my shoulder is beginning to tighten.

I turn to face the lady.

She is beautiful. I've always thought she was beautiful, even when I was like to die from the horror of her, from the nothing-ness of her face, from the uncanny brilliance of her eyes. Her hand lights the corners of the woods, throwing shadows here and there, a playground of movement and hidden places, laugh-ing at me, inviting me to come, to explore.

The lord next to me stands frozen. He will not stop me if I go.

"Tulip." She says it in a way that says she knows me, every bit. She knows the thoughts in my head. She knows the itching in my fingers to launch me over these stones and leave things like castles and uncles behind.

Yes, I want it. I want to forget every sleepless night, to be-come a thing not swayed by human troubles.

I brush a leaf from the wall; I watch it fall. I think about go-ing over to talk to her. I could ask about my mother, and maybe this time she would tell me something of what happened to her in the woods. I could ask about my father, even, the nameless monster, the dragon I've met only in stories.

She holds out a hand to me.

And I near leave right then, never mind my magic needles back in the castle, never mind my uncle, never mind revenging my Gramps. I almost leap across the wall and run to that lady. But as I'm bending my knees, as my hands are pushing against the stone, the Lord of Ontrei's fingers tighten a bit more on my shoulder.

I stop.

I turn to him, and he's looking at me, and there's not just

fear there, and not just awe. Behind that, there's a sadness in his eyes, and I think, without knowing quite why, that he's sad for *me*. And I can't leave. That takes my very breath. That pulls me so firmly back into myself that I don't even look out at the lady again, but I take this man's hand from my shoulder and I lead him away from the wall, through the fading garden and into our old, cold hut.

The voice follows me there, of course, still murmuring its offers into my blood, but I ignore it best as I can, and I pile some logs in our blackened fireplace. I take the tinder still sitting on the mantel, and I build us up a grand fire.

I drag in the chairs from out on the porch, but they're near as bad as Gramps's cane, so I pull Lord Edgar down to sit next to me on the rug. Time was, Annel and I sat just like this, and as her words spun and twirled, rose and fell with those flickering flames, I imagined sorcerers riding big brown horses and women crying themselves into flowers.

It's not until the first log is burned half through that the lord stirs himself.

"You didn't follow her." He's not looking at me. He's looking into the fire; his lips are barely moving with the words.

I don't tell him how close it was. I don't ask about that sadness, neither. He hasn't looked my way since then, and I'm thinking maybe I imagined it. Instead, I say, "Did you expect I would?"

He doesn't answer.

"You think that was the first time she's called me like that?

You think she's never tried for me before?" I shake my head. "My Gramps never knew, so if you thought I'd never been to the woods, I shouldn't be surprised. But I went. I went every day, nearly, as long as it wasn't knee-deep snow." I don't know why I'm telling him this, except that I've never known anyone else to see that lady, and I want him, somehow, to know more, to *see* more.

Still, he doesn't answer, and now he's shivering, as if he's come straight out of a blizzard himself. I fetch the dusty blanket from my bed and wrap it around him before settling back down, my arms holding my knees.

"You came back," he says.

"Yes. Like I said, it wasn't the first time she's done a thing like that."

"I mean before. You went to the woods every day, and you always came back."

"Well," I say, "we lived so close, and there wasn't much to do with just my Gramps and me around, and—and it's pretty in there. It calms your head, if you know what to stay away from."

He nods as though he understands, and I find that I'm holding my breath, waiting for something, I'm not sure what.

"I like to go riding in the meadows up north, where you can go for miles without seeing a village or a field. I imagine it's something like that."

"Sounds like."

Now I'm all tense. He's not said a thing to put my back up, not a thing to contradict me or to make me mad. I figure it must be coming soon.

"Meadows are different from the woods, though, aren't they?" he says.

Ah, this will be it. "They don't have faceless women reaching out glowing hands, I suppose is what you mean."

Again, he doesn't answer right away. He pulls the blanket closer around his shoulders, refusing to look at me, still staring into the fire. Then, "They've come in so far now, Marni. All over the kingdom. And the king has been looking for someone to blame."

"For the woods moving in," I say.

He nods. "He's been saying it more and more, louder and louder. That he should have killed you when he had the chance, that you'll be the kingdom's doom."

"But I've nothing to do with it."

He shrugs. "It's what the king thinks."

"Isn't it enough that they want our land?" I hear the anger in my words, and I stop to breathe. "Isn't that reason enough for them to be moving in?"

"Maybe you're right. Not everyone agrees with the king. There are plenty who still carry that guilt you were mentioning, plenty who have no wish to see the past repeated." Now he turns to look at me, straight into my eyes. "The king still blames you, though, and what the king thinks matters."

Outside, our horses are snorting and shaking their heads; we can hear the reins slapping against their backs. "They'll be wondering where we've gone," I say, standing. I don't want to talk of this anymore. "We should get back."

"That's why you mustn't be seen here, Marni," he says, looking up at me. "Not this close to the woods."

Not with that lady reaching out a hand for anyone to see. He doesn't say it, but I know it's what he's thinking. I shake my head. "If I cared what the king thought, I might as well have thrown myself from the castle walls by now."

"He is the king. He has the ears of many powerful lords, and he is more dangerous and more desperate now than I've ever seen him."

"He's a bully and an idiot."

"A bully with a sword."

I reach down and pull him to his feet. The blanket slips off to lie huddled on the floor. I say, still holding his hands, "Don't you have a sword too?"

He goes all still. I see the thoughts churning again in his head, and I see him looking at me, his eyes sweeping from my hair to my cheekbones to my smile. "Yes, lady, I do," he says, quiet.

"Then what do I have to care about the sword of my old, stupid uncle?" I say.

"Not a thing," he says, still looking at me.

So I keep on smiling, and I let him take my arm as we walk out to the porch and down the steps, and if he stands a bit close as he lifts me onto my horse, I don't say nothing to that, neither, and he's smiling too as we turn our mares and start back up the path to the castle together.

HE THING IS, this Lord Edgar, head of the Ontrei family, confuses me. He's an arrogant, stubborn man, and he's closer to the king than almost anyone at court. He's asked for my hand not once, but twice, in the most insulting way both times, and still he doesn't seem ashamed or see any reason why we shouldn't be friends.

But he also laughs with me in this open, unworried way when I poke fun at him, and he taught me to ride, and he saw the lady in the woods without going mad. He doesn't tell anyone about that, or about our visit to the hut, or about the way the trees there haven't moved in any, even though all around the country they're leaping forward, a whole row of them every night.

In the days since that ride, the king has started to scowl at him instead of smile, and I think it's because this lord has been paying his attentions to me. And that scowl is the best mark in his favor so far.

"You could tell my uncle you're controlling me." We're out on another ride. There won't be many more of these before the snows wall us in. We've gone to the east; we don't take the road with the path leading off to my Gramps's and my hut anymore. There's no discussion of this; it simply never happens.

"Why would I do that?"

It's too cold to race, even. We plod along through frozen fields, huddled up in our layers and coats, the horses huffing big steaming breaths.

"Well, so he'll like you again."

Lord Edgar laughs. He does that, too, laughs when I'm as serious as can be. It's a less endearing trait, I think. "What do I care if the king likes me, Marni? We're allies, you and I. The king's my friend as long as he's yours."

I think this over. I may be new to court games, but I know who's the boss there and who's the boss of this lord. "Seems treasonous, that."

"Are you going to tell on me?"

He's grinning, but I only give him a frown. "I'm nobody still, you know. The king won't scarce speak my name. You'll do yourself no favors by linking up so openly with me."

"I think the king can decide who's nobody when he has a prince of his own to put on the throne."

I'm shaking my head. "So you're in it for the power," I say. "Aren't we all?"

I give him a look, hard and searching. I want to know what's lurking behind that smile, whether it wants to help me or to bite off my head as I sleep. "It's a dangerous game you play," I say, but the teasing is back in my voice now too, and before I know it, we're laughing and pushing the mares into a gallop, never mind the weather, and I'm forgetting, anyway, why I should care about the king when there are hills to thunder across and a sky to run and meet.

After that ride, the cold gets to be so much that we wouldn't want to push our poor brave mares out into it, and so the friendship, or the alliance, or whatever it is between the Lord of Ontrei and the king's niece becomes less a partial secret and more common knowledge for all the gossiping nobles.

The country lords and ladies begin galloping in on their stallions and rolling in on their carriages for the start of the winter festivities. At first these lords try their luck with me just as the court lords have been doing for weeks now, fetching me things and hanging on my words and in general turning themselves into fools. I don't mind so much with these new ones, to be truthful. They listen eagerly, but they don't simper. They flatter, but they don't compose poems like the moody Lord Nakon or wave handkerchiefs like the pale Lord Lesting does, with his runny nose and his red eyes. And they talk, too, about more interesting things than the courtiers: their neighboring farmers and their own fields, the weather patterns this fall and what they mean for the spring planting — the woods moving in.

They don't talk much of that, though, of the woods. Seems the moment they bring it up, it's brought back down again, with a look at me and a kind of unease that makes me all fidgety. I want to know. I want to hear every bit about the woods, but I also don't mind them stopping, neither. I think of what Edgar said that day in our hut, and somehow I don't care to hear how far the trees have come, how many miles the shadowed places have crept into our land now.

It isn't long before these new lords see what the castle folk have been whispering about for days, and they give up on me.

"Will it be soon, then, lady?" my maid Sylvie asks one morning as I'm letting her put up my hair in the twists and curls the ladies are wearing this week. It's the first day of the festivals, and I'm to go to a dance in the city's main square, as castle folk do every year, at midday, when the sun is high and the air is as warm as it gets. The city folk come and dance too, though not with the castle folk, as far as I can make out.

"Will what be soon, Sylvie?" I ask. It's a pretty fashion, this new hairdo. I tilt my head at my reflection, and my maid turns me upright again with the tips of her fingers.

She leans down next to my ear, catching my eyes in the mirror. "The announcement," she says. "When you tell us of your engagement." She raises her thin eyebrows at me, as though this is our secret, as if we've planned it all out, her and me, and our triumph is at hand.

I keep my face blank, but there's a twisting in my stomach. "No," I say. "No, there won't be any such announcement."

"He hasn't asked, yet, then," Sylvie says, straightening up to finish with my hair.

"I haven't said yes."

Then I wish I could take that back, because I can feel her hands pausing in their task, and I know I've given the servants, and through the servants the ladies and the lords, a new piece of gossip.

"You'll be wanting the king's blessing first, of course," Sylvie says, but it's a question more than a fact.

"Mmmm," I say, not yes and not no. The instant she's finished tying back the last loose curl, I'm up and grabbing my things, and she gets nothing more out of me that day.

But everyone's thinking as Sylvie is, I can tell. Why shouldn't they? Lord Edgar asks me for the first dance in the square that afternoon, and he spins me so fast and grins at me so happily I can't help but laugh, and when my hairpins fall, what do I care? But ladies always care, unless they've lost their mind to love or some such. So what are they all to think?

And I won't say he's not handsome, not even to myself, not with those dark eyes and that infectious smile turned right on me. He's charming when he decides to be, and he holds me close and sure as we spin through dance after dance.

As the head of the House of Ontrei is offering his arm to walk me back up to the castle, and I am taking it without even a protest, shaking my hair back over my shoulders and lifting my head to glory in the bright blue sky, the king is watching. He has his men around him, the ones who ride with him all about the kingdom — all but my escort, of course — and there are always lords and ladies near the king, ready with a flattery on their tongue or a simper in their eyes. But my uncle stands as though alone. It's more than a frown upon his face; it is a hard and present anger. As I hold his eyes for those few seconds, the queen comes up beside him and touches his arm. He looks down at her. He says something, low and quick. When she turns to look my way, that sparkling smile of hers is not to be seen.

By the end of the day, not even the newest-arrived of the country lords is paying me his attentions anymore.

But after a few days of these festivities I scarce remember that look the king gave me or how dangerous it is to let Lord Edgar spend as much time with me as he does. I even think less on that empty place inside where my Gramps is supposed to be.

Gramps and I had our own celebrations, of course. We'd bring in holly leaves and berries and drape them around the fireplace. We'd cook honey cakes and sunflower-seed bread, and long into the night we'd tell each other stories we made up on the spot.

We used to go to the nearest village for dancing, too. When Annel was there, I'd join in sometimes. She'd swing me around, and I'd get passed from villager to villager, on down the line as if I were one of them.

It was something, to twirl and smile and pretend I was one of them.

But we never went more than once or twice in the festival weeks. Gramps would have brought me as often as I liked, but I never was good at making friends with the village lads and lasses. I didn't go to their school; I didn't play with them in the evenings.

And—I'll admit it—as I got older, I grew more and more to like the way I didn't fit in. I wasn't a villager—not just because we lived outside the village, but because I was born for other things. They didn't get close to me, because they knew I was different. And I didn't get close to them, those later years, because I didn't want to become the same, to forget the life that had been taken from me.

Here, though, where the ladies laugh and talk with me as though I'm a princess in truth, and where a great lord courts me, and where to wake in the morning is to remember the thousand happy things that are coming to me today—here I am having myself festivals galore. We hold parades across the hills outside the castle, the ladies throwing dried flowers this way and that, the lords reaching high to catch what they can; we sing songs and tell stories, hours of them from anyone who cares to sing or speak, in a great circle in the castle's main hall; and we have feasts and dances and more feasts all week, and we will all the next week too, before the country nobles return to their estates for the winter.

It surprises me at times to think on how much I'm enjoying myself, how much I'm enjoying being around the Lord of Ontrei. I've scarce had time for knitting these last few days, even though the king is here and I'm eating dinner with him every night, so every night I'm reminded of the reason I came to this castle. But I'm finding that I don't want to give up thinking on Lord Edgar's laugh, or the way he looks at me. I want to hold on to this sweet sense of happiness, so strange, so unlike anything I've ever known. When I get to my room at last, after dancing half the night away, and I know the needles are there waiting for me, tucked beneath my mattress, more times than not I let them lie. More times than not I crawl into bed at once and let my dreams take me away.

These days seem to last forever, and that is Edgar's fault. With him, I'm thinking always of the moment, of the cutting remark he's just made about the king, of his laugh as we break off from the rest of the nobles to run over the hills together, of the fleck of yellow in his deep brown eyes, and how, when he turns them on me, I don't think that he's judging or afraid, but that he knows me, with all my wishes and my yearnings, and he likes me even so.

Everyone knows for certain now that he's after me.

I forget sometimes the power he holds at court. I forget the way the nobles are splitting, some rallying round the king and the queen, some following the Lord of Ontrei to my side.

When we gather all together in the hall for a story or to mingle before we go in for dinner, the king's nobles stand on one side of the room, Ontrei's on the other. The queen doesn't come over to talk to me anymore, and for that I'm sad. I smile at her when she looks my way, but either she doesn't dare smile back, or she doesn't want to. She turns her head, and I'm left smiling into empty space.

"I didn't ask them to do it," I say one evening as I take Edgar's arm to walk into the dining hall. We're bringing up the pack tonight; I've held him back so there's no one left to hear us as we walk. "I didn't ask them to pit themselves against the king."

"You didn't need to," Edgar says. "They were ready; they were ripe for it. There are plenty of us who never felt right about what happened to your mother or how he abandoned you. A king who can kill his own sister . . ." He shakes his head, and I near love him at that moment for what's in his eyes as he looks at me, all fierce and bright. "And now that there's trouble with the woods, and the king hasn't been able to stop it —"

"You said they blame me for that."

"Some do. It's not your country, though, is it? You're not in charge of what happens to its people."

We've reached the entrance to the dining hall; the others have found their seats, and the king will be arriving soon. He won't look kindly on us if we're dawdling outside the doors. "Well," Edgar says before we walk on through, "it's not your country *yet*." And then we're making our way to our seats. The nobles are watching us, wondering, no doubt, what we've just been speaking of, and I feel a thrill despite myself, to be this center of attention, to be the subject of their thoughts.

I love that, too, the sudden power of being courted by him. I love his talk of me taking the kingdom for my own, even though I know — I *know* — he's thinking that when I have the kingdom, he will be king.

He pulls out my chair for me as I sit down, and he whispers into my ear, "It won't be long now, Marni, before the king gets what's coming to him and you get what's yours." He raises his eyebrows at me as he slides into the seat beside me, and I smile back at him.

When the king walks in with the queen on his arm, I let his glare wash over me. Edgar's words, his nearness, and his friendship keep me safe, and for a moment I believe him. I believe in the truth of the future that he's offering to me.

OME THE SECOND week
of the festivals, Edgar starts trying
again to get me to marry him.

He asks me in silly ways, in
breathtaking ways, and in serious ways. He asks me in the main
hall as we're passing out berry tarts that the ladies have cooked
up as a midwinter treat; we both reach for the same blueberry
one, and we're standing like that, holding the tart between us,
and he whispers, "Marry me," and I shake my head, laughing.

He asks me while we're dancing; every time he spins me
around, as I turn back to face him, he says it quick, then spins
me away again. I don't have the breath for answering, even.

He asks me when we're sitting by my fire after dinner with

only my maid Sylvie for company, and she's knitting and muttering to herself about something, and I don't know if she sees when he edges his chair over next to mine, takes my hand from where it's resting on my lap, and says, as solemn as anything, "Marni, I know I've made light of this, but I wish you would give in and marry me."

The firelight is painting his face in orange shadows. His eyes are dark, darker than the corners of the room, and I want to look away because I don't know what I'm to do when he looks at me like that.

"I won't," I say, but I keep on looking at him. I like the dark of his eyes and the light on his face. I like the seriousness in his voice. I've even grown familiar with the arrogance in every inch of him. He keeps asking because he knows I'll say yes. He owns near half the court now, their loyalty, their fear. It's not just him who thinks he'll win me. It's everyone who thinks so. They're only split on whether they like the idea or not.

"You think I'm asking only for the throne," he says. He folds his other hand over the first, so that my fingers are cocooned between his warm palms. I'm not sure I've ever felt this way before. I think, *As long as he doesn't let go, I'll be safe. I won't have to watch out for myself anymore.*

"Yes," I say.

"I'm not," he says. "I don't like what the king has done, and I'd be happy to bring him down. I don't think I'm imagining that you feel the same way."

"No," I say.

"But it's more than that." He's looking at me so softly, as if he cares — not just about my rights as a princess, but about me, the girl who thinks and dreams. "I like you, Marni. I want to love you. There's something pure about you, though you keep yourself hidden away. There's something unwilling to yield to any injustice, any untruth. I like that about you."

He's so close now, and I'm not leaning away. Why am I not leaning away?

"I like a lot of things about you."

And then — then he's kissing me. I suppose that's what this is, the warm rush of his skin, the taste of his tongue, the melting all through me. My fingers are tingling, and now his hand is on my waist, and now my hands are in his hair.

I don't want to stop. I want to keep on like this forever, and not care what it means, and not care whether he's lying or what the king will do about it. My eyes are closed, and I'm someone I've never been — free, certain, disconnected from the world. There's no thought of the woods and no thought of any vengeance.

I love it, this feeling. I love the melting into nothing; I love the fierce refusal to care anymore.

But it also terrifies me.

"Marni? What is it?"

I'm up; I'm standing by the fireplace, and Edgar's still sitting on the edge of his chair, leaning over my empty one. I'm breathing fast; there's tingling through me, still, but it's sharp, as though I've just shaken myself awake.

Sylvie's chair is empty too. I didn't hear her leave the room, and I wonder if he started kissing me because she left, or if she left because he'd started kissing me. Then I wonder what the queen would say if she knew I was all alone in my rooms with a man—a man the king near hates by now. I smooth my skirts out, avoiding Edgar's eyes.

"Thank you for your visit, my lord," I say. "I'm afraid I had lost all sense of the time, and I should be well abed."

The fire crackles. Edgar rises from his chair slowly, and I force myself not to back away, and I watch his feet as they come near.

He lifts my chin with a finger. He's smiling, that cocksure grin. "Too soon, my lady?" he says.

I'm not certain what that's supposed to mean, but I'm flushing, and I pull away from him. I sweep to the door. "Good night, my lord," I say pointedly, and as Sylvie's not here to do such things, I open the door for him.

For a moment I even think he might refuse to leave, but then he's walking past me. He grabs my hand before I can flick it out of the way, and he bows over it, brushing the back with his lips. There's no tingling now, though, no warm rush of abandon. I'm cold all the way through, and when he murmurs, "Good night, lady," I give him my politest smile in return without a shiver or a flinch. When he passes out into the hallway, I shut the door at once and turn the lock, and I stand with my back against it, wondering why I still feel so afraid.

*   *   *

Later that night, after Sylvie's helped me into my nightgown and gone off again to her room, I sit in my window seat and look out toward the mountains. The moon is full. I've pushed the window open even though it's dead cold and I've no wrap.

It has only just, in the last few days, begun to snow regularly, and the mountains are sparkling a thousand different colors in the moonlight. As I'm looking out over this world, which is almost as bright as it is in the day, as I'm leaning out and breathing it all in—a dragon flies across the moon.

I know it for a dragon; I know it without question. It near takes my heartbeat, the spread of its wings and the power, the downright royalty of its shape. There's nothing like a dragon. I've never seen one before, and I know already there's nothing to match its fierce beauty. As I watch it swoop across the sky again and once again, my ears resound with a cry they can't possibly be picking up this far away—a piercing cry, a roar like the boundless black sky all lit with the moon's cold fire.

I don't know how it is, but I'm standing, and then I'm up on the window ledge, outside the room, bare feet on gray stone, hands holding tight to the shutters.

I think if I wanted to, I could let go and balance perfectly. I think if I wanted to, I could jump and not fall. I could make that sound, the one that's still echoing through my body, and it would turn me into something bold and beautiful, something more like who I am than I've ever been before.

Then the dragon's gone, disappeared back into the bright white expanse.

I stand there a moment more, and then I leave the sky, leave the sparkling snow to take my needles from their place beneath my mattress. They are singing to me. Not in the usual gentle quiver, but with a loud hum I feel right down to my toes and along the nape of my neck.

And it's not just the needles, is it? The dragon's flight has done something to this whole room, has cast a spell over it so that the fire diminishes, the shadows melt away. The stones are thrumming softly. There's a tension, a breath, and when I close my eyes, I think I feel my mother's hand upon my hair.

She did this. She turned men from her room. She watched a great, wild beast fly across the moon. She had everything you'd think she could have wanted, and she gave it up to jump from a window, to run until she scarce could remember her own name.

And I would too. I would be running and running, forgetting all this and remembering a truer, older part of me, the part that knows the language of the woods. But the needles prick against my palm, and at long last I sit against the windowsill and I know what it is I am to knit. I call out to the moon; it answers with a skein of light, bright and strange. I wind it around my fingers. I know my uncle's gaze. I know how he hates me, and I know the bitter pain he steeps in daily, and through that I reach the deepest part of him. I tie it into the song I've started to sing, and I lace it with the sharpest tip of a claw, the hottest flick of a flame, the empty nothing of a moonlit sky.

I knit until the winter birds are starting their morning

songs, and then I slip my vengeance back beneath my bed and sleep for the few last hours before the castle wakes.

The next day, when we are going out to the river to test the new ice for skating, the Lord of Ontrei offers me his arm and I turn my head and keep on walking.

I hear the whispers. I hear the rumor starting through the court already, that the princess and her favorite have quarreled. I hear Edgar's laugh behind me, and I near turn back, angry, but I'd rather avoid a real fight in front of everyone, so I keep on.

I stay away from him as I poke about the edges of the ice with some of the ladies, but I can feel him watching me all the same. Turns out that the river isn't solid enough after all. We spend the afternoon throwing rocks out into the center to see if they'll stay or slide off into a hole and disappear, and we race one another up and down the riverbank and watch the lords trying to push one another out onto the ice.

When we're all trooping in for dinner, I find I've somehow lost my scarf, and I peel back to search for it along the banks, telling Lady Susanna to go in without me, much as she tries to come help.

I was thinking it would be nice to have a few minutes on my own out in the winter silence, but I should have let her come along after all, for as I'm fetching my scarf off a bush and lifting my head to the gray, dense sky, Edgar says, "A hand, lady?" and reaches out to help me back up the bank.

I blink at his hand and want less than anything to take it. Behind, the river murmurs, and I've a sudden wild wish to run out to the middle until the weight of me shatters the undeveloped ice and I fall into the rushing blackness and sweep away, far from anyone.

Or if I jumped, maybe the sky would take me, swoop me into scatterings of wind and leaf bits, toss me across the land until I melded with the roll of the hills, the rustle of the trees, the sharp, unyielding mountain peaks.

It's only a hand, though, and what harm will it really do? I take it, mumbling my thanks as he pulls me up onto the castle lawn, and when he tucks my arm within his to lead me back to the castle, I don't protest.

But when we arrive at the steps up to a side hall where the nobles are gathered like a bunch of chirping birds, waiting as their servants rush around, plucking the layers of coats and hats and mittens from them, Edgar stops me from going in.

"Are we friends still, Marni?" he asks. "Are we allies?"

"Yes, of course," I say. "Why wouldn't we be?"

He's looking at me, again with that intensity, and I wonder where my frivolous companion has gone. Where is the man who spun me around until I was dizzy? Where the whisperer of scandals, the daring horseman? "I think you have been avoiding me since last night," he says. "I think you are frightened of me, maybe."

When the firelight was playing across those eyes, it seemed right for them to draw together so, to be that serious. But the sky is wide and open, the breeze is teasing at my hair, and the voices of the nobles are drifting from the hall. He's as out of place as a daffodil in the snow.

I laugh, as naturally as I can. "I'm not frightened of you, mighty Lord of Ontrei." I toss my head, even. "I'm not frightened of anything."

There, the sparkle's back in his eyes, his smile. "Good," he says, and I'm starting to relax when he bends his head toward me and kisses me soft on the lips.

Again, there's that immediate melting, that urging to kiss him back and let us see what happens next. But I'm not the girl I was last night. The sun is full upon me, and I've sleepless hours and the memory of a dragon against the moon to separate me from the part that wants only this, only him.

After the briefest of moments I push him back, harder maybe than I need to, and he trips over the steps and sprawls into the hall, bumping a servant who has her hands filled with coats, who loses her bundle and trips as well. The coats go flying in all directions, and the nobles suddenly find themselves busied with catching the girl and holding themselves up and turning around to see Lord Edgar on his backside and me, standing just outside the door in the snow, gaping at them all and looking as guilty as anything.

The silence spreads through the hall like honey over a cake.

Lord Edgar's laugh rings out. He's pulling himself to his feet, brushing off his legs as though it's all a great joke.

But I've never seen that look on his face before.

I've never told him no quite like this, neither.

He comes over to where I'm standing and reaches out a hand to help me up the steps. I don't want to know, somehow, what would happen if I refused it, so I let him pull me inside, though I drop it as soon as he eases his hold. "My lady," he says, still with that laugh in his voice, but it's not the laugh I know, not the carefree joy when we dance or ride, not the surprise at what a different sort of girl I am. "I am sorry if I have caused you any offense."

He's not keeping his voice down one bit. He's letting the whole court hear, and while my uncle isn't in the room, there are plenty who will tell him anything we say, so Edgar must not care that everyone will know our business.

There's a ringing in my head, and my hands are trembling something fierce. "No, my lord," I say, and I can scarce hear myself. "I should be the one to apologize. I never meant to be so rude."

He smiles at me, but it's a smile the way a winter gale is a warm breeze. "There are things a lady doesn't want the world to see," he says. Oh, how they are listening now. He's kept us near the door, so it could be thought we're trying to have a private conversation, but in this silence not a scuffle of a shoe is private. "I understand. I will keep my distance until I can come again to your room tonight."

And then, the knave, he's bowing to me and walking away. Walking away!

The rage is a freezing fire running through me, and for

three seconds, four, I cannot move or speak or think, and he's on his way out, and all the court will believe what he wants them to believe, and he must know — oh, he must be so sure! — that I will do whatever he wants. That I will marry him tomorrow, even, just to keep them quiet.

And it won't be long before they know, because this court always knows such things, that he was in my room last night in truth, and that we were alone, long enough — long enough for whatever they want to say.

There's no dark river or bright sky or dragon against the moon in my mind now, only a clear, cold anger that throws me after him to grab his arm.

He's raising an eyebrow at me, so calm, so certain.

I don't bother with the ladylike responses I've been taught. I don't berate him with well-turned phrases. I don't give him a haughty glare. I don't even slap him across the face, as I've seen the Lady Elinor do to Lord Lesting when he became particularly forward after a few too many drinks at cards.

I am not a lady. I'm the heir to the kingdom if my uncle will ever admit it, and I'm my Gramps's only granddaughter, and I pull back my arm and punch him, as hard as I can, straight on the nose.

Now, I'm not one to condone pointless violence. But if there was ever a thing to show all those nobles that I'm not the sort of person to get myself into a romantic tryst, if there was ever a thing that would stop the rumors of how I'd thrown myself into this man's control, it's that savage punch, and the crack as my fist connects, and the blood that starts dripping at once.

He doubles over before pulling himself upright. I've never hit a man before, and I have to say I'm pleased with my success. He's holding his nose with red fingers and blinking at me, tearing up, I think.

"My Lord of Ontrei," I say, and again I'm pleased, because my voice is steady, without a trace of fear. "I don't know who you think you are, but I'm the king's niece, and the closest blood he has left, and you'll keep a civil tongue or I will cut it out."

I can feel them, the looks, the way nobody in the room is breathing just now. A serving boy has taken a step or two toward us. I don't know if he means to protect Edgar from me or to help me beat him up. The loyalties of the court must be all confused — the king's men will love to see Edgar brought low, but they won't want to support me in it; my men — well, are they mine or Edgar's?

Nobody says a word, though, and at last he bows to me, wiping his hand on a handkerchief from his pocket and holding that to the blood. "I am," he says, "as always, your servant, lady."

I go up close to him, until we're as near as we were last night, that moment before our lips touched and he almost swept me away from myself. "I'm not afraid of you," I say, so that only he can hear it. I'm looking into his eyes so he knows I mean it. "And you can ask, and you can threaten, and you can start up whatever rumors you like, but none of that is going to make me marry you."

He hasn't looked away; he barely seems shamed, in fact. "Marni," he says, "I didn't mean—"

I don't let him finish. "You made a grab for power," I say. "I can understand that. But I won't be used, Edgar, and I won't be rushed, and I won't be forced into anything I don't want."

He's shaking his head. "I would never—"

"Or coaxed into it, or enticed, or what have you. I won't be *persuaded*."

I hold his gaze. My blood still rushes, and my fists are itching to hit something more, but I keep them quiet.

At last he nods. "Yes, lady."

It's not enough. I know it won't be enough for this man, and what's more, I know it won't be enough to keep me from him when my anger's ebbed, so I step back again and say, so everyone can hear, in the clear, calm sort of voice my aunt would adore, "For the last time, my lord, I will not marry you. Not for all the gold in the kingdom, not if wild horses were to drag me to it. You have not the slightest hope, and I wish you would stop trying."

He's looking at me all stricken, and even through my rage my heart is near to breaking. I turn and walk away from him, and the nobles part to let me pass.

After that, there are only a few days left in the festivals, but they are the dullest, the longest days of the last two weeks. Lord Edgar does not come near me. I don't go to him. The court is still split, but it seems halfhearted, the way the nobles go to their opposite sides of the room and cast the others looks and whisper secrets. By the end of the second day, they've started to meld back together again, and I even see Lord Theodore, who was a staunch supporter of the king, laughing jovially with Lady Beatrice, who'd been part of Lord Edgar's circle. When Beatrice catches my eye, she flushes and looks away.

I talk with the lesser nobles and stay as close as I can to those from the country, who have the least to do with this drama. They are kind enough, and I smile more than not during these final dances, feasts, and games.

But the spins have lost their sparkle, and the stories, races, and sweets, which so excited me only days earlier, are bland, uninteresting. I let the nobles sweep me along from each event to the next, just putting one foot in front of the other.

My only joy these days comes late at night, when the others have gone to bed and the moon shines full through my bedroom window. Then I take out my bright knitting, and I dream of death. I don't see the dragon again, but I've no need. I can hear his roar all through my skin. When I close my eyes, I can feel my mother's hands, too, placed over mine, guiding me along as we finally, bit by bit, create her vengeance.

On those nights I can forget that I ever knew the Lord of Ontrei. I can keep from wondering, as I do on dark, cloudy nights when I've nothing to take me away from my thoughts, whether I did right, in truth, to reject him.

EIGHT

HEN THE COUNTRY nobles have gone, when it's only the king and queen, the court nobles, and me, the real cold starts creeping in. Every other day, it seems, it snows, until our world is white. This is the snow that still looks fresh and clean. This is the snow we catch our breaths at, watching it from the floor-to-ceiling windows in the main hall.

The ladies and the lords go out into this snow, and they are like little children, throwing snowballs and kicking up great big drifts. The lords roll about on the ground with the real children, the ones the nannies usually keep hidden away in the children's quarters, and these boys and girls laugh and scream, thrilled to bits.

I walk by myself when I get the chance, smiling up into the sky as well. I know this is only the beginning. I know that by the time the river shudders and cracks, opening itself to the sun again, we will be well sick of it all. The snow will be gray. The cold will have entered our lungs until we're sneezing and coughing, every one of us, and we'll be yelling and snapping at the slightest irritation.

It was always that way with Gramps and me: the beginning of winter was glorious, and we smiled at each other more in the first snowfall than we did the rest of the year, almost. By the end, we'd keep to opposite corners of the hut, barely holding on to our tempers and our wits.

I guess the lords and ladies know it will be like that too, but none of us cares during the first big snows. We can't, can we? If we think about what's to come, we'll want to run off and hide ourselves under our covers, to sleep until spring. We've got to keep believing it will stay like this, even when we know it can't.

Then, only a few weeks after the festivals, the real cold settles in, the bone-freezing cold, the kind that seems near alive, we get to hate it so. The snow doesn't stop falling. The mountains are mounds of white, scarce distinguishable from the nearer mounds that cover the castle lawns, the river, and the streets of the city. The winds come down from the north, howling around my tower room all night long. All day they blow, too, whipping the world until it's as though nothing exists but the castle, as if beyond our triple layers of clothing and our foot-thick stone walls is only a white, frozen void.

Nobody goes out; nobody comes in. If our entire population of villagers and farmers has gone and died, we'd have no way of knowing. If the army from the queen's country has taken up the notion to invade, its soldiers could be knocking at our door before we would realize they'd entered the kingdom.

The king keeps to his rooms, and the queen attends him there. The nobles gather in the main hall every afternoon, though our breath freezes there and tinkles onto the floor as so many icicles. Yet there's something more awful about staying in our rooms, each with our own servants, reading or sewing the endless hours away. The nobles near loathe one another now, and when they're not talking of the weather, they're picking fights, lashing out in ways they'd never do on a warm, sunny day.

Edgar stays on one side of the room; I stay on the other. My knitting comes to an all-out halt. There's no moonlight to spin, what with the clouds and blowing snows.

It's on the tenth day of this cold, when the winds die down for the first time and some of the city folk make their way to the castle to beg for coal and to deliver our flour and milk, that the rumor starts.

It's midmorning. We've all gathered, impromptu, in the hall to catch up on the news from the city and to marvel over the white, sun-sparkling heaps that we can see now, near up to the hall's windows. I've just come down from my rooms; I'm walking toward Lady Susanna and Lady Hettie, who are talking together by an eastern window. They grow quiet as I walk up, even though a minute ago they were whispering to each other something fierce.

I reckon it's some secret love affair; there've been a load of those the last week and a half, what with there being nothing better to do. But when I tell them to let me in on it, they shake their heads and won't meet my eyes.

"I won't tell anyone," I say. "You know I can keep secrets."

"It isn't anything," says Hettie.

She's so willing to spread the juiciest rumor, usually, and she loves to tell me things, to be the one who lets the princess know. "Come on," I say, "give it up. I've been bored all morning. What—has Lady Flan finally given in to Lord Theodore?"

Hettie gives Susanna a panicked look. I can see it poised on the edge of her lip, the rumor, her desire to let it out. Susanna grabs her arm, and she smiles at me, her sharp, sweet court smile. "Isn't it a wonder, lady, how the snow has stopped at last?"

I scowl at them, folding my arms just as the queen says I'm never to do, and Hettie gives a little yelp and takes herself away, murmuring about promising Lady Charlotte a ride in her sleigh through the fresh snow. Susanna continues with her smile, though it's growing more brittle by the second. I sigh. "Something personal, then? All right, I'm sure I'll hear it somewhere else soon enough." I let her talk about the weather for as long as I can stand before moving off.

It isn't just Hettie and Susanna, though, who are acting odd today. The ladies aren't meeting my eyes, or are moving away as I get near, or are stumbling over their words. And the lords are giving me looks like to turn me to stone, and speaking only in short, clipped sentences, and laughing at none of my jokes. Not one! Even though you'd think now that Ontrei's out of the picture, they'd be trying again for that marriage and the kingship.

In the end, it's Edgar himself who tells me what's gotten into them all. The king and the queen have come down to dinner for the first time since the deep cold began, and there's an air of festivity in the dining hall, or there would be if the nobles didn't keep glancing toward me and away again with something like fear or suspicion—I can't tell quite what. When the king gets up to leave, and we all stand with him, he says, as if he's decided all of a sudden to make a speech, "We will support those who aid our cause. Those who are against us needn't look to us for help." Except it's an odd sort of speech, if that's the whole of it, and as he says it, he's looking at me with that same fear or suspicion, and there's a scattering of applause at the end, as if the others know what he's talking about.

The queen sends me a small, worried smile as she follows him from the room. She, at least, hasn't lost her mind. But after dinner, as the nobles gather again in the main hall for one last round of gossip and repetitions of how marvelous it is that the snow's finally done with its tantrum, I walk from group to group, and everywhere I meet closed circles and am presented with silent backs. I give up, and I've made my way halfway up the stairs to my room when I hear Edgar—"Wait!"—and turn to see him hurrying after me.

"What do you want?" I ask as he stops a few steps down from me. "Want to give me a look like to kill me, do you? Or a brushoff, or a nasty, cryptic speech?"

He says, "They are saying the northern woods moved in ten miles during the storm, one for each day."

"What?" My arms drop to catch the railing. I've heard of the trees moving in leaps and bounds, but miles? Ten in as many days?

"They're blaming you for it."

I shake my head. "They've always blamed me. Everything that goes wrong, they've always blamed me."

"No, Marni. This is different. They're saying the dragon's come to take back his child."

I laugh, but it's verging on a sob. "Sixteen years he could let me alone, but now he decides it's been too long?"

Edgar shrugs. "That's what they're saying."

Five months trading gossip and laughter, playing games and going for walks with these folk, and one rumor throws it all to the wind. "Well," I say, in a weaker voice than I'd like, but the light is doing funny things in my eyes, gleaming bright and going dark. My ears are numb with an echo of a fierce roar. I take a deep breath and wait for it all to settle. "Thank you for telling me." I start my way up the stairs again, concentrating on putting each foot in front of the other, on holding the railing only as hard as is needed to pull myself up.

I stumble anyway when Edgar says, "I thought you should know," and I look back down at him there. I wonder how this day would have gone if I'd given in to him and he were promised to marry me, and defend me, and love me. I wonder what he would say if I gave in now, this very moment, and threw myself into his keeping. Would he toss me out into the cold?

"Yes, thank you," I say again.

He nods and turns to go, and I let him.

I reckon if there is any time to put my plan into motion, this is it. I'm near done with the knitting, and over the next few nights I work like mad from dusk until dawn, as long as there is a sliver of moon to see.

It is three days after the rumor begins that I finish it.

It is beautiful. Its wings shimmer; its beak gleams. It moves like liquid, flowing from the window to the bed to the fireplace and back again. It sits on my hand and rubs its head against my cheek as though it loves me, and I love it.

"Sweet one," I say, "you lovely sweet thing. Welcome to my world."

I hold out the piece of paper I've been keeping beneath my mattress all these months, the one with Gramps's handwriting and my own face smiling. I kiss it, the place he would have rested his hand as he drew. I offer it to my creature.

"This is my heart," I say, "and you are to kill the man that took it."

It flicks out a tongue, thin and sharp and bright, and it snatches the note out of my fingers. It takes it into itself. There's no chewing, no swallowing, but it gleams white suddenly, a flash that lights the whole room. When it looks at me again, I know it knows me — and what I want of it.

Then I tuck it into my left sleeve, and it molds against my skin so that beyond a slight glisten it shows not at all. Come the right moment, I'll let it out. Come the right moment, we'll fly free.

If I'd thought myself lonesome before, it was nothing compared to what happens now.

When I come into a room, all backs turn. When I smile or ask how someone's been, I'm given only the bare minimum courtesy before the courtier makes some excuse and walks away.

The king is still stuck in the castle with all his army. Every day we hear more news of the trees that are galloping now, it seems, across the landscape, though no one ever actually sees them move. But the king can't ride out when the snows are still so deep, so he paces the halls and snarls at anyone foolish enough to get in his way.

We all have started to wonder what will happen when the spring comes, if it ever does come again. Will there be fields enough left to feed our people? Will there be anything to trade for wood and coal? I imagine the queen even worries about her kingdom by the sea. They depend on us to make up what they lack in grain. If our crops are lost to the woods, her people, too, will suffer. Her people, too, will starve.

And if the woods keep coming, if we've nowhere left to go, how long will it be that we stay a kingdom? How long will any of us stay human, when around each tree there'll be a monster, and the voices of the woods folk won't ever let us alone?

I sometimes think it's already happened to me. Ever since Edgar stopped me on the stairs and I felt the echo of the dragon's roar, I've been hearing the lady's voice in my head again, even here in the castle, even through all this stone. I'll be waking from a dream that my Gramps is still alive and we're sitting on our porch together, cutting up peppers for soup, and her voice will slip its way into the scene, singing of the mystery, the wonder of deep, dark places. I'll look up from my knife, and instead of my Gramps, she'll be sitting across the table from me. Hand held out.

Or I'll be at dinner, listening to talk of the weather or some such, and between one blink and the next the lady will be whispering of how the snow shines, cradled by pine needles. I'll be there for a moment, standing with her in an open place encircled by trees. I'll turn my head up to feel the sun, and the dragon's shadow will sweep by overhead, and my legs will twitch to throw myself after him.

Then I'll be back in the dining hall, and Lord Nakon will be asking me if I'm quite all right and handing me a glass of wine. They'll all be looking at me, paused in their chatter, and

I'll wonder how much they guess, how much they suspect about the monster in me, pulling at me, growing in power every day I keep myself inside the castle walls.

As the days go on and the snows begin to melt, the faces of the nobles turn from blank civility to open contempt. Lord Beau near spits in my eye when I ask him in a corridor how his daughter does, the one who is recovering from a cold. "No good if you have a say in it!" he calls after me as I rush from him down the hall. Elinor and Flan sneer at me as I pass them by. "Witch's brat," they hiss, and it takes something to keep from turning on my heel and slapping them as hard as I can or clawing their hair from their heads. Lord Edgar says nothing more after that moment on the stairs, and I don't go near him, neither. I see him watching me, frowning, but he doesn't say nothing, and the lords who keep to his side glare at me like the rest.

And then, as the river begins to creak with the waters rushing by underneath its winter ice, the king starts trying to kill me.

I'm not surprised, exactly, but I don't realize it at first, and there are two close calls. One night after dinner I retch out my entire stomach, and I toss and turn for hours, a fire running all through me. Sylvie brings me glass after glass of water, and I feel I'm near to die before the morning, but somehow I pull through.

I don't figure it out then, but just two days later, a lord who's always stayed close to the king asks if I'll go ice-skating with him. I'm so starved for attention I stupidly say yes, even though I know the river's not safe for that anymore. While we're skating and laughing and I'm thinking maybe they've finally decided to stop blaming me, the ice opens out under my feet and I see how it's been hacked at with an axe and the lord was leading me this way. I near to drown and get saved only at the last minute by some servant who'd been walking by and hadn't been in on the plan, apparently, because he sticks in a branch and pulls me out as quick as can be. And as the lord comes up now, all concerned, I see the look he shoots the servant, and it's like to burst him into flames right where he stands.

That very afternoon, once I'm warmed and dry, I go to my rooms to set the vengeance free.

I don't know quite why I've been hanging on to it this long. In part, I like knowing it's there, just inside my sleeve. I like the secret power and I like the thought of what will happen when I let it go. I like the memory, too, of my mother's hands laid over mine. Even if this is only a thought, a wish, it's the closest I've ever been to her. The soft grasp of the vengeance reminds me of that, and if I let it fly, I'll lose that feeling against my skin.

And in part, I think my days in the castle, even these days when no one has a smile or kind word to throw my way, have softened me. I'm someone, here, more than I ever was with my Gramps. I have a title. I have a purpose. I belong.

When I set this thing after my uncle, all that will change. I haven't thought on it much until now, but I'm starting to. I've started to wonder in the last few days what will happen once my lovely thing has killed him. I'm not sure they'd give me the throne after all, not now. Even if they did, would I want it? To sit in my uncle's place, to rule over all these lords and ladies — to take up an axe and try to fight back the trees?

But I can't hesitate any longer. My uncle is trying to have me killed, and I reckon I owe it to my Gramps, to my mother — to the flower girl I was — to take him down first.

I stand in the middle of my bedroom, facing the window, feeling the breeze that is melting the snow sending its tendrils in. I hold out my left arm, the arm with my vengeance wrapped around it, and I say, "Come out, my beauty." There's a stirring along my wrist; it unfolds itself, pulls itself over my palm and up, up to perch on my fingertips. If it has eyes, it's looking into my face now. The breeze flutters its wings to rise, and it hangs on to my skin only by the slight tips of its talons. They hurt, as insubstantial as this thing is. They will hurt my uncle much more.

I lift it to my lips and kiss its head. It shudders. It knows me. It knows what I want.

Magic is knowing what you want. The lady, the little ones, the speaking owls — they never hesitate. They would have set this creature free many days ago, as soon as they'd knit the last stitch of moonlight thread. They wouldn't have held it close against their skin. They wouldn't have waited one moment longer than they had to.

Ah, well. I'm still half human, after all. And the king will die today as well as any other day.

I raise the thing up high; its head turns this way and that, seeking its target. I know the word to let it go, and it hovers at the edge of my mouth. My tongue forms its shape.

He knocks at the door.

"Marni!"

I falter. I shut my eyes until I feel the word rolling out along my breath again.

"Marni, I know you're there! Open the door."

And who does he think he is, to be coming round after all these weeks? "Go away!" I say, and the creature looks down at me, tilts its head.

"I won't. They're saying you nearly died."

"I'm well and good now, so you can trot off again."

There's a silence. I let my breath out and lift my eyes to the thing once again, smiling at it. It raises its wings high, ready to jump.

"Marni, I'm coming in."

I growl, a short, low growl the queen would near kill me for, it's so unladylike. I think of saying the word, quick, before he enters. But the moment's not right; I can't very well be arguing with the Lord of Ontrei while my uncle dies. I want to savor it; I want to think of it every moment it's happening. It won't be long before I kick this lord out.

I coax the vengeance back under my sleeve, and I pick up some piece of sewing, some horrible-looking curtains. I'm sitting down all placid when he walks in.

He shuts the door. I don't look up at him; I'm getting my breathing back, slowing my blood down. He says, "I hear you had a narrow escape."

"You might call it that." I bite the thread I'm measuring to tear it, more violent than need be, maybe.

He says, "What would you call it, then?"

I make the mistake of looking up. He's not sat down; I've not offered him a chair. He seems earnest, with his dark eyebrows drawn close, and I haven't seen him getting chummy with the king, so it could be he has no idea of what's going on. I want to tell him, suddenly. Just as I wanted to tell him about visiting the woods, when we were out in my Gramps's hut, I want him to know. I want someone to know. "Twice now," I say, "the king's tried to have me killed."

He sits down, though I glare at him. "Once when you were a baby," he says, "and then again—"

"No," I say. "I mean twice in the last three days." I stick my needle into as ugly a flower pattern as I've ever seen, gritting my teeth.

"In the last three days . . ."

I swear, if there were a real flower that looked like this, I'd never let it into my garden. I look up to see where he's trailed off to, and I sigh. He's frowning, all worrisome. "It doesn't surprise me," I say. "Why should it you?"

"Well," he says, "for one, he's your uncle."

"Yes, and my mother was his sister."

"He was younger then."

"He's the king, and he thinks that when he's done with me, the kingdom will be saved."

He's shaking his head. "That was only coincidence with her. There's no proof it worked before."

"What do you mean?"

"When he killed your mother and the woods stopped coming in. Why would they have stopped just then because of that? She had been living so close to the woods. Surely they would have taken her long before, if she was what they wanted—"

"What do you mean, *the woods stopped coming in?*"

NINE

THERE'S A BIRD singing out-
side the window, probably in the bushes
along the riverbank, and we hear its
bright, sweet song in the sudden silence.
It's winter still, no denying it, but there's something of spring in
that breeze today. It won't be long before the king can ride out
against the trees.

"What do you mean," I say again, "the woods stopped coming in?" My fingers are white against my needle. The ugly flowers
have dropped to the floor, I don't remember when. Sometime between when Edgar was looking so annoyingly worried and naïve,
and when he said the thing that made time stop.

"When your mother, the princess that was, came back from
the woods," he says, and pauses. "You don't already know this?"

I shake my head. "Not all. Gramps didn't like to talk of it."

"Well," he says, "I suppose I don't like to either, though for a different reason." He stops again, and we look at each other for a long moment, neither of us saying a thing.

"Edgar, please," I say. My voice sounds strange in my ears. "Tell me."

He nods. He takes a breath and lets it out slow, and then he speaks. "When she came back, it was spring. All that summer, as she hid her pregnancy, the trees were moving in. Just like this summer, really, bit by bit, nothing to cause alarm. But when she was found out and ran away with you to hide, the trees started coming in leaps and bounds."

"Like this fall," I say. I look down to see whether I still hold the needle. I can scarce feel it between my fingers, but I'm gripping it so tight it's making furrows in my skin. I place it, carefully, on the table beside me.

"Yes," Edgar says. "And that winter, while your uncle and the men your grandfather couldn't placate paced the castle halls, planning their attack on her, the woods came in farther and farther, until they thought they might not have any kingdom in the spring."

"They rode out in the spring," I say.

"It was a long winter, but when they could ride, they found her in no time. She'd been living with an old servant who'd moved up north near a village against the mountains. For whatever reason, her house hadn't been overrun by the woods, even when all the neighbors had trees growing right through their kitchen doors and vines closing off their wells, so they couldn't find clean water without walking fifty miles."

"I thought—" I begin, and then can't go on.

"What is it?"

I don't know what's on his face; I can't look at him. I close my eyes against the drifting breeze.

"I always thought she was so clever, to keep away from them so long. I thought it was her that kept me safe, not just that they couldn't ride out in the winter."

He doesn't say anything right away. I wish I could push down the shaking in my hands; I wish my voice hadn't wavered so. "She was clever," he says, "to hide her pregnancy as long as she did. And where was she to go?"

"Across the mountains, to another country," I say.

"With a newborn, when the pass was closing up with trees? She did what she could."

I make myself breathe, deep, long breaths, and it calms me. Some. "Go on," I say. "They found her there, and they killed her, and my Gramps was crippled when he tried to stop them. What did they do to the servant?"

He sighs heavily. When I glance up, there's that sadness in his eyes again. He looks down into his hands, held open in his lap, as if reading the palms for his next line. "They killed her, too. It wasn't the king who did that. It was the Lord of Ontrei that was."

"Your father," I say.

"The king's right-hand man."

"And the woods?" I whisper. "When my mother was dead, the woods pulled back again?"

There's a long silence. Edgar doesn't look up. "You looked about at all of them with such eerie round eyes, my father and his men used to say. All those noble, brave soldiers used to say you were casting a spell on them, that you were thinking already how you could take your vengeance." His hands are curling into fists. "As if a baby girl was anything to fear. As if seeing your mother killed wasn't enough to make anyone look eerie, enough to stop up anyone's throat."

I say, "But the woods pulled back?"

Now he does look up, and there's a sharpness in his face, and in his voice, too. "So what if they did? She was so far north, surrounded by trees on three sides when they found her. Why would the woods have needed to come any farther? No, it had nothing to do with her. It was coincidence, that's all. It was the woods folk playing games with us, or just random, just something that is bound to happen now and again no matter what we do."

"Do you really believe that?" I say. I'm remembering the lady, what she said to me before I left for the castle: *We will be coming for you. Every one of us will be coming after you.* I know they want me. They've sent their dreams, their voices; they've shown me the dragon, stark against the moon.

Edgar is telling me something. That it's not my fault. That

the king is out of his mind trying to blame someone for a thing that's nobody's fault. And again, about those soldiers looking at that little girl, so convinced she was already plotting revenge.

But he's grown up with the festering of his guilt, with a hatred for what his father did. He's no more levelheaded than the king.

I stop him. "It's no matter, my lord." I bend to pick up my work, and I grab the needle from the table again. My hands have finally stopped their shaking. I stick the thread straight into the center of a misshapen flower's eye, smooth and certain. "He didn't kill me then, and he hasn't killed me now. Now, if you'll excuse me, my lord, I've sewing to do—"

"Marni, if he's trying to kill you—"

I wave one hand at him. "I have it under control. No need to worry about me."

There's a pause, and then he laughs, short, under his breath. "As my princess commands," he says, "I shall now cease to worry about her uncle chopping off her head."

"What do you want, Edgar?" I say, stabbing my curtains with the needle again, though maybe less accurately.

"I could protect you. You would have the support of half—at least a fourth—of the nobles, and we could keep you safe. Watch your back, taste your food, make sure you live long enough to take the throne."

"That's sweet," I say, "but really there's no need—"

"You could marry me."

My breath catches. Not just because I thought we'd gone over this, but because as he says it, for one crazy instant I think about saying yes. I think about living with this man, who's always taken my side, who melts me right away with his kisses, who believes in me and my innocence even when he really shouldn't.

He really shouldn't.

Before I can stop myself, I throw my sewing back on the floor and push myself out of my chair. Edgar rises to his feet as well, wary. "How many times is this?" I say, my voice shriller than I mean it to be, but I push my anger on, fall gladly into it. "What is it with you, my Lord of Ontrei, that makes you think that when I'm telling you *no*, and *no*, and *no* again, what I really must be meaning is *ask me again*? Could be I'm crazy, but I've no wish to be the stone you step on to reach the throne. If all you're going to say, again and again, is *marry me*, then I reckon you'd better leave this room and not come back."

"Don't you like me, lady?" he says, weak, when I've done. The stones are ringing with my words. I remember the open window and hope, belatedly, though without much force, that no one was outside just then. It's the most beautiful day yet this winter, and at the very least the children and their nannies will be running about in the melting snow, and what the nannies hear, the nobles will know of by dinnertime.

"Oh, perfect," I say, falling back into my chair.

Edgar makes a move toward me — to — to *comfort* me, or some such. "Get out," I tell him, quiet. From the corner of my eye I see him hesitate, then make me a bow. It's a correct bow, the bow of a lord to a princess. He goes then to the door and lets himself out of the room.

The birds are still chirping. They, at least, aren't bothered by my screaming. After I can bear to take my hands from my face, I go to the window and sit on the seat there, leaning out.

Sure enough, there are children playing a game of hide-and-seek, and their nannies are gathered in a group near the castle wall, talking excitedly about something. As I watch, one looks up at my window and, catching sight of me, does a little jump in the air and turns back to her friends, gesturing even more.

I wrinkle my nose at them, though I scarce care. My vengeance is itching against my arm. It knows we're alone again. It knows it's time for it to fly. But a memory is trickling into my head, something I'd forgotten — just as I'd forgotten the way I used to knit magic things with the lady — something that the Lord of Ontrei's words set free. As the sun takes itself off to the west, this memory holds me tight. I watch it all the way through, waiting as pieces fill themselves in, as bit by bit it builds itself into the story of the very first time I went to the woods.

I was out alone in the garden. That much is clear, and that much makes sense. Something called to me — maybe it knew my name, the little man standing on the edge of the wall, or the bright light pulsing in the tree branches, twinkling my way. I don't know exactly what it was, but I remember the pull, the sense that if I climbed over the stones, dropped myself down onto the pine needles on the other side, there would be magic waiting, a magic that would belong to me and show me wonders.

And I remember the lady, my first sight of her. Some children would have run at that sight, I reckon. She's not a comforting presence. She leaned over me where I'd tumbled down from the wall, and she held out her hand. The way I'm remembering it, she said, *Welcome home, little Tulip. We've been waiting.* Again, that might have sent me running, except — it wasn't just that what I knew of myself was tied to this lady, to this place. My mother had gone to the woods, and here was a woman reaching out her hand to me. My father had come from these woods; I knew that before I knew anything else about him. So the fact that there was a place for me there where the magic seeped and sparkled didn't surprise me all that much.

But it was always more than that, wasn't it? It was deeper. It was much more dangerous. The lady's words and her voice, and that face that would scare any normal child — they felt *right* to me. That little man, that twinkling light didn't seem strange so much as a part of me that I was just discovering. It was the dragon's blood, even then, rising in me, pushing me toward the woods.

Those soldiers, the ones Edgar talked of, they said that little girl was already plotting her vengeance. Even when she scarce could walk, she had already become what she was going to be. And maybe, I'm thinking as the children and their nannies go inside and the cold air crawls into my skirts, maybe they weren't so far off. Maybe the king isn't so far off, or the lady or the dragon, even, all the ones who want me to come home. I'm the dragon's daughter, aren't I? Blood will out, even when you don't know a single thing about yours.

I don't go down to dinner, and I'm shivering when Sylvie comes up with a tray from the kitchen.

I smile at her as she puts it on my table. She fusses over me, pulling me from the window, bringing me to my chair, and tucking a blanket tight around my lap. I study her. She doesn't seem fearful of me, or suspicious.

"I know I'm not a normal princess," I say, and she turns from closing the shutters to look at me, eyebrows raised.

"What's that, then, lady?" she asks.

I smile more, ignoring the chattering of my teeth. "I talk funny."

"Less and less so every day."

"And I walk funny, and I won't marry a great lord."

She sniffs. "No reason you should marry yourself off so soon, when you could have anyone you'd like."

"And no one knows who my father is."

"Well, that's true." She locks the shutters with a click, and she moves over to take the covers off the food for me. "Eat up, lady," she says. "You're going to make yourself sick, sitting in the wind like that, especially after what you went through today."

I lean forward to sniff the food. It smells delicious, but then so did the food the king tried to poison me with. Sylvie is watching me. She dried me off so thoroughly this morning, made me sit by the great fire in the main hall for hours. I ask anyway. "Are you trying to kill me?"

She pulls herself up to her full five-foot height. "Lady," she says, "you are my princess, and I am your maid. I would no more kill you than I would kill my own sister."

"That's not as comforting as you might think," I say, but she's already moving about the room again, muttering to herself as she plumps a pillow here, straightens a tapestry there, and anyway, I guess the first person they would blame, should they need someone to blame, would be my maid.

And I'm dead hungry, so I eat.

The next morning, the lady's voice wakens me, sliding into my head like one of my own thoughts, stronger than I've ever heard it, and I look, my heart beating sudden wild, into the dark folds of my bed's canopy, and I see a griffin flying in for a kill, and a spirit dancing around an ancient tree, and eyes I've never seen before, all deep and black, with a thousand sparkling reflections, looking right at me.

When I go to the window, the sun is only just brushing the sky with white. It's warmed up considerable overnight; the river is flowing smooth, with only chunks of ice drifting here and there. Pockets of snow dot the castle grounds, but nothing like the heaps that still stood yesterday. The king will be able to ride out this morning if he chooses.

I blink into the morning sky, breathing the scent of fresh spring grass and pine. I've been telling Emmy she should get out to the garden soon. Maybe I can go along and help her, make sure she plants things the right way. Maybe there I can find a place away from the nobles' glares, away from Edgar's worried looks, while I figure out what I am to do with the thing around my wrist. Maybe there — *pine.* I'm smelling *pine.*

It takes a second or two for the sun spots to give way, for my eyes to look that far, beyond the castle lawns, beyond the river, over several hills, but still in sight, still not a ten-minute ride from the king's front door.

Dark green in the early sunshine, as tall and proud as soldiers, and reaching north in a jagged carpet all the way to the mountains. No wonder the lady's voice is so strong. The woods are here.

There's a knock on my bedroom door, but I can't move, I can't think to answer it. There's a song in my head of flying above the clouds, and there's an itching in my feet to go, to jump from the window and run until the shadows eat me up. But the knocking is getting louder, and now I can't keep from hearing the shouting, too, the deep anger in the soldier's voice: "Open up! In the name of the king, open this door! You're under arrest for treason!"

THIS IS THE KING trying once more to kill me.

This is the king seeing his sister come home with a baby from who knows where, threatening his kingdom, tearing out his trust for her and his compassion all in one fell swoop. This is the king doing what he's always done—protecting his lands by throwing his own blood on sharp steel, by hardening his will, his purpose, until he is nothing more than a tool for cutting down those in his way.

I am thinking this as the guards break down my door, as I stand there unmoving by the window and they grab my arms, pull me away as though I'm like to scream and struggle and spit at them, when I'm barely moving my feet to keep from dragging along the floor.

I am trying to remember the anger I hoarded for so many years, the bitterness I planted along with each flower bulb. The vengeance is tucked in against my sleeve still. It is crying out to me, high, desperate. It wants me to set it free. It's telling me that this is the time, now, here, at once. But I've nothing left anymore, no hatred, no resentment. It's all gone.

Could be Edgar's story yesterday sapped it out of me — the certainty that I am right, the will to tear my uncle's eyes clear from his head.

Could be last night's memory took it from me, that something shifted inside when I remembered how easy it was to go that first time to the woods, and now I can't keep from wondering what I have to do with their advance.

Could be, too, that the smell of pine and the memory of those piercing eyes drove any vengeful thoughts clear out of me. That sight of the woods and the heady smell of wildness pulsed all through me, like a fire, like a dip in freezing river water, and could be when I came out, I was someone else, someone entirely new.

Because as they drag me uncomplaining from my room and down the tower steps, as we hurry along the corridors and the lords and the ladies come out to stand and watch, none of them saying a word and all of them looking straight into my eyes as if I'm already no longer there, as if I'm something they've dreamed up in the early morning — as we slip across the main hall and there are faces, the eyes of the servants watching from half-closed doors, and there are Emmy and Sylvie, and they are holding each other, pale and crying, but they don't call out to me, they don't come and take my hand—as we rush through the open castle doors and into a warm (warm!) spring breeze that lingers promisingly along our cheekbones and pours itself like honey into our lungs—as we make our way out the castle gate and through the city streets, and here, too, the city folk are at their doors, so someone must have spread this news so fast it seems impossible, and then we're at the steps to the city's prison, and a bailiff is opening those doors for us, and I think briefly of all the doors we've seen on our way, the doors of the lords and the ladies and the servants and the castle and the city folk, and this door to this prison—and then, as we're stepping real careful down cold stone steps and stopping before another, final door, with iron bars and a great cold padlock, I'm thinking about how all those doors are the freedom I will never feel again—

And as I step alone into this cell and I hear that sharp, sweet clang of the door and the clunking of the padlock and the stomps of the soldiers moving off up the stairs, I'm not protesting. I'm not thinking of ways to chop the king into little bits. I'm not seething in my anger or wallowing in my despair.

I'm scarce upset at all.

I sit myself down on the thin, hard bed and look up into the thin, hard light streaking through the window at the top of the cell, and I listen to the lady's song until the day is a pile of dense, uncountable minutes. I pee in the bucket when I need to, and I eat when they give me food, and when the light softens and disintegrates, I slip underneath the covers and fall instantly asleep.

I am dreaming I am winged.

The sun sweeps across my back, and I lift my beak to drink it in, dazzle in it.

I can go anywhere. I can do anything. The quickest fleeing prey and the strongest leaping predator must stop short and tremble when I scream.

And how I scream!

It gathers in my every feather, in the tips of my talons and the edges of my wings. It smolders in my lungs until I roll it along my throat and out over my tongue. It's in the heavy downbeats of my wings. It's in the air that whistles past my ears, and far below, it's in the mountaintop that blurs and shifts as I shoot forward and sharply twist, chasing bursts of wind.

The world is my scream.

It's a disappearing thing, isn't it? It's the letting go of everything you've ever been and turning into something that doesn't care about the future or the past, but only this one moment, only this one flight and swoop and cry.

Something that doesn't care about the people she doesn't have or the people she's driven away. Something that doesn't wonder if they are right about her ruining everything.

Because if you want it this much, if it calls to you this

strongly, maybe you aren't even half human. Because if they killed your mother because of you, and your Gramps lost everything because of you and died alone because of you, maybe it's time you stopped thinking about what you think they owe you.

Maybe it's time you start thinking about disappearing in truth.

ELEVEN

I COUNT THE DAYS this way.

The first day, I scramble up the rocky back wall, gripping tight with my fingers and my bare toes, leaping to grab the bars of the window. I pull. I yell. I shake them, but they don't even rattle. I stare out at the brown dirt street until my arms grow numb and I can't hold on any longer.

The second day, I keep a knife from the food they give me, and I dig away at the corner of my cell behind the bed, where the ground is soft and fine.

The third day, I keep on digging.

And the fourth.

And the fifth.

And the sixth.

On the seventh day the knife snaps, and the hole I've made is only big enough to fit my head and shoulders.

On the eighth day I throw a fit, a crazed, shrieking fit that brings the guards running to make sure I'm not dying or some such. They call for a doctor, and when he says the light isn't bright enough in my cell, they take me out into the hall and up the stairs and through the prison's main room, and I'm blinking in the sun when they open the door.

The guards have me by both arms, held tight, and I'm shouting nonsense still, pulling this way and that.

When we're full in the street and the doctor is leading us up the road toward his house, I go limp, and the guards stop in their surprise, and before they've a chance to tighten their holds again, I've torn away from them and am running back down the street toward the city gates.

I run maybe a hundred steps before they have me again, and I'm back in my cell two minutes later.

The ninth day, I sit and look at my hands and eat no food until my head is filled with dizzy black spots and my throat is closed and dry.

The tenth day, the queen comes to visit me, and she gives me the key.

TWELVE

SHE COMES to tell me that the king is saying he'll kill me this very week.

"I've held him back as long as I can, Marni," she says. "But he's saying he can't afford to wait any longer. It's almost spring, and the farmers need to be planting." She's come all unannounced, scooting through the door the guard held open for her, waiting until he closed it again before she threw back the dull gray cloak from her head. I reckon there aren't many who know she's come to visit me. I reckon the king himself doesn't know.

I've felt the weather changing, even in my stone cell. The air is defrosting; the light from the window is growing warmer, softer day by day. Only tonight there's a bite again in the drafts that circle always through the prison. Tonight the stones are freezing to the touch.

"What are the lords and the ladies saying about it?" I say it low. I almost don't want to know, but I can't help but ask. I think of Susanna and Hettie, how they'd grasp my hand, giggling with me over some nonsense. I think of the lords who courted me before Lord Edgar, how they listened to what I said as if they cared, pulled back my chairs, asked after my health.

I don't think of Edgar or of Sylvie or of Emmy. I wouldn't think of the queen except here she is, her perfect hair tousled by the cloak, dark circles under her eyes.

"They don't say much," she says. "They're scared, Marni. The woods . . ." She loses the sentence. I see her look down at her hands where she's holding them, properly folded as always, in her lap. I see her shift them, grip them the tighter.

"I thought it was only a fairy tale. I thought the whole country had lost its mind."

We're sitting side by side on my mattress. She's brought me a new blanket, and I've wrapped it round myself. It's keeping out some of the evening's chill.

"How close are they now?" I ask.

"Every day," she says. "Every day they are ten rows closer. We fall asleep each night hoping the city will still be ours in the morning. We think — we wonder whether the king will get around to killing you before they arrive."

Hearing it out loud, so simple, my mind goes blank in panic.

She notices something about the way I look, or maybe I make a sound without realizing it, because she reaches over and takes my hand. "I'm sorry," she says. "I didn't mean to say it like that."

I shake my head. "Seems I've been waiting for it my whole life. Seems I should be ready for it by now. Only — I thought my Gramps would be here as well. Not that I wish he was, not to go to the axe with me, but being alone, you see. Being alone at the very end." *Like he was,* I think, and then I can't say any more.

"I'll be there," she says, "though I suspect that's not a great comfort."

We sit in silence for a bit. There are a thousand things I could tell the queen, a thousand words of thanks and a thousand accusations. I could tell her of the vengeance, the one I scarce feel anymore, though it's still clasped tight to my wrist. I could tell her of the lady's voice, and those sparkling eyes that so fill my head these days I can hardly care about being locked up or worry about my death. I'm only longing to get back to the woods.

"There are *things* in the gardens now, and all along the river," the queen says abruptly, in a different tone of voice. "Little men who disappear when you look at them straight on. Wisps of smoke where there is no fire. And voices, singing songs or chanting rhymes, with words not one of us understands, but they make our skin crawl. Things that aren't supposed to exist, you know?"

I've turned to stare at her.

She shrugs. "You'll think I'm making it up, but it's true. It feels less and less like the world is ours. I'm starting to think I dreamed up things like fields and meadows. I'm starting to think the woods have already taken over."

"Aunt," I say, "there are things *in the castle gardens?*"

"Yes, and near the river. And no one dares go into the flower garden now, not with that monstrous plant — why, you might know what it is. It's all vines and little blue flowers, carpeting the ground. It's spread from one end of the garden to the other. There's no room left for other plants."

"That's the dragon flower," I say. "Nobody plants it. It just grows."

"Yes." She nods. "I daresay nobody *would* plant it, when it takes over everything so."

"It never has before."

"I suppose it's never tangled up a gardener so much that she broke her leg and had to be hacked free with axes, either."

"No," I say.

"She said she was following the pretty blue lights, that they were leading her from one step to the next." She shakes her head. "Poor thing."

I don't ask the gardener's name, but I reckon I don't need to. It was only a few weeks ago that I was telling Emmy she should get out to the flowers soon, and with me locked away, she'll be feeling it's her duty to take care of the garden.

"Tell her to leave it alone," I say.

"The gardener?"

"If you can get a word with her, tell her it's all right, that she can let it be. Tell her I said so."

"I will," the queen says. Moonlight has begun to seep into the cell. It falls across our knees and turns the queen's rough cloak into silk. She raises a silver-edged eyebrow at me. "Is there anyone else you'd like me to take a message to?"

"No," I say at once; then, "Yes. Tell Sylvie she's not to fret."

The queen laughs, and it's the same laugh I've heard a hundred times before, incandescent. I stare at her. I always thought she'd created that laugh to seem ever happy and sociable, as if none of the court's cruel gossip could get to her. But what reason would she have to laugh that way now if it weren't real? "I'll tell her, dear," she says, "but I don't think it'll make any difference." She stands, and I look up at her numbly. She says, "It's late, and if I don't get back soon, Roddy will wonder where I am."

I whisper, "Don't go."

She looks down at me. You know that way a person can look when she's done with pretending anything anymore, when she's letting you see what all the years of worry and struggle have done to her — you know how, when there's nothing but this one moment before it all goes away, so there's nothing left to do or say or hope for, and you're bare to the storm — that's how she's looking at me, and I reckon that's how I'm looking at her.

"Do you want me to take any word back to *him?*" she says, and the moment, if it was such a moment, is over.

"No," I say, "I've nothing to say to any *him.*"

"Well," says the queen, "I have a message for you, if you'll hear it."

I look at her, startled. "From him?" I would have thought he'd be forgetting me as fast as he could, now the king had won.

"He would have brought it himself, but he's watched even more closely than I am these days. Here, stand up, Marni."

I let her pull me to my feet. I've not the energy to fight the queen, not when she's got that purpose in her voice and is tossing her little head in such a way. She looks downright regal.

When I'm standing, she grasps both my hands. "He sends his love," she says, and I swear there's an evil glint in her eyes.

I'm about to snap at her — how dare he send his love? Does he think that's like to make me *happy?* But then she's wrapped one arm around my shoulders, and she's whispering in my ear: "Along with this." And she's slipping a hard, cold key from her sleeve into my nearest hand. "I may have been wrong about the woods," she continues, only just loud enough for me to hear, "but they are not going to kill a lovely young woman out of misguided superstition. Whatever the reason for the griffins and the phoenixes and the shy little men and everything, it's not you, Marni." Then she folds my fist around the key and steps back, and I've just the strength of mind to bury it in my skirts as she calls for the guard.

The door is clanking open when she says, "I daresay I'll ask the guard to walk me back to the castle. It's long past sunset, and I could use the assistance."

"Go safe, lady," I manage, and she scoots out into the corridor. I see her wink at me, and then she's gone. The padlock clunks back into place; the guard's boots clomp off down the hall. I wait one minute. Two. I go to the door, peer into the dark of the prison. I listen hard. Nothing.

In a flash, I stretch my arms through the bars and get the key in the lock, and then I'm taking the lock off, as quiet as I can, and placing it down on the floor and swinging the door open, smooth, smooth, smooth. I leave it to hang, and I pad my way down the hallway, up the stone steps. The queen's blanket is still around my shoulders, and I wish I'd left it behind to free my arms, but I dare not leave it here. They'll see it, a minute before they see the empty cell, and that's a minute I might need.

The main floor of the prison is empty too. I don't know how she's managed that; could be that only the cells are staffed this late at night. It doesn't matter; all I care is that not five minutes after the queen leaves me in my cell, I'm running down the city streets, and luck is with me for once, because the moon has been swallowed up by a whole fleet of clouds and everywhere is shadows.

PART THREE

IN THIS STORY, the dragon was a man.

Don't ask me how that works, but he was a man; he came riding up on a great black horse as a girl was collecting berries and roots and such in a basket to bring back to her ailing mother and four younger siblings.

This was back when the woods were everywhere, and one of this girl's little sisters was just old enough to be playing about outdoors, and the girl had noticed how the fairies and the spirits swooped around more when her sister was nearby.

Well, and the girl was worried about the child's getting snatched away by the forest folk. When the dragon rode up, fire in his eyes, she dropped her basket and held the point of her little gathering knife against her chest, so that he pulled up his mare and stared at her, sitting still, so as not to startle her none.

"You'll be wanting to take me away," the girl said.

"I reckon I will," said the dragon. "Now, don't you go and do nothing foolish."

"I won't if you won't," she said.

And the dragon he shook his head because now there wasn't nothing he wanted more in the world than this girl.

"You're not understanding me," she said. "I mean I'll go with you, and gladly, and stay as long as you'd like."

"Good, then," said the dragon as cautiously as a dragon could.

"But you and your folk will leave my family alone, and my people alone, and you'll pull back your trees so that we've space and sky and land to call our own."

He might have laughed at this; some people say he did.

"I mean it!" she said, and held the knife tight against her skin. The blood beaded there, and her chest fell up and down with her breathing, and there was such life in her; the dragon had never seen such passion, such spark. How could he let this one get away?

"I so swear," he said, and moved to pull her up onto his horse.

The girl kept the knife steady. "Not for a hundred hundred years," she said.

"Not for a hundred hundred years," he said, and what is that to a dragon anyway?

The girl threw her knife down next to her basket, and she ran and jumped up on the horse behind the dragon, and he took her away all for himself.

And the woods gave up the space and the sky and the land to the people, and they began to look around and blink their eyes and see one another, how many they were, and that was the beginning of our country.

The thing with this story is, who would have told it if it were true? It was only the girl and the dragon that day, and no one to hear them speak.

But others like it for the cleverness of the girl and the love in her heart, and they say it explains why the woods have been moving themselves in: our hundred hundred years are up, and the dragon's coming back to take what's always been his, and was ours only as long as the girl's bargain held firm.

Oh, and I forgot to mention — didn't I? — that when the girl's family found her basket and its contents strewn over the forest floor, they found a patch of flowers, too, growing all through the basket weaving and around the berries and over and under the roots. The knife was well buried beneath the creeping green vines and hidden by the bright blue blossoms.

In that story, it's how the dragon flower got its name, and depending on the teller, it was either a promise that he would keep his end of the deal, or a threat that one far-off day he'd be back, or just something the ground couldn't help but send up when the drops of the girl's bright blood fell and mixed with the leaves and dirt of the dragon's woods. The girl's brave heart and that dragon's harsh will, they say, made themselves a flower garden.

I GO TO THE WOODS, of course. Once I'm out the southern gates, I circle round and run north. The air grows cold and colder with each step. Soon I'm over the river and running across the open hills, and just as I see the first line of the trees — a dark mass on the horizon, closer, sure as sure, than ten long mornings ago — I catch the first sharp snowflake on my nose. For a second I don't know what it is, and I stop there in a valley between two hills and I touch it, the cold, wet sting. Then another falls into my hair, and as I lift my head, a soft flake lands on my tongue. I breathe it in, swallow. It tastes like something I've forgotten, a dream I used to have of impossible things.

They are falling all around now, big and slow, each one

separate from the rest. It's not unheard of, to get a snowfall this late. But the ground is hard, and there are grasses pushing up already. It's like the first snow of the fall, not the wet, miserable snow we get in spring. It's as if we're outside of the seasons tonight, on the cusp of something uncertain, something new.

I hold out my hands, watching the silence drift around them.

I look up, and she is there.

A twist of wind in the blowing snow, a glint of the rising moon.

Hand held out, as always. Needles at her side. Face fractured; eyes stark and inescapable.

I step toward her. When I'm only an arm's length away, she says, "Tulip, it's time to come home."

I close my eyes, thinking of the way the shadows stretch out long beneath the trees, of the chittering squirrels throwing acorns just above my head, of the days I could run and never see another person, of the griffins and the phoenixes I could ride so high we almost would touch the sky.

Back there is all the doubt and fear, everything I've never had and everything I'll never be. The last dregs of it are falling away from me. Finally, there is only this moment, and finally I can answer her.

I reach out and take her hand, and we run, as light as the clouds, across the fresh white hills, on our way to the woods.

✻   ✻   ✻

I imagine there are a thousand reasons girls take themselves to the woods.

Cruel parents. Ugly betrothed. A wish, a dream of something they'll never have out there with those rules and probabilities, and they can't accept it anymore.

A thousand reasons, and a thousand choices, and a thousand fast-beating hearts and quick-stepping feet and deep breaths of their first moments of freedom.

This lady can run.

She doesn't let go of my hand, not all that night as we're racing through the trees that stretch like columns in every direction. Could be it's snowing still out there, but we don't feel it. Here, the ground is dry beneath our feet. The twigs snap and old leaves crunch, and I can smell them, the clear, musty smell.

There's nothing before this. I've become the wind, a flash of light, a spurt of magic. I'm laughing as we run, and the lady looks back at me, and if she had a mouth, I know that she'd be smiling.

There's a long way to go.

We're heading for the mountains; I know that without the lady telling me. It's the north of my compass, and it's pulling me as much as the lady's hand. These woods have spread themselves out so far, though, that we don't even reach the foothills by the morning.

There used to be farms all along this way, I think. There used to be families living here, safe and happy. Not anymore.

"Why have you moved so far into the kingdom?" I ask her as we're stopping to catch our breath. My breath, I guess. I don't reckon the lady needs such things.

She's bending down to look into the hole at the bottom of a tree. She pokes one of her long needles into the dark; there's a squeal, and she takes the needle out again, a mouse squirming on its end. "Does it matter, Tulip?" she asks. She plucks the mouse from the needle, cupping it in both hands so I can't see it. Her hands glow bright, and the squealing stops. When she opens them again, it's not a body she reveals, but a finely roasted bit of meat, skinless and steaming.

She hands it to me. I bite into it. The tangy, juicy charred flesh burns my mouth and seeps down my throat. It tastes like nothing I've had before, like sunlight, like power. I blink at the lady. "Does what matter?"

She holds out a hand again, and I take it. "Off we go," she says.

It takes us three days and nights of running to reach the mountains, and all that time I am remembering those things I learned so long ago when the lady and all the folk of the woods were my teachers.

I'm calling out to birds and squirrels as we go, and they're calling back, welcoming me home.

I'm throwing myself into whatever guise I choose, leaping

over logs as a deer, flipping through leaves as a bat, bounding along as a great gray wolf, panting and shaking my ruff in the midnight dew.

The lady follows alongside always. She doesn't lead anymore; I know full well our direction. But she accompanies me, sits by me when I stop to sleep, and finds me berries and meat when I've not the instinct for it.

As we get closer, the folk of the woods grow numerous. Seems every way I look, they are poking their grotesque heads out of a hollow log or flicking from trunk to trunk, trailing sparks, or swinging from branch to branch, gripping hard with tiny hands and screaming war cries with tiny voices.

The lady sees me looking. "They've come for you," she says. "They've come to escort you back."

I don't ask what she means by *back*, when I've never been here before. It seems right, somehow, the word, the idea that this isn't a leaving, but an arriving, not a first visit, but a return from a long exile.

We reach the first hints of the mountains to come: foothills rising from the gentle waves of the lowland into sudden steep slopes and drops. We follow a riverbed, climbing up and up. I turn mountain goat and cougar, picking and padding my way ever higher.

As we step into the true mountains at last, the final wide-leafed trees disappear and the pines grow thinner and farther between. We're walking in the open at times now, and the sun falls, unfamiliar, on my skin and fur and scales. If I stopped in a clearing, climbed a rock or a tree, and turned to look behind, I would see the kingdom, I imagine, all spread out for me like a map. I would see the edge of the woods, and the king's city, and the rivers flowing free along the fields that are left. I would see how far it's shrunk now, the land of my people.

But I don't look back, and my mind is on what's in front, on what is waiting for me at the end of this race northward.

Half a day into the mountains, the first of the phoenixes comes rushing overhead, arrowing down through trees, to land, feathers furling, beak glinting, eyes narrowed, right in front of me.

I'm startled out of my wolverine self and shudder back up to a human, stepping away from the bird.

Like a sunset, this creature is, all over red, orange, and gold. It's twice my height, and I reckon its wings would span right across the main hall of the king's castle. Used to be, I'd run right up to a phoenix and stroke its feathers, and it would take me on its back for a ride up into the sun, and I would laugh and hold tight.

I'm grown now, though, and I've not the trust of a little girl. Nor, would I guess, does it have the trust in me.

"Don't fear," the lady says. She stopped when I did and looks back at me now. "She'll not harm you."

It's a she, then. She shifts from one talon to the other, keeping her eyes always on me. She's waiting for something, I think. She opens her beak, and her throat moves, and I'm covering my ears before the cry comes, the shriek that resonates through the woods.

Still shaking with the sound, I bring my hands back to my sides. The phoenix has dipped her head down low, and she looks at me sidewise, laughing maybe.

With a light head I step my way over to her until I can hear the rasp of her breath and see the quiver in her feathers. There's wildness in the depths of each black eye. But there's something else, too, a question, a puzzle—recognition.

"Hello, my lovely," I whisper, and she ducks her beak to nudge my left hand, gently, almost a caress. Could be we know each other from way back when. I trace a finger across one long, silky feather, shining and glorious in the forest light.

She grows still under my touch. We're breathing together, almost, and again I nearly know her. As though it's been a thousand years and I only just awoke, I feel the answer swimming up through my mind, and I close my eyes, waiting, feeling her warmth beneath my hand.

"Tulip," says the lady, right by my ear, "we must go." Then she's taken my hand and for the first time in days she's leading me again, away from the phoenix, and the thought sinks beyond my reach.

But she doesn't leave us, that great, beautiful bird. When I look up, I see her shadow across the treetops and hear the echo of her shriek in my mind. Her sisters join us one by one; they land and touch their beaks to my hands or hair or shoulders, and I touch their feathers, and on we go. With none of the others do I feel the recognition of the first one, though. I always know where she is, even when there are so many I scarce can tell her shape from the pack.

Later in the day, the griffins start coming too, with their hawk heads and wings and their cougar feet and tails. Where the trees are thinnest, they run along beside us. I hear their heaving and panting, strangely feline from a bird's throat, and their cries are deeper than those of the phoenixes, more powerful, not as piercing.

Darkness pushes the sunshine across the rocky slope until it tinges only the top peaks of the western mountains and then slides down, off the edge of the world.

I'm human, still. I've not changed since the creatures started arriving. The lady has let my hand go again, but she stays so close by my side that I fret I'll trip her up or push her off a cliff without meaning it. She doesn't suggest that we stop, and I've nothing but energy, a thrill that sets my legs always on, always up, a strength in my lungs as though I could keep going forever.

All around us, griffins scramble up the mountainside, and above us, phoenix wings beat the black night air.

There's no moon, but I figure it's round about midnight when the pines give up the climb for good and the bare face of the mountain, dotted here and there with snow, rolls out before us, gray and gleaming in the starlight. Not fifty paces from the tree line, a cave gapes, boring down into the mountain.

In the entrance, his head tucked between his claws, his tail wrapped around his side, and his eyes open, black and deep, glittering with a thousand reflections as they focus on me, is the dragon.

THREE

E LIFTS his head from his claws, and I can see his muscled neck. He is so long, so huge. I remember him, dark against the moon, and his mind-shivering roar.

The griffins have stopped at the edge of the trees, just behind me. The lady is there too, and the phoenixes circle overhead. There are little people poking their heads out of the grasses by my feet, and balls of light every color of the rainbow dart and twist among the rocks down the slope a few paces.

It's me and this beast. Nobody, nothing stands between us.

I breathe in, out. It's taking near to everything I have not to turn and run down the mountain, through the foothills, back across the miles of wooded fields.

Seconds go by; they last forever. The dragon gestures with his head, and I know he wants me to walk up the slope toward him.

I take another breath, steadying myself. If this dragon had wanted to eat me, he could have swooped down out of the sky anytime in the last three days. Running wouldn't save me from that.

It's insanity, but I clamber up over the rocks to the mouth of the cave and, keeping a good ten feet away, look the dragon in the eye.

His breath is hot, of course. I scrunch up my nose to keep out the scent of sulfur. I can see myself a thousand times in his pupils. There's no familiarity here, no urge to reach out and stroke his razor scales. There's the quivering of the prey, and the terror of the unknown, and there's the thrill, too, the same rush that near made me jump from my bedroom window when last I saw this beast. Yes, there's his size, and his teeth, and his claws, but he is beautiful, pure, and I near wish he *would* eat me up and make me part of him.

He pulls his head up, and up, and up, and his front legs are stepping back. His wings rustle, settling into a new position. He draws a great breath in; I hear it whistling through his lungs. I think, *This is it. This is when the dragon burns me to bits,* and I close my eyes without meaning to, without wanting to shut out the sight of him, but I can't help it for that one moment, when the fear is sliding all over my skin like oil and I can't even scream.

There's a whooshing sound, and the hairs on my arms prickle. I seem to be alive, so I open my eyes and look up, and the dragon isn't there.

"Tulip," says a man. I bring my head back down. There he is, just in front of me where the dragon used to be. I don't need anyone to tell me they're one and the same. His eyes are black and glittering even from this distance, even in this dim starlight. He's wearing some sort of leather pants and shirt, and his feet are bare and tough, as tough as the rest of him, I'd guess. "I hear that's what they call you," he says.

I somehow get myself to nod. "Some do," I say. My voice is clear. Seems my body's caught up on its own, or there's some spirit taking over my speech while my brain's still babbling incoherently at being near fried to a crisp, and seeing a dragon turn into a man, and hearing the man speak my own name.

He's tilting his head at me. "It's an odd name for a dragon's daughter."

"Yes," I say. "Yes, I reckon a dragon wouldn't name his baby that."

The griffins have crept up from the woods now, and the phoenixes are landing, too, in sliding thumps all around us. "Could be he didn't have the chance to name her anything," the man says. He speaks like me, like the villagers in the kingdom. I would have thought, if I'd thought anything, that he'd talk like the king.

I see the first phoenix, the one I almost recognized, coming toward me, stepping with her backward-bending legs across the stones, sending miniature avalanches down the slope. When I look back, the man is only two feet from me. He's tall, taller than any lord at court, taller even than my Gramps would have been, if he had stood straight.

"I loved her, Tulip," says the man. The phoenix is right beside me now. I can feel her breath on my shoulder. The soft edge of a feather trails along my arm. "I don't suppose you'd believe that, me being what I am. And maybe my love is different, but I loved that princess so much it hurt sometimes. Should love hurt?" He's tilting his head the other way. He's looking at me as though I'd know the answer to such a question.

"I don't know," I say. "I think it often does."

"And then she ran away. And I was like to tear up her kingdom looking for her; I was like to take the whole land, risk losing any affection she had for me, to get her back. Does that sound like love, Tulip?"

The bird is nudging my hand again with her beak. I reach out absent-mindedly along her neck, grasp the down beneath her wing, feel her beating heart thrumming through my fingers. "Some folk love that way," I say.

"Well, then, I loved her," says the man.

I nod. "I believe you." It's like a story I've heard a hundred times in a hundred different ways. The phoenix gives a soft cry, much softer than before, so soft I've no need to cover my ears or step away. I look at her, and she's looking at me. And she knows me, and then I know her.

"Dragon," I say.

"Yes?" he says.

"What happens to all those girls, the ones who leave their homes and run away to your woods?"

"They get what they want," he says.

"What do they want?" I whisper, and I'm looking at him, so I feel it first, the sudden heat through my hand, and then the shrinking, the feathers pulling away, leaving smooth skin and rough cotton. There's a rush, like the rush when the dragon disappeared, and when I look her way, my hand is on her shoulder, and she's smiling at me.

"We want our freedom," she says, my friend, my long-lost Annel. All around, the other phoenixes and the griffins are shrinking into themselves as well, and I see it happen, the impossible transformations, there and there and there, all turning up as girls at the cusp of their lives, all those girls we've lost through the years to the siren song of the woods.

She reaches out to hug me, and I bury my face in her shirt, not quite knowing why I'm crying. "Welcome home, Marni," she says.

"Which am I?" I say when I can manage to mumble the words through the wet and the cloth. "Am I to be a phoenix or a griffin?"

"Neither," says the dragon. Annel pulls back from me, lets me go. He takes my hand, and the heat of him crawls up my arm, but still I shiver. This was always going to happen. There was always going to be this night, with the stars to shine and a hundred lost girls to witness, and the lady of the woods, always at the edge of the trees, to see her mission finally complete. The dragon leans in close to me, with my reflections all sparkling, and he says the magic words, the ones that will change me, every bit of me: "You, my dear, are to be the dragon's daughter."

He tells me a story. It seems he must tell me the story now, at once, before anything else. He doesn't wait for me to sit down on a rock or on the dirt of his cave. I listen standing up, watching him in the midnight dark. He's hypnotizing, so I don't notice my weary legs. He gestures in the oddest places and pauses in the oddest places. He speaks like a human, but his every breath and twitch give him away. He's nothing like us.

But oh, he can tell a story.

He tells my mother's story, the story of the princess the dragon loved.

The girls who run to the woods, they are all of them wishing for something they couldn't have where they were. They are all of them avoiding some necessity, breaking free of some future they don't want. My mother came to the woods like the rest, but she was something else altogether. The dragon had seen her in her bedroom window in her father's castle. He'd seen the look in her eyes, and it wasn't desperation, and it wasn't some irresistible longing. This one had everything she could want, and what the dragon saw in the princess's eyes was happiness, anticipation of a life she would choose for herself, every day she lived.

She saw him there, too, the dragon against the moon. She was happy, sure, but she was curious, too, and not feared of anything. She wasn't one to let a mystery go untouched, and she ran after him, just like so many of the ordinary girls of the kingdom—and not at all like any of them. And when she came to the mountain and should have turned into a phoenix or a griffin, the dragon saw her standing here, hair all tangled around her silk gown and her last string of pearls.

There was a fierceness in her eyes, and he knew she wouldn't have run from poverty or cruelty or even from a marriage—this one had come for the thrill of it. There was a flower in her hand, a white rose she had plucked as she darted through some garden or along some hedge. She'd carried it all the way up the mountain until it was drooping and sad. No flower grew like that in the dragon's woods, and he knew that she wouldn't have brought it all this way if she hadn't been holding on to something else, too, and when she demanded that he give her what all the other girls had been given, that he let her feel what it was to fly free, he wouldn't do it.

It wasn't fair, he said; it wasn't the bargain. No voice had tempted her. No spirit had called her name and led her on through twisting trunks until she forgot who she'd been, until she was nothing but instinct and hunger, as feral as a wolf. She'd come all on her own, and he couldn't change her—could he— when she was still so much herself.

Well, but she wouldn't go back, neither, not when there was so much to discover out in the woods.

She made herself a nest in a corner of the dragon's cave, and she foraged for food, and she rode on the backs of the griffins and the phoenixes, and she walked with the lady of the woods, and the dragon didn't let any of the woods folk harm her.

And he spent more and more time as a man and less and less time as a dragon, because he knew from the moment he'd seen her in her window that this was a girl he loved.

One thing led to another, and the princess must have known one day that she was going to have a baby. She didn't tell the dragon, but she had kept that one white rose, had let it lie on a stone until it was thin and dry, and he saw her, more and more, sitting at the edge of the cave looking south, holding the rose to her nose and breathing in leftover whiffs of its scent.

And one day she was gone, and the dragon near went mad with grief.

There's something to do with the magic that runs all through the woods, something without which none of the uncanny folk there can live. They can send their voices out, some of them, and they can step a few feet beyond without any harm. But if they go too far, it's not only the archers of the king that need worry them. If they stray too far and too long from the woods — the little folk, the lady, the griffins and the phoenixes that used to be girls, even the dragon himself — they lose all memory of what they were in the woods and are nothing more than beasts, rampaging and wild.

So the dragon couldn't just swoop down out of the sky and scoop my mother back up. He couldn't just send a centaur to throw her over its back or a griffin to grab her in its claws. He had to send the very trees.

Turns out that my uncle was right after all. Turns out that he was right to kill my mother, and he should have killed me, too. Turns out that my Gramps, the hero of the piece, who thought he'd saved a baby, saved a monster.

When Annel takes me up on her back and we fly out above the trees, I can see that already they have started to pull back from the king's land. Already the villagers will be returning to rush in the spring planting, rebuild their homes, and give thanks that the end of the world never came. The dragon has his daughter, and all is well.

"Go back," I murmur into Annel's soft neck. She banks, turns around, and brings me to the mountain.

I slide off into the sharp morning light, shrugging away the last of the bitter pain, the final niggling anger. The dragon is waiting at the mouth of the cave.

I go to meet him.

FOUR

T IS A YEAR before I speak human words again.

I run with the little winged ones; they take me as their captain on their raids, and one day I fight for one side, and the next I fight for the other, and no one cares. The little ones shoot up like blades of grass from the ground. Just as we cut one down, another takes its place, and they don't take petty things like death at all amiss.

I knit with the lady, masterpieces, and we hum dreadful songs all the while. Our fingers move in sync, and we throw our projects to the wind together and watch them flap away, gleaming new chances and final breaths, together.

*　　*　　*

I turn myself into a wolf and run with them for a time — a week, a month; afterward I'm not sure quite how long. It's the middle of winter, and we race across the mountains, chasing fat rabbits and sleek weasels. At night we howl at the moon, and I almost hear it howling back; it's so bright, it shoots through my wolf mind with such brilliance.

I romp with my pack in the snow. We've a litter of pups, born just last spring, and they pull at my ears, tumbling across my back. I sit and grin at them, my tongue tasting sharp air.

We cross over onto the other side of the mountain once, and we make our way down, farther and farther. The fairies disappear as we go. The scent of magic fades away by the time we're at the foot of the mountain, and the woods are giving way to rocky ground, patchy bushes, and, far in the distance, an endless shifting mass I think must be sand.

My brothers and sisters keep on, out into this land, chasing a rabbit with ears so long I scarce can see the body. My wolf heart wants to follow them, but I've a stronger urging, to get back to the woods.

I give them up, leaping into a sparrow, and I angle back toward the mountain.

I turn myself into a tree in summer — grow roots, spread leaves far into the sky. I'm the sort of tree that hides a dozen faces, the sort that whispers songs and riddles in the dusk.

I listen to the other trees. I can hear them, now, as I've never heard them before. They've a whole society. They've a whole history, and I hear such things as I'd never imagine, of how they can trick a bobcat into leaping after a rustle it thinks is a mouse, or sing a song to a nesting bird so that it gathers up all the rocks it can find and sits on them, hoping every day to hatch a chick. They laugh, these trees, more often than not. They have more stories, more jokes, more fun than I reckon the jolliest lord does, even in his richest house.

The lady comes and sits by me at times to keep me company. She forms a tinkling bell out of sticks and stones and ties it to my leaves. I make music from it, and the other trees stop their chatter to listen, and I become friends with them this way.

We feel the birds flying overhead, and the phoenixes and griffins, too. And the dragon. It's him what gets me to come back to myself at last. When he swoops by, I feel my roots not as comforts, not as anchors, but as ropes tying me tight, keeping me chained to the earth.

I tumble back onto the forest ground. The lady is waiting there, holding out a hand to help me up. For days after that, we don't stop running and leaping and laughing out loud at the joy of moving through the woods.

I turn myself into a thousand things, everything but a griffin or a phoenix or a dragon. For days, for weeks and months, I lose myself in the woods.

Time doesn't matter here. I reckon I may live forever now; I reckon the dragon has lived longer than he can remember. It makes no difference. One day is all the days, and when it is summer, it has always been summer, and when it is winter, the snow will never leave.

T'S IN THOSE in-between times — the first chill wind at the end of long months of heat; the quiet leaf bud poking out from a frozen bush — that the tinges of uncertainty creep in. I'll be chasing down a vole as a fox, and I'll see a robin hopping through a patch of grass where last week — or was it yesterday or last month? — were mounds of snow. In a flash, I'll be myself again, in a tumble on the ground, staring at that bird as if it held the key to some great essential mystery.

For an hour or a day, there will be thoughts in my head again, human thoughts formed with human words. I'll look at my hands and name them: *hands*. I'll breathe in the scent of the sun and remember that it is a thing to be treasured, this warmth, this opening up of the world.

I'll walk about and notice things. Little things: the pattern of fallen pine needles, the shine of a feather. I will be separate from it all, when for months I've been a twig on a sapling, a rock on a mountain, blowing and rolling with all the other twigs and rocks. It will be beautiful to me, in a separate way again, and it will make my eyes tear, and then the tears will keep on flowing, now from the loneliness of being all myself.

And my wrist will itch, and I'll look at it and see what I haven't seen in weeks: a shine, a gleam, something I wanted once. I will remember. My mother, my uncle, my aunt. The Lord of Ontrei's laugh. My Gramps's smile, the one he kept just for me. It will be too much, too sudden. I will run up the slope, around the trees, and over the streams starting to trickle free, until I reach the dragon's cave. I'll go in, so far that the sunshine fades away and it's winter again, as damp and as chill as yesterday or a month before. I'll stand there until my skin goes numb, until I can't think or feel the shining thing wrapped around my arm.

The dragon will find me there.

He'll fold his arms around me, his warm, rough arms. He'll whisper in my ear, the first words I've heard in as long as I can think. "Tulip, my Tulip, you are safe now. You are home." He'll hold me and rock me until my crying turns from sharp pain to dull relief that here, finally, I am where I'm supposed to be. That after all those lonely years, I have made it home.

* * *

Home, I think, is forgetting who you are. Home is knowing that nobody expects anything of you but that you get up in the morning, and you feed yourself during the day, and when you lie down in your leaf-strewn corner of the cave at night, you fall asleep as soon as your eyes close up.

The cave is filled with phoenixes and griffins the nights I'm there. As the sun is setting, they come flying in over the trees and land on the rocky slope, shaking their fur and settling their feathers before turning themselves human and filing into the cave. They nestle down here and there, calm and businesslike, not minding if they get a pile of leaves or only a bit of dirt floor. In human form, they wear their old village dresses still. It's something, to see a pack of monsters turn themselves into a bunch of village girls.

Except they're not just village girls, are they? No village girls walk as they do, smooth and feline, almost gliding across the floor. No village girls dart their heads from side to side, ready to pounce at any moment. Village girls don't carry the power these girls do in every inch of them.

And village girls chatter.

Annel and I, we don't talk after that first night. She sleeps near me; I watch for her at times, and at times she catches my eye before we fall asleep, and maybe she smiles quick, and maybe she gives me such a long look it's almost like a message all its own. But she doesn't come any nearer, not to tell me stories or to ask how my Gramps is getting on, or even to talk of the faraway lands she used to dream about. I don't try going over to talk to her, neither. It's always such a flutter of wings and tails coming into the cave, and they all seem to arrive just at the same time, and they all go to sleep almost at once. And I never wake earlier than when they're getting up again, running to the mouth of the cave, jumping into the sky. I'm always left on my own, shivering in the sudden chill, listening to the pounding of the air beneath their wings.

The dragon, who's been coiled in his beast form in the center of the cave, opens one eye, then the other. Stretches his muscles, sending a shiver all the way down from his head to the tip of his tail. He unfolds himself and pads out into the morning light.

Sometimes he takes off as well, without so much as turning to look my way. But sometimes he stops and slants an eye in my direction, and I scramble up out of my corner and run to him. He stands perfectly still as I climb my way up his front leg and slide into the groove of his neck, behind his ears and before the start of his wings.

It's something, to be sitting on a dragon when he rolls out his wings for flight. It's something, to feel the tendons tensing in his chest as he lifts his back up and takes his great running steps down the mountain. The rocks slide toward you and the trees rush up, and you think it's impossible, no matter how many times he's done it—you think there's no way in the world we're going to get ourselves off the ground this time.

But the wings are beating windstorms, and he's snorting

loud, smoky breaths, and between a moment of vertigo and a wild, crazy hope, we're going up, as high as ever we want.

Those are the days, when I'm clinging to the dragon for all I'm worth, that I feel the freest. Those are the days I never miss the sound of speech, not even in the deepest corner of my mind, not even in the empty space right before I sleep.

When the dragon brings me back to the cave after a day of flying, he doesn't say a word, but he changes to a man sometimes, and he sits with me on the rocks as the sun goes down.

When it's dark, when the phoenixes and the griffins have dropped from the sky, slipped back into their girl shapes, and filed past us like apparitions in the twilight, and the sun has dripped itself out, we stand, the dragon and me, and walk together into the cave.

You'd think it would be awkward, or lonely maybe, to sit in silence like that. It's not, though. It's a sort of conversation, to share space, to hear each other breathe. Times are that I'll lean against his burning shoulder and he'll put his arm around me. There's something I know in him. He doesn't question things; he takes them in; he becomes them. He takes in the rivers and the trees, the mice and the spirits. It makes him more himself to be all those other things too.

I recognize that because it's how I feel too. Some nights, sitting by him, it's almost as though we're sharing thoughts, I feel I know him so well. I match my breathing to his — deep and calm and steady. I listen to his heart beating next to me.

It's that—his heartbeat—that reminds me that I'm not yet quite like him. His heart pounds, a never-ending drumbeat, sending blood enough to power a dragon's great wings. And I've a simple, human heart still, that flutters and races and dully thumps away. Even when I'm a wolf or a tree or a talking owl spinning riddles through the wind—even then I've not a heart like his. I run and I swim and I fly, but I've not his sheer majesty. Nothing else comes close to the rush I feel when we jump together into the sky.

Could be if he'd change me to a dragon . . .

But he doesn't.

He takes me flying, and he holds me in the cave, and he sits with me as the sunset brings his creatures in. He watches me, too, as I'm watching them spread out, dark against the draining light. It catches my breath every time I see it. I almost feel then that I could do it too, could leap up into one of them, and when I look back at the dragon, he's grinning a wild grin. He knows what I'm thinking. He knows what I want. But he doesn't change me.

And I don't ask him to.

I've no rose from the lowlands clenched tight in my fist. There's no reason not to ask, and there's no reason he wouldn't give it to me: the wings, the scales, the fire.

Still, though, I don't ask for it. I guess I figure there'll be time enough. Maybe I like the closeness that comes from riding with him; maybe he likes that too.

And anyway, I know that once it comes, there will be no more turning back. See, I never let the dragon know it, but there are other times, not just when the seasons are changing, when I fall out of this new life into my old self. They aren't as dramatic as the others; they don't hit me over the head. They slide in, peaceful-like, so that I scarce know they're there until I find myself staring at the stars and humming a lullaby my Gramps used to sing when I was but a tiny thing. Or I'll be knitting with the lady, and I'll think if I turn my head, the queen will be there instead, telling me how all the woods' magic is nothing but the crazy dream of a backward people. Or I'll be sitting in a sunny clearing, eating berries, and think someone's touched my hand, though when I look, there's only the grasses blowing across my knuckles.

Not as dramatic, these times, and not as painful. They ease themselves in, the sensations, and then they ease themselves out again. They're like the rain on my fur or the claws scratching along my bark.

And I know that when the dragon changes me, these moments will disappear, too.

I've seen it in the others. I see it in Annel's eyes, the distance she's gone from who she was. She's gotten what she wanted, sure as sure, and she's given up the girl that wanted it.

I want it too. I'll ask him soon enough. I'll turn to him as we're sitting there on our rocks before the cave. He'll look down at me, and I'll see my determination a thousand times in his eyes. "I'm ready," I'll say. "Make me one of you."

He'll smile, because he'll have been waiting for me to say just that. He'll know that I'll mean that I want to stay forever, and this will make him happy. He'll turn into his dragon self, and he'll do whatever it is that makes a girl a monster, and I'll be free, finally, from all those memories that tie me down, that make me less than what I could be. I'll rise up into my new shape. I'll breathe in, a bigger breath than I've ever breathed, and I'll feel my heart settling into its never-ending thunder. The fire will race along my sinews, pour into my muscles, temper my bones. I will scream. And we will kick the ground away and rush, tail to talon, toward the stars. We will sweep across the full white moon. Somewhere in a bedroom window, a girl will see us and hear our cries, and she will want to jump as well, want to throw herself into our flight, to risk the chill air and the jagged rocks for a chance at what we have.

Someday I'll ask him, soon enough. But not today.

T'S A YEAR before I speak to a human, a year and a season. It's the height of summer again when a miller's daughter from the western edge of the kingdom takes herself to the woods. She shows up on our mountaintop one morning, torn by brambles and breathing hard.

The phoenixes and the griffins haven't been back since the day before. The dragon's been waiting at the mouth of the cave all night, and I sleep there too. The air's warm enough for it, anyway, especially with his heat next to me.

While the sun is rising, we don't move from the spot. I turn myself, now and again, into a ferret or a butterfly or a lizard just to pass the time. Doesn't take any thought to change now, hardly.

It's like standing up or switching from walking to running. I can do most any animal, anything but a griffin or a phoenix or a dragon.

I'm a wild boar when the girl comes out of the woods flanked on all sides by her winged escort. She's dead tired, you can tell, but when the dragon gets up and picks his way down toward her, she straightens and even walks a few paces to meet him.

He touches his nose to her forehead, and then his great bulk is in the way, so I can't see a bit of the girl. It's as though he's wrapping her right up in his wings. When he pulls back, the girl is gone and a griffin stands in her place, pawing at the ground and tossing her head this way and that, sniffing the air.

The other griffins cry, a deep, guttural cry, and run up the slope to surround her. When they rise into the sky, I can't tell who is who anymore. She's become one of them.

But late that night, a full moon night, when I'm human again and the griffins have come back to the cave, the new girl ends up in front of my corner, staring.

"Who are you?" she whispers, as though the rest can't see me, as though I've slipped in unnoticed.

It's dim in here, but my eyes are as sharp as any hawk's, adapted for the dark as any fox's. I look her over. Already she has that poise, that grace, her every movement fluid. But there's a hunching of her shoulders, still, and a shy, slanted look; and her hair is a yellow I know, and I've seen her face many times. I wait for her to gasp, to recognize me, too. When I was small, she came with her mother often enough to our hut; she used to peek round her mother's skirts at me, staring as she is now. But no light comes on in her eyes. "I am the dragon's daughter," I say.

She scrunches her nose at me, considering. The wind will be in her blood now, and there's only so much room for thought after that. After a moment she shrugs and lowers herself to the floor, curls up next to me.

The other girls have gone to sleep, and the dragon is rising and falling with each great breath before I get up the nerve to say, "Why did you come, then?"

I know she's awake. I can hear the unevenness in her breathing; I can see the whites of her eyes, blinking in and out. She's not yet all the way gone. She's not yet left it all behind, and I figure this is the only chance I'll have to ask it.

She doesn't speak right away. I wait. People like to tell their stories, you know. If she's human enough, still, and if I wait long enough, she'll tell me hers.

And she does, real quiet and careful, almost as if the words are being pulled from her, so that she doesn't know what they'll be until they come out. As if they aren't hardly words, even, but bits of herself, tears maybe, or blood dripping from a cut. "We'd gone away when the woods came in," she says.

She says, "Father, Mother, me. My sisters that weren't yet married. There were lots of us girls, too many for one family. When we left the mill, it was hard to keep us all straight, to watch what we were doing."

It's as though we're our own country, here in our corner. The girl's voice fills me up so I can see the grain she would have ground, the road she would have taken when the woods came, and the blanket she would have carried, bundled tight with pots and food and clothes.

She says, "The one closest to my age, she was Nerida. She fell in with a boy that was running with his family too. We'd all gone to the camps round the king's city. There were so many people there. It was a year ago now, wasn't it? I can see them still, the people spread out all over the ground on rugs and in makeshift huts. And the fear — you wouldn't believe it."

"I believe it," I say.

Her eyes gleam my way. "Would you — and you the dragon's daughter?"

"Wasn't always," I say. "I was there then."

"Well then, you know how every moment we thought the land might vanish, the sun might get wiped away, the city might crumble. And what do people do then but all the things they might never get to do? What do they do but grab hold of all the things they're worried will disappear?"

"Nerida," I say.

"She up and had herself a baby." The girl shakes her head, looking up into the dark. "Not for months and months, of course, and we were back home by then. The woods were on their way out. But the boy was gone too, wasn't he? And my father, it's not that he's mean, exactly, but there were so many of us. So he told her, he said she'd have to go off and find this boy of hers, and now it was winter, and the snow was three feet deep. They said she should wait; they said she could stay until the spring, but she wasn't about to stay where she wasn't wanted, and she left anyway.

"I tried to go with her. She'd have none of it. I watched her and her baby boy walking off into the snow, her dress fading into the gray of the sky until there was nothing left of her.

"Never heard from her again.

"When the sun came up in the spring, I went out searching. They told me to stay home, said there was no point."

The girl stops. She says, real slow, "There was no point in anything else, was there? Nerida had gone and melted away into the snow, and nothing else mattered anymore. But I didn't find her, and I didn't find her, and I knew they'd be right in the end. We'd never get her back again.

"And when I went with my mother to visit the flower man, and that voice came creeping out of the woods like the only real thing in the world, and there was that lady, holding out that hand, it was the easiest thing to do. It was the only thing to do. And here I am."

"You went to visit the flower man," I say.

"Yes."

"In a hut by the woods?"

"Yes. He came back, too, when the woods went back. I reckon he got pushed out, just like the rest of us."

She doesn't know. She really doesn't know me, or her voice couldn't be that calm. I am used to transformations these days, but this is something else. This is the world, the whole of what I know, changing all about me while I stay put.

When I can breathe, I say, "Wasn't there a girl that used to be there too?"

She has to think about it. "I guess there was," she says. "You lived round about there?"

"Round about, yes."

"She's not there now. Maybe she got herself a family, something more than that old man."

I can't help but mutter, "You mean that old man who was the *king*."

"There's a girl who comes down from the castle at times, though she's a different one. She helps with the gardening. Emily? Emma?"

"Emmy," I say.

"That's the one. How would you know that, then?"

"Just a guess," I say.

"She called out to me, she did, when I was running back through the flowers, over the wall. She said, *You take a message to my lady! You tell her we've not forgotten her — you tell her to come back home!* I didn't say nothing back. I was just running and running then, you know?"

"Yes."

"Not that I'd know her lady if I saw her."

"No."

"Anyway, that's what happened. That's how I ended up here. That's how I found myself a dragon and turned myself into a—a griffin, I guess." She's trailing off. Her story's done; her words have all run out. Come the morning, she won't even remember we spoke, I reckon. "That's how I flew so high my feathers near touched the clouds . . ." Her eyes are closing now. Her breaths are evening out. She stiffens, looking straight at me. "Is it a dream, dragon's daughter? Will it disappear tomorrow?"

I shake my head. Could be she'll see it even in this dark, with eyes grown already sharp. "It won't disappear," I say, and I know it is true. "It'll be here tomorrow, and the next day, and the next, until you don't even remember what tomorrow means, until tomorrow won't exist."

She breathes in, out. "Good," she says. "That's what I want." She murmurs, "Good night, dragon's daughter."

"Good night, Thea," I say, because I've remembered her name now, the yellow-haired child her mother brought on her visits to me and Gramps. She had a pack of sisters, true, but she was the youngest, and the best loved. Her mother's whole face lit up when she looked at Thea. The little girl used to sit on the porch steps, just behind her mother's skirts, and she'd hold a daisy in her hand, and she'd pluck the petals one by one and watch them drift away on the breeze. Gramps gave her the flower so she could do that, never charged her nothing. Thea. I used to watch her, wonder what it would be like to have her life.

She doesn't answer me back. Could be she's asleep already. Could be she doesn't realize she never told me her name. Could be she's started to forget, already, that it's hers.

*　　*　　*

Something makes me turn my head only a few moments later. It's a silence that wasn't there before, a heavy presence. Thea sleeps, but there, in the center of the cave—the dragon watches me. We are the only ones awake, and I hear, as though I'm dreaming it, a voice, harsh, low: *"Tulip."*

It's what they've always called me, the ones who don't want to remember who I am, and the ones who don't care.

The dragon lifts himself up, scales glinting darkly. He pads, careful, about the piles of girls toward the entrance to the cave. He looks back at me.

I know that look. It's the one he gives me in the morning when he's of a mind to take me flying. It's a look that sends a thrill right through me, makes me think of the glorious hours to come.

I've never denied that look.

But I'm frozen. Thea's face, her childhood face, peers at me from behind my eyelids, and the petals of those daisies drift and drift through my mind, and a voice, a voice I know as well as anything, as the taste of rain, as the language of wolves—is saying something through them, something about me. My left wrist quivers, and the voice seems to flow up my arm to my ear: *My Marni, I'll love you always. Be safe.*

I shake my head at him.

He blinks, and blinks again, then swings his head away. I hear a great, frustrated snort, and then he leaves the cave and flies off into the full white moon without me.

SEVEN

T DOESN'T WORK anymore.

Tomorrow won't exist, I told her, and for me it had been true. You get so you'll forget there was a yesterday, that there's anything beyond this moment. In the sun, you forget the touch of a shadow; in the rain, you forget the brush of the sun. It's a merging, a becoming part of everything so that you're never separate anymore.

But it isn't working now.

Thea doesn't talk to me again. I'm not expecting her to. She sleeps nearby, as Annel does, so could be she's still holding on to who she was, at least a bit. Or maybe it's only habit.

In any way that matters, she's gone; she's lost; she's buried all her yesterdays and doesn't care about the tomorrows. She is free.

Around me, it's closing in again.

They run through my head, the memories, the questions. I can't get rid of them anymore, not even for a day or an hour. Now, whenever I glance down at my hands, I think I see my moonlight creature looking back from my left wrist, gleaming, asking me what I want, murmuring the words from that note I fed it, over and over again. I hear his voice, my Gramps's voice, and I know he is alive. But I don't know why he left me, and I don't know what it means for me, and I don't know what I am to do about it now. And the memories rush, and the questions do not stop.

I'm sitting at the entrance of the cave, perched upon a rock, looking out over the woods. The dragon flew off this morning and made no offer to take me with him. I'm relieved, somewhat. A week ago now is when Thea arrived — I've been counting the days again, as I've not in months — and I've not gone flying since.

I've not been running thoughtless through the woods as all manner of folk, either. Not for more than a bite to eat, a wash in a spring. I've been sitting here watching the sun move across the rocks, watching the shade dance under the trees down the slope.

I've been thinking, or trying to. Whenever I shut my eyes, I see my Gramps's face looking back at me, and my heart flips over to think he's yet alive. And when I open my eyes, my heart drops all sudden, as though I've lost him again.

The lady's down at the edge of the woods, sitting and singing on an old black stump. The wind drifts her notes up the mountain slope. They play through my head, twisting this way and that. I shut my eyes to see his face again, and I think on the way the world has shifted, and I almost know what that shift means for me. And then the lady's tune darts into my head, and that knowledge slips away, and I open my eyes and gasp again at the loss.

Again: closed eyes, my Gramps's face, what it means for me. The lady's music floats through my mind again, emptying it, and my eyes snap open. And I try to grasp the thought again, and again. It itches at me.

By the time the griffins and the phoenixes fly in, I'm all over nerves. I watch them come, watch them settle into their old selves, file into the cave. Soon after, the dragon comes, and he gives me half a look before going inside as well. I've not slept deeply the last few nights, and my bones are weary, my mind all eager for a break.

Still, the lady keeps on with her song, and I can't bring myself to go in yet. There's something waiting, I think, some idea, some purpose just beyond my Gramps's face. But every time I shut my eyes to think, the lady's song twists, and my mind empties, and I'm left holding back my tears.

The moon rises. I bunch over myself, rocking to and fro.

The dragon comes out as a man and sits next to me.

"Tulip," he says, "what's troubling you?"

I let the question settle inside me, and I find another

coming out to meet it. "What troubled my mother, then?" I say. "When she sat with her flower and looked off south, what troubles picked away at her mind?"

He is intense; he always is, in whatever he does, and now he is intense in his frown at me. "She was thinking on you, inside her, I reckon."

"Oh, yes?" I'm feeling my way, searching for the thing that seems best, the right thing to say. "And nothing else? Not the father she left behind, not the girls she might have known from that life who'd run to the woods and, when she found them here, wouldn't speak a word?" I'm thinking of Annel, of course, and maybe Thea. "Could be she had a friend here, one she'd loved. Could be she couldn't stand it, the space between them now."

I stop to pull in a breath, and it gets caught in my throat. *My Marni, I'll love you always.* I shut my eyes.

"Is that it, then?" the dragon says. "It's that girl you knew, the one who's here?"

I open my eyes, focus on him. "Annel," I say, remembering.

"Annel," he says, and it's scarce a human word, how it trips on the way across his tongue. "You'll be missing her."

I shake my head, not to say no, but because I don't know if that's it. "I guess," I say. "Yes, sure, I miss her."

Then he laughs, a great, warm dragon laugh. He slings an arm around me. I can feel my face at once going pink from the heat. "*That's* easy," he says. "I'm not surprised you're lonely, Tulip. You're the only one of your sort up here."

"So are you," I say.

"Well now, and I've got you, haven't I? I've got the dragon's daughter."

I look up at him from the crook of his arm. The lady's music is drifting over still. She's having herself a right long concert. I frown. "I guess," I say again at last.

"Well, and I know how to fix this for you, don't I?"

"Do you?" It seems impossible.

"Yes," he says. "I would have ages ago if you'd said the word. Just you sit right here and wait."

He slips away from me. The lady's song is getting louder, if anything, faster and more insistent. The dragon moves back five paces, shakes himself all down, and stretches up, slides into his beast shape. I find myself looking straight into his bottomless eyes.

"Hold still."

It's that harsh, deep voice again, but I haven't the mind to decide where it's coming from, because I'm prickling all over; my hairs are lifting, my breath coming fast.

The dragon takes a breath. I see his wings lifting out and coming close to fold around me, and I remember the morning Thea arrived, how he seemed to envelop her before —

I lurch to my feet. There's a ringing in my head, so I've scarce the balance to look behind, to see how the space is closing in, caught between his wingtips. He's beginning to breathe out now. The tips of my fingers and the point of my nose are shivering, twitching as I've never felt them before, and it's spreading — to my cheeks, along my hands, lighting on the ends of my toes. I hear the cry, the dragon's cry, piercing, unforgettable. I'm beginning to lift. I'm beginning to melt, to turn into just what he wants me to be — a dragon or a griffin or a phoenix, I don't know. Something to make me more than one of a kind.

And I've wanted this, yes, with everything I am. But there are thoughts I have to think first, and there are questions that need answering, and I can't let him do it.

If I were an ordinary girl, I'd have no way of stopping him. I would be caught, and by the time it was over, I'd be lost forever. I'd be exactly what he wants.

But I'm not an ordinary girl, am I? His wings are near around me now, but they're not yet touching me. His spell is turning me away from myself, but I use that urging, I use the twitching through my skin, and I throw it in a different direction, down, into itself, smaller and smaller.

When I look up again, the pebbles are boulders. I scamper, squeaking, out from under his scales and race down the mountain.

EIGHT

I RECKON I've come through this place a hundred times in the past year and a half. I reckon I flew right over, or jumped past these tumbled walls, or darted under the old leaning table in the center of the clearing, and I never once saw it for what it was.

I was gone then, lost in the flying and the jumping and the darting. I didn't have my thoughts to catch me up, to snag on the quiet that settles here, strange and stagnant. Nowhere in the dragon's woods is as quiet as this. I don't mean the quiet of animals sleeping or the wind dying down. I mean that the very leaves, which crunch so deliciously in the woods, are muted here. I mean that the air here is dense and colorless. The tingle, the heady scent of magic, is nowhere here.

The trees lean in all around, but the ruins of this cottage and its garden aren't part of the dragon's woods.

I'm down off the mountain, on the northern edge of what was once the king's land, almost to last of the dragon's retreating woods. It's been two or three days since I first ran from the dragon — two or three days I've spent at the edge of my ability to outrun, outtrick, outscamper, and stop quite still in a burst of sunlight, a speck of shade, so that for a moment I'm near invisible to passing eyes. I've been leading the dragon's folk in a merry chase.

Could be that's another reason I see this place today. I've been paying so much attention to the fairies and the spirits and so on that their sudden absence shocks, like a bowl of ice water splashed in my face, like a great hand that reaches down and trips me up, leaving me sprawling on the ground, nose just inches away from something glinting, half buried in the dirt before the square rock that I now see that was once the step to this place's front door.

I sit up. I've been jerked out of a lynx shape, and my eyes are straining, missing the cat's precision.

It's been a long while since anyone lived here, longer than before the woods started moving in two years ago, I'd guess. There are plenty of abandoned homes and farms all through what's left of the retreating lowland woods, but none of them has crumbled the way this place has. And none of them stands separate from the trees, in its own spellproof clearing.

Over there, that would have been a shed for the chickens or

a cow, now just a pile of boards rotting. That heap of stones up the hill a bit would have been the well, with a footpath running back through the garden. And here where I am, there would have been a road, or a trail at least, going off toward the farms and the villages in the valleys a hill or two away. They would have come up to this exact spot, whoever visited this hut, and they would have stepped up onto that rock and rapped on the door that stood just there, and passed into the room beyond, an entryway by the look of it. Not a hut, then, but a house. Someone would have lived here, milking the cow, chasing the chickens, drawing water from the well, and helping up whoever was clumsy enough to trip themselves at the front door.

I reach out and grab the sparkly thing just in front of me in the dirt. I shine it with my fingertips.

Someone must have lived here or come visiting who had some money. This isn't a fake metal thing you might buy at a market. This is gold.

I know I ought to be leaving straightaway. I've almost made it through the woods. One more quick dart and I'll be in the king's land, and the dragon won't be able to get at me there.

I'm even picking myself up, brushing myself off, but now, as clumps of dirt fall away, this gold ring is beginning to shine, and the words wrapped around the band stand out, black from the bits of earth still wedged in their grooves. I've not forgotten my letters, not even after all this time, and I lift the ring to read it.

☞　☞　☞

Sometimes, when a person is about to tell you something that's going to change your life, or make you cry, or make you leap for joy — sometimes you know it before they say a word.

It's in the way they look at you and in the way they open their mouth. It's in the tilt of their head, the tension in their hands, or the slump of their shoulders.

Times are, you don't need words to hear a thing.

I look at this ring, and before the letters fit together, before they sound inside my head, I know what I'm going to see, and I start trembling all through me.

"*To my daughter*—" it says. My hands are shaking so, it's hard to keep the ring turning, to keep squinting at the words: "*a darling princess.*"

And who else would have had a golden ring out here at the edge of the world? Who else would have come to this isolated place, and her a princess?

Who would have lost her ring and never returned to find it?

I fold my hand tight around the ring and turn my back to the woods. I walk around the ruins of the house, not through; it doesn't seem right to go through. I step across the garden, where I figure the paths might have been, looking here and there, always searching.

At the back, near the tumbled well, I find the stones. Two of them, grown over with grasses but still unmistakable in their meaning. On one, there is carved a woman's name I don't recognize. On the other, there is the name of my mother.

To my daughter —

I wonder, I can't help but wonder, who put them here. My uncle? Villagers? The soldiers who showed up on that very door-step, who knocked with their leather gloves and made the baby inside cry, so that they knew they had come to the right place after all?

And I wonder, did her ring fall off when she rushed out, trying to get away, or trying to reason with them or to beg for her child's, her servant's, lives? Did she lose it in the struggle — grappling with the men, with her own brother? Did it jerk its way down her skin and drop to the floor of the house and roll, unnoticed, out the open doorway into the dirt?

Or did it slip from her trailing hand as they dragged her out to her grave?

Yes, I am trembling. My very thoughts are trembling. Some-where above me the dragon flies, and here in this corner of the world, in this bit of space that doesn't belong to him somehow, that doesn't belong to anyone but the ones underneath these stones, I am trembling, and my thoughts are running wild, and there's nothing here to see or hear me.

My mother was here. She stood in this garden just like me. She held this ring in her hand; she looked off into the woods. She thought about the dragon and she thought about my Gramps, who wouldn't have known where she'd gone.

But there the sameness between us ends. She had a baby, first small in her arms and then crawling about, getting itself into the vegetables or the flowers no doubt, maybe rolling a ball across the floor of the house. She had someone else, too, her old servant who she would have talked to about things, who she would have worried about late at night when she'd put the baby to bed and couldn't keep from remembering that half the king's army was on her trail.

She would have been afraid for her life, and she would have had nowhere left to go. Not home, to her enraged brother. Not to the woods, not with her baby. This was her final hope. This was her last chance to be free.

And me? There are a thousand places I could go. I could go back up the mountain and let the dragon turn me into some great wild beast. I could continue south until I make it out of the woods altogether, and then I could run back to my uncle and spit in his eye.

I could stay here in front of these stones — stare at them until the rain and the wind wear me away, or until I grow roots, like a girl in a story, and turn into my namesake tulip, bright and bold and helpless.

Then, with the wind blowing through the trees and the sunlight glinting on the two stones, it comes to me: a memory so deep it's been well buried for years and years, so long I'd think I was making it up, except I know it's true. I've become so still inside, so empty in the last months that now I can touch each thought within me, feel its texture, its importance. This one is bright and sharp and real. This one makes my heart beat fast, before I even know what it's about.

*　　*　　*

First, there was a sword. It scraped from its scabbard, harsh, like the first loud sound on a day when you've had no sleep. It shone in the sun, clean, bright. It was mesmerizing. I was watching from the doorway, and I saw it all, and I saw the way the lords, my mother, my Gramps, even my uncle watched the steel gleam, as if it wasn't theirs to control, as if they'd nothing to do with it.

The body of my mother's servant already lay on the ground.

My mother didn't try to run when my uncle swung the sword her way. My Gramps did — not away, but toward her, dropping his horse's reins, pushing through the lords, who stood silent, as if turned to stone.

The woods were whispering my mother's name.

My uncle drew back his hand, and a spark struck from the sword's tip. My Gramps screamed. I remember that. It wasn't my mother. She stood straight, maybe in disbelief, maybe in acceptance. But my Gramps screamed, and it was a sound that made my breathing come fast, as it hadn't before, not when these visitors rode up all grim-faced, not even when that sword scraped free — and I left the doorway to clamber down the steps, stumbling as well, toward my mother.

It was so fast, I could have missed it. As my uncle slid the sword forward, my Gramps reached him, grabbed at his arm, and my uncle swung the sword his way almost without looking, as hard as anything, and my Gramps crumpled to the ground. And then, easy, as if it were nothing, my uncle swung his sword back again and then forward, one steady motion. When he drew it back once more, my mother folded with only a sigh, and it was done.

My uncle turned toward me then. I'd stopped before reaching them, as my thoughts had stopped, as the world had stopped, as the whispers through the woods had stopped, cut off with my mother's breath. My Gramps — though I'd never met him then — said, through his pain, "Roderick, let the girl live . . . I'll give you the kingdom."

My uncle looked down at his father and around at his men, who were shifting now, their eyes wide. He held his sword to the side, and a lord came to take it from him at once. Then he looked at me again, long and steady. I saw that darkness in his face for the very first time, and there wasn't a speck of guilt there, and he didn't come over to comfort me or speak some gentle word. Still holding my gaze, his voice flat, he said, "We'll see. If this is enough to stop them, she can live." Then another lord came forward to lift my mother, and I didn't see anything more because someone was raising me onto a horse, and my Gramps behind me.

"What's your name then, little one?" he said into my ear. I could hear the scream left over in his words, a harsh scrape like the scrape of that sword as it slid out into the light.

"Marni," I said. His arms were tight around me. I watched the soft spot between the horse's twitching ears.

"Marni," he repeated, bending round to look me in the face. "I am to be your Gramps." I saw for the first time those deep, intense eyes, that already silvering hair, the determination that never once faded, that saved me then and kept me living all those long years to come. It's an expression I've never seen in the lady's face, nor in the dragon's, nor in any of the woods folk's. Those of the woods can't help what they do. If they say they can't live without you, or that they'll make a bargain but otherwise they'll take your land and your people, or if they send you tempting dreams to draw you out of your dull, everyday life, through the woods, and up into the wind-strewn sky — well, you can't much blame them for it. It's who they are, and they can't go and change it.

But people, now. We're not as strong as they are, or as clever, or as filled to dripping with all sorts of unnatural powers. We can't lead them to their deaths with a light so bright and beautiful it's like to make you cry. We can't promise them impossible things and then deliver, hand them their every wish on a golden platter.

Could be, though, that we've got something just as terrifying, something just as likely to confound them.

It's what my Gramps had when he stepped in front of my uncle's blade and when he spoke for me, a crying little thing he'd never seen before, and gave up his throne to keep me safe.

It's what my mother had when she ran as fast as she could from the dragon and all his people, and the prince and all his army, for the sake of the tiny spark inside her that was going to be me.

It's what the queen had when she freed me from the city prison, well knowing that the king would near to kill her if he found out.

It's what I had, I guess, when I turned the dragon's spell inside out, and when I told the Lord of Ontrei I'd not marry him, and when I stayed with my Gramps all those years when I could have gone off to the woods.

It's our choices. It's our changing, every day, into creatures who might do something completely different from the day before. It's our stupid stubbornness and our constant unpredictability, and the irrational way we have of holding on to our love, our anger, our hate, letting them grow within us until they're a part of us as sure as our hands and feet, as sure as the laughter that catches on our breath, the moonlit tears in our eyes.

It's a magic too, in its way, and times are I reckon the dragon's happy to leave us our kingdom, happy to stay away.

After all, it didn't do him much good to send his trees after her, did it? She was only right next door, and he didn't dare come get her. The woods were whispering her name that day, so why didn't he send them in to save her? It bounds around inside my head, that thought, that question, and I can't get rid of it, no more than I can make the names on these stones leap up into people, laughing, smiling at me, knowing me for the baby girl that learned to sit up and clap her hands, and made herself dirty digging in the flowers, and watched the leaves flutter on the dragon's trees for the first time right in this same garden.

I open my palm and look down at it, at the ring gleaming

softly in the sunlight. I lift it between my first finger and my thumb, and I slide it onto the middle finger of my left hand. I twist it round. It's snug; it will stay.

As I pull my right hand away, I brush against my vengeance. It unfolds itself, drifts out from my arm. It hovers, looking at me. It's still wondering what I want. *The king?* it asks, and somehow I hear it clear in my head. *I'll kill the king?*

And yes, it is his fault. It wasn't hers, the woman who stood so still before that sword. It wasn't mine, the tiny thing that watched and then buried the memory so deep I only now found it again.

But it wasn't as simple as just being his fault, neither. And anyway, here, with those stones staring back at me, I've not the will to wish for death. There's only one thing I want, and no magic could give it to me.

So I shake my head at my making. It's soft in the light, insubstantial, drifting like a kite or a thought. I say, "I want the woman this ring belongs to," and I lift up my hand for the vengeance to see.

It comes closer. It wraps itself round my finger, curls between the gold band and my skin. *A princess?* it says. *A darling princess?*

"She was," I say. "She was a princess. Not anymore."

I will bring her to you. It unwraps itself from my finger, pulls away. *Wait here.* Then it's gone, up into the sky, over the woods, lost in the bright white sun.

It makes my eyes tear up to think on that moonlight thing

traveling the world over, looking for a person who doesn't exist. Could be it'll keep on forever. Could be it'll pull itself to bits and fade away and disappear, still searching for nothing. My wrist is bare without it, but I twist the ring again, and I don't miss it.

There's something else I ought to be doing. Cutting flowers or some such to leave with them. But there's nothing here, only weeds and rocks. I don't even feel the urge to clean their stones, to make the words show clear. It's right to let the grasses cover them over. It's right to let them fall back into the way of things.

So I only kneel down and press my cheek against their names, first the one I don't know and then the one I do, the one that threads its way into my dreams and hopes and tears. I stay like that as the air grows cool, warming her stone with my skin.

NINE

AM WAVERING.

I don't leave the clearing all the next day, or the next. I don't know what I am to do.

Or, I know what I am to do, but I don't know if I can do it. I escaped from the dragon, yes, but that was only barely. I ran from his folk, but I got away only because I never stopped running, never turned to look back at them, never gave them a moment to get inside my head again.

Could be, if I darted to the south, I'd make it out through the last of the trees before the little ones surrounded me, before the lady grabbed me tight. That's where I was running when I landed here: to the king's land, back to my mother's kind, back to my Gramps. Then, I thought only of getting away, nothing of what happens after that. Nothing of what happened when *she* went back.

Now, though, sitting by my mother's stone, I can't stop thinking on it, and I know I can't go south. Instead, I'm readying myself for that last climb, where I might well lose myself forever. I'm readying myself to answer the question that needs answering.

When you've been running for so long, it's not an easy thing to stop, to turn yourself around and look clear at what you've been running from. It's easier to sit, and twist your mother's ring, and feel the breeze drift past. It's easier to wait today, and then tomorrow.

It's the next day, not long before midday, that I hear crashing through the trees off to the west. The dragon's folk have been flitting here and there in the woods round about the clearing since I arrived. They make their own sorts of noises, but those blend in with the wind and the soft padding of the ordinary beasts. This crashing isn't from a fairy or even a griffin or a phoenix. It's the sort of clumsy noise that sounds all through the woods — the sort that comes only from someone not caring if anyone hears, or not aware enough to realize what they're doing. The sort that comes only from a human.

Could be it's another girl, another Thea, running off to the dragon. But it's a louder crashing than one young girl would make, and girls never run off together. Then I hear a whinny, soft, but it threads its way through the trees to me. And then I hear a voice, calming: "It's all right, girl." It's a voice I've heard in my head many times since I left the castle, as I'm knitting with the lady, as I'm sitting in the cave looking out over the mountains and remembering conversations, laughter, the warmth of velvet chairs and a fire.

It's not a voice I've heard in truth, though, for many long months.

I'm standing before I think it. I'm across the clearing, to the edge of the western woods. The speaking owl there swivels its head to stare at me. The little ones push themselves almost out of the woods' grasses, gnashing their teeth, waving their weapons.

She's moving northward. She's almost past the clearing.

"Aunt!" I call. "Aunt, over here!"

I wait, straining to hear. I think of turning my ears into those of a bat or a wolf, but I haven't changed myself, not a bit, since I came to the clearing. I haven't risked it.

There's silence in the woods. The owl swivels his head back; the little ones turn too, all still.

And then: "Marni? Marni, is that you?"

"Yes, it's me!" I call. "Come this way!"

The crashing starts again, but it's moving toward me now, and then she comes into view, my uncle's wife, dressed all in plain dark cotton, her hair piled up on her head. She starts running as soon as she sees me, or as near to running as she can get through the underbrush. She's leading two fine mares—the gray I used to go out riding on with Edgar, and a white.

They come into the clearing, and she throws out her arms, reins and all, to fold me into a hug.

"Aunt," I gasp. "Aunt, what are you doing here?"

"Oh, my dear," she says, pulling back to hold me at arm's length.

For half a moment, looking at her brilliant smile, it's as though I never went to the woods at all, but live still in my uncle's castle, in the care of his queen. I find my eyes tearing up for some fool reason.

"Oh, my dear, I wasn't sure I'd ever find you."

I shake my head. "In these woods, Aunt, you'd be lucky not to get yourself lost instead."

"Yes, well." She lets me go. "To be perfectly truthful, Marni, I didn't feel there was another choice."

"You haven't — you haven't *run away to the woods?*" I'm gaping at her, I know. It's the most unlikely thing I can think of — my uncle's practical wife, taking herself to the monsters.

But no, she's shaking her head, giving me a half smile. "No, not like that. I've come to find you." She looks around the clearing, at the ruined house, at the tumbled well. "I never expected to succeed so soon."

"You wouldn't have if you'd come a few days earlier." I take her arm and lead her farther into the clearing. She sits next to me on a broken stone wall and lets the reins lie loose in her hands. The horses start nibbling at the grass.

She's looking somewhat like I feel — stunned, unbalanced. I

give her a few minutes, but my curiosity's raging, and soon I say, "Why did you come for me, then?"

She looks over, rueful. "It's not enough just to want you back?"

I only hold her gaze, impassive, until she says, "No, I don't suppose it would be enough. I always hoped you'd found a place to be happy out here, even if it hasn't been easy at court these last months." Her words fill the clearing, make it even less magical than before. I near forget the many eyes watching from the trees as she goes on. "After you left . . . well, at first there was a sort of peace. The woods began drawing back, and the lords were so relieved they forgot that without you around, the king had no heir." She stops, and then says, "In the last few months, though, they've remembered."

"There's been trouble?" I say.

"Not yet," she says, "not full out, anyway. Still, hardly anyone listens to Roddy anymore, and it's only a matter of time. A few nights before I left — we were at dinner, the whole court, and there was a scuffle over who would sit where. Ontrei's been at the king's right hand again, and no one disputes that. But Roddy has been keeping old Handon in the chair to my left, and Lord Beau of Cavarell decided he had something to say about that. He took poor Handon's seat before the man could totter into it. Of course, the whole Handon clan rose up, and the Cavarells rose up against them — they were pulling knives, Marni! — and I don't know what would have happened if Ontrei hadn't shouted them down. He had his own men there, enough of them that when he gave Handon back his seat, Lord Beau only muttered dark things to himself and went to sit elsewhere.

"It won't last forever, though. One day there will be violence. Possibly against Roddy, even, or—or me, though at the moment they hardly view me as a threat." Her voice is wavering now, so soft I scarce can hear it. "A good joke, maybe. Not a threat."

"Aunt—"

She cuts me off. "That's not why I've come."

"It's not?"

"No, Marni."

I wait. She's looking away from me, and there's something there, in the way she holds herself so careful, so tensed. She says, softly, "It was the dreams."

My skin prickles, and I think of the dreams I used to have, waking and asleep—of the woods, and the dragon, and the lady beckoning me away. She said she didn't come for the woods. "What dreams?" I say.

She says, "It was only three days ago, that morning before I woke. You were there, as real as you are now. You were standing in a clearing just like this one, and you were telling me to come find you.

"No," she says, and she's shaking her head, and her hold on the reins is tightening, tightening so the horses look up at her, twitching their ears. "It wasn't as straightforward as that. You were there, and looking at me, but you weren't saying anything in words. You might have been crying. Or singing. You held a golden ring stretched out toward me, so I could see the moonlight glinting off of it. And I knew — *I knew* — that you wanted me to come to you. It was a compulsion so strong that when I woke, I was out of bed and through my door almost at once.

"I didn't go that day. It was difficult. It was an ache inside me, as though I had lost something terribly important and the only way to find it was to leave for the woods immediately. I ignored it as best as I could, until that night when I was falling asleep, and I could see you there again, behind my eyelids, even before I had drifted off. I knew you would be calling me all night long. There were tears on my face, and my heart was racing. Roddy was still at dinner; I had begged out early with a headache."

She stops. I'm afraid to reach toward her, afraid to startle her out of her memories. But she's staring so blindly, and I put my hand over hers. She turns to look at me. She says, still staring, her voice gone all low, "Instead of sleeping, I forced open my eyes. I don't know how I didn't scream. There was a — a creature. Not a living creature, Marni. A thing of white light and air, glowing. It was sitting on my chest. I didn't move. I've never seen such a thing. I've never heard of one, not even in the stories of the sorcerers from my land.

"It wasn't living, but it seemed at the same time somehow *more* alive than you or I. It seemed truer than we are, more essential. I didn't scream, and I couldn't breathe, either. It was looking at me, and I knew that if it wanted to, it could kill me with a thought, maybe with a dream. It must have been the thing sending me those dreams. I knew that at once, too.

"But it didn't kill me."

"No," I say, before I know I am saying it. "It never would."

"It flew from my chest," says my aunt, "and I breathed in and out, and followed it over to the window. It hovered just outside. I heard — Marni, I *heard* it saying, *Find her.* It waited, and what could I do? It wasn't a thing you could refuse, not without tearing a hole inside yourself, not without going against the deepest part of yourself. I think I told it that I would, or maybe it could tell without me saying anything. It turned, and it shot off north toward the mountains, and I watched it go."

"And you came to find me."

"That very night," says my aunt. "I came to find you."

I let go of her hand, and I take off the ring I've twisted round my finger. I hold it out to her.

She reads it. "This was the ring you were holding in your dream."

"Yes," I say. "The creature you saw was of my making."

She shakes her head, turning the ring so it catches the sunlight. "But why?"

Now the tears are hanging at the edge of my lashes, and I blink, hard. "It was meant for a vengeance, but instead it brought me what I wanted."

"You wanted me?"

"I wanted a princess," I say, "a woman who used to be a princess."

She hands the ring over, and I slip it back onto my finger. "Your mother," she says.

"Yes," I say. "A thing not possible."

It's then, as the queen tilts her head away, that I see it, the flower she's stuck into her piled-up hair. I reach out a hand toward it, brush it lightly. "Aunt . . ." I say, and my voice is near to breaking.

"Yes," she says. She tugs it out, holds it between us. "A tulip. That's what they call you sometimes, isn't it? I brought it to remind me, you see. I brought it to keep the voices away, to help me remember what I'd come for. I didn't know how long it would take me to find you."

She hands it to me. I cup the flower in my hand, feeling its heft, its silky smooth petals. I worry that it won't stick itself in my hair, and I've nowhere else to put it, so I thread it through the buttons on the front of my nightgown, the same nightgown I was wearing that night I ran from the prison, the night the queen handed me the key. I've been wearing this dress a year and a season, and it still holds together, and it still shows white in places, the places left clean after ten days in a city cell. Woods magic, I guess. The same that takes the dress away when I turn bird or beast and gives it back the moment I'm human again.

"Well, Marni," the queen says, "I'm not your mother, but I've come all this way, so I will ask anyway. Will you come back with me? The king has no reason to kill you now. One lord at least would welcome you home. And—I don't suppose you've heard—"

"My Gramps is back at our hut, and alive," I say. "I've heard. Where did he come from, then?"

"You can ask him yourself if you come with me."

And I near say yes, just like that. It would be easy. To get on that gray mare and leave it all behind, to forget my year in the woods, to give up the question this clearing put into my mind.

But she's looking at me so appealingly, as hopeful as a green spring bud, and instead of convincing me to follow her away, she's reminding me of all the things that choice would put at risk. There, in my aunt's kind eyes, I'm finding the strength to go back up the mountain.

"I can't come with you yet, Aunt." I say it slow. I'd rather not say it at all. "There's something I have to do beforehand."

She sighs, but she doesn't argue. "And what will that be, Marni? Please tell me it's something outside these woods."

"No, it's here," I say. "There's no need for you to come. We're near enough to the king's land; if you go back a few dozen paces, you can wait outside the woods. It shouldn't take long, not more than a day, I'd think."

But she slides off the wall and shakes out her skirt, and I love her more than anyone in the world, almost, as she raises an eyebrow at me and says, "My dear, the sun is rising higher every moment. Shall we be getting on?"

She hands me the reins to the lovely gray. I pat her down, and she snuffles at my hair. When I mount up, a piece of me settles back into place. It's not all forgotten, then. I could ride this beauty all day and never want to stop.

When the queen is mounted as well, we share a long look, not smiling, but each as determined as the other, and then we push off together, out of my mother's clearing and back to the shadows.

HE WAS RIGHT next door, and *he didn't dare go get her.*

This is what I'm thinking when the woods sends its soldiers after us. The woods' soldiers don't use swords or spears. They don't rush up at you all violently, so that you have to fight them off with fist and steel.

They use beauty. They use curiosity.

There runs a centaur, a bit off to the right, and I've never met one before, not in all my months with the dragon. He looks back at me, straight into my eyes, and I know that if I follow him, he will take me to hidden glens and breathtaking views, the like of which I've never seen even in my dreams.

There flies a tiny winged girl between my horse's ears. She

zips and tumbles, and her laughter dances like raindrops. I could join her. I could twist through the wind like that; I could laugh like her.

There gleams an opening to a tunnel beneath the woods, to caves I've visited before, where crystals shine with a light all their own and your echoes in the greater chambers speak to you of things you've never said.

There floats a spirit, all shimmering blue and white. Spirits know such things, they've been around so long. If you can coax them close, they will tell you stories so strange you'll forget to sleep or eat. And this one's only inches away, drifting along beside my mare, keeping pace with us.

I think if I were walking on my own two feet, I wouldn't be able to resist them. I wouldn't be able to keep from leaping up and sprouting wings, or throwing myself forward into a beast with paws and a mouth full of teeth, or just running, mind lost, after the nearest wonder.

But every step my mare takes is slow, careful. They don't have power over her. She's as solid, as steady as they come. She'll run her heart out, and she'll whinny for the joy of a springtime day, but she's not so easily lured away from her path, away from her rider.

And the queen's every bit as unflustered. I know she sees the things I do. Her eyes are darting all about; her mouth is tight. But she's not the sort who would have ever been seduced by the woods. That helps too, to have her next to me, my clear-sighted, reasonable aunt.

I keep one eye on her, and I concentrate on the feel of my sturdy mare beneath my legs, and I hold on to that thing I need to remember about the dragon and my mother.

Once, a bird nearly does me in. Not a human-faced bird, not a magical bird in any way, just a starling sweeping over my head so I feel the air move. When I look up to see it shooting away in front of me, I rise out of my saddle before I know what I'm doing, and I think the queen sees it, sees the way I'm turning all over feathers and beginning to shrink, because she pulls up in front of my mare and says my name, sharp: "Marni!"

She jolts me into myself.

I sit back on my horse, who's turned her head to roll an eye at me. "She was right next door," I say, stamping it into my head, "and he didn't dare go get her."

The queen eyes me. "Should I know what that means?"

"No." I smile at her. "Thank you for that, Aunt. Without you here, I would have flown away."

She looks me over for a long moment. "I don't suppose you ever knew what those days were like for us, when you were locked up in the city prison. Or knew how many girls were tricked away by the monsters the woods kept sending out into our gardens, over the river." She pauses. "Not that any of them turned into *birds*."

I ignore that last part. "He doesn't take the ones who don't want to go anyway."

"Who doesn't? The dragon?"

I nod. I don't want to name him aloud, not here. It's only

superstition, but in a magical woods, I reckon superstition counts more than usual.

"Is that what's going on here, Marni?" she asks. All around us the woods folk are poking their heads out, listening in, no doubt. "Are they tricking you into what you want anyway?"

I glare around at all the eyes and teeth and tails. Some scurry away out of sight; more only blink and keep on staring. Cheeky little things. "It's not that simple, is it?" I say, and pull my horse to the side to get around the queen. "Not for me, and probably not for the girls he lured away, either. You can want a whole slew of things. It's what you choose that ought to matter."

Then we're riding on again. The queen stays nearer to me now, I notice. The woods folk keep on with their songs and wild beauties, but there's no more need for the queen to bring me back from the brink. I get the sense that they aren't trying as hard now, maybe because we've resisted this far — maybe because they can see her there, jaw set, ready to punch the first one that comes too close, as hard as ever she can, straight on its crooked nose.

I knew the lady would be waiting. I've never entered the woods before without her there, just around a tree or beyond a rise, ready to keep me company through my rambles if I would let her, wanting to take my hand and draw me off through the trunks.

She leaves us alone as we ride through the last of the low-lands and across the foothills. She's nowhere to be found either as we begin to climb the mountain, but when I know we're getting close, when the trees start to thin and the air grows cool, she's there, standing just out of our path beneath a tall pine, hands empty for once. Her dress falls like another sweep of needles from her shoulders to her feet.

She doesn't call out to me. She doesn't slide her voice into my head, even. She watches us make our way up the slope, and I think we could ride right on by without her stopping us.

It would probably be sensible to do exactly that. I know that's what the queen would think, and she makes a grab for my reins as I stop my mare and dismount.

I hand them to her. "I'll only be a moment," I say.

"Marni—" she starts, but without her usual conviction. I remember how the lady froze Edgar up when he saw her out by Gramps and my hut. Seems she's too much for the queen as well, who's looking from me to her in a sort of daze.

I've wondered sometimes what role the lady plays in these woods. The dragon is king, that's sure enough, and she, too, seems something more than the ordinary magic folk. For one, there's only her. No cousins, no sisters. Even the griffins and the phoenixes have one another; even the rarest of the creatures, like the centaurs, aren't one of a kind. The lady is just the lady.

And for another, she's the only one I really know. I'd recognize a little one or a hawk, maybe, that had run or flown with me. But the lady's the one that talks to me. She's the one that waited by my Gramps's and my hut, day after day, and taught me curses and showed me how to wrap a sunbeam round my finger, how to sing her songs.

She's the one who knows who I am more than anyone else in the woods. More than anyone outside of them too, excepting my Gramps. She knows the part of me that loves this place. She knows the bit that rejoices in the mystery, in the strangeness. She knows because she rejoices too.

I step over to her, across the rubble and the tough weeds of the mountain. A mouse darts between rocks. I've come upon her a thousand times like this, her waiting beneath a tree, watching me. I used to laugh, running to her, jumping up next to her on her log. Time lasted forever then. Those afternoons, they smoothed out long, filled with adventures, wonder, the lady's crafts. She called me Tulip, and she taught me half the things I ever knew.

This walk is all of those walks into the woods toward the lady — and nothing like them.

She doesn't speak or move when I get up close. She doesn't try to take my hand.

I say, "Aren't you going to ask me what I want?"

She's so still, I start to wonder if she's real or just a spirit playing tricks on me, taking up her form. She opens her mouth, the mouth I never can see but always somehow sense. She draws in a breath; it rushes through her as though she were all hollow. "You used to sit with me," she says, and her voice is high and sweeter than I have ever heard it. "You were perfection, my dark flower."

I've heard that before, and I've said this, too: "I grew up."

She shakes her head at me, back and forth and back. "You don't have to."

I smile at her, a small smile, not because it's funny, but because I know it's true, what she says, and I taste salt from the tears I didn't know were sliding down my face. "I know," I say. "But I grew up anyway."

She holds out a hand to me, an ordinary hand that doesn't glow but feels all cold when I take it. She shivers. She looks at me with those tiny suns, and when she speaks, the sweetness is gone, and it is so eerie, so thin, little hairs stand up all over my skin. "Come along, then, Tulip," she says. "I'll take you to the dragon."

I beckon the queen to follow behind with our mares as the lady leads me upward, and after a moment I slide the flower out of the front of my nightgown and hold it tight in my hand.

The lady leaves me at the edge of the tree line. She drops my hand and steps back into the woods. I wait for the queen to come up alongside me. She's down from her horse now as well, leading both of them by their reins.

She looks at me, doesn't say a thing.

All along the slope up the last bit of mountain to the dragon's cave, griffins and phoenixes stand and lounge, and all of them watch us.

I hold my flower, my tulip, like a talisman, and I start through them. I don't look to see if the queen is going to follow.

I scarce care now whether she does or not. But I can hear the horses' hooves on the rocks behind me.

Brave, that woman is, to follow me out among these beasts. And brave, those horses, to come along with her.

I look at them as we go, the shaggy griffins and the brilliantly feathered phoenixes. I see the glint of their beaks. I see the curve of their muscles, the tendons in their long necks. Annel is among them, over to the west. She's watching me, too, but there's nothing different about her gaze, nothing to separate her from the rest. Except I keep on looking at her, and after a bit she does turn away.

They don't stop us. They don't cry their shrill cries or flap their powerful wings. They let us clamber over the rocks to the mouth of the cave.

We stop there.

I can hear the harsh breath of the dragon. I can smell the fire, too, of his great belly. I turn and meet the queen's eyes.

"Stay here," I say.

She looks as if she's about to argue—she looks round at all our company, and I see the thought of being alone with them clear on her face—but she stops herself and nods.

"I'll be here," she whispers. She's holding the horses loosely, but they're backed up against the wall of the cave; they look as though the last thing they want is to go down that hill.

I leave them there, watching as I slip into the cave.

*　　*　　*

It's dark. I stand for a minute, waiting for the shadows to trans-form into nooks and boulders.

He's in dragon form. I know it from the sound of his breath, and soon enough I see him, a gray shape against the black. I pick my way over near him. He's lying on the floor of the cave. His head is down on the dirt. He peers at me out of half-lidded eyes.

"She was right next door," I say, "and you didn't dare go and get her."

There's no response. He doesn't even blink, just keeps on breathing in and out.

"It's a question, isn't it? *Why* you didn't go get her, not even when her brother was running her through with his sword." My hands are cupped around the tulip. I know he sees it. He's not one to miss a detail like that. But he says nothing about it, doesn't flick his tail to knock the flower out of my hands.

"I've thought about it, and I think I've figured it out. You *couldn't* have taken her back. You never could take anyone who didn't want to come. My mother . . ."

There, he shuts his eyes a moment, he does. I see him.

"My mother knew it better than most, didn't she? The others, the villagers, the lords and ladies, even her brother, they didn't know not to fear. They thought you could take their land away, and that thought let you come and take them. But my mother had gone into the woods of her own free will, without even the voices pulling her along. She wasn't going to let you take her away, not once she had a baby to protect. Not once she had *me*."

I'm wondering why he's still a dragon. Seems he'd have a

better chance of swaying my mind in his human shape, and I think he does want to sway my mind. Didn't he send his army after me? But he keeps still, and he keeps his eyes all slanted at me, as if he's getting more and more dangerous—or as if he thinks I am.

I go on. "And then, when she was gone, you couldn't take me, neither. First there was my Gramps, protecting me with his determination to keep me safe. Could be you thought it over, too, and realized you didn't know much about raising a baby. After all, I wasn't going anywhere, and my Gramps had chosen the perfect spot for us, right where your lady could watch me grow day after day. So you waited.

"But then, when I was finally turning from a girl to a woman, and the woods were drawing me deeper and deeper in, and I was ready to run myself wild, my Gramps up and disappeared, and I went to the castle and slipped from your grasp again.

"And then it turns out I never did like being pushed one way or the other. Turns out I've more than a bit of my mother in me, doesn't it? Because the more you all tried to make me run, or stay, or marry, the more I pushed back, didn't I? And there's nothing you can make a girl do if she doesn't want to. Not even if you're a great big dragon."

Still, he looks sidewise; still, his head rests on the ground and his tail wraps around him, his wings folded tight. But I think, I sense, he's growing angry.

It's not that I think he couldn't do anything to me. I'm a soft-skinned human, after all, and he's got teeth and claws the size of plow blades. Doesn't matter to him that I'm his daughter, maybe. Or then again maybe it does.

Either way, I fold my legs up right there on the cave floor, and I lay the flower across my lap. I'll be less likely to run if I'm sitting.

"Here's a story," I say. I rest my hands on the dirt of the cave, feeling it soft and dry beneath my fingers. "There was this girl. She was rich and beautiful and all that. She wanted some adventure, so she ran away to the woods and met a dangerous creature there, all fire and power and passion, and she loved him, in a way. But she was young, and when she knew she was going to have a baby, she ran from him.

"Well, and can you blame her? The woods are exciting, sure, and magical and so on. But what does a baby want with excitement or magic? A baby wants a warm bed and lots of food and a mother to love it.

"It was too bad this girl's family didn't welcome her back home, but she found a place anyway, with an old friend in a safe house, and she had her baby. And she raised it up to be a child, and then a girl, and then a woman just like her. And everyone left them both alone, because they might not have liked what she did, but it was her choice, wasn't it? The mother kept her daughter, and the daughter kept her mother, and maybe one day they went back to the woods together, and maybe they didn't.

"Nobody sent their armies after her, not armies of trees and not armies of people. It's not what armies are for, is it? They left her alone to live her life as she wanted."

The dragon is breathing harder now. There are puffs of smoke coming from his nostrils; they float to the ceiling and around in the air currents there, this way and that, before they find their way out of the cave. I don't know if he's thinking this story over or if he's near ready to gobble me up in one bite.

I get up now. I've found my courage, and I want to be right close to him when I say this. As I step before his front claws, his tail gives a mighty twitch. I scarce breathe for a moment. He lifts his angular head so that we're face-to-face. There are the thousand reflections of me, all spiraling through his eyes.

I say it quiet, because it is dangerous, and because could be that this will hurt him, and I don't mean to hurt him, not more than I need. It's just that this has to be said.

"You killed her, too," I tell him. Now his whole being is still. Even the breathing, even the smoke puffing has stopped. "You sent your woods out after her people, and they knew it had to do with her, and they killed her for it. If you'd let her be, she'd still be alive, maybe even standing here. She might have come back on her own."

He looks away from me, swinging out that great neck to turn his head.

"If you loved her . . ." I say.

"Go away."

It's a deep, scratchy voice; it sends a shudder through his scales, and the air drops out of me. I can't talk; I can't breathe.

"Go away," he says again, *"and don't come back."*

I've heard this voice only twice before, and both times it

came as though from far off, as though he were whispering his words into my bones. I've never heard him speak this full, not as a dragon. I wonder if she did. I wonder what else he can do but has never showed me. I wonder what I'll never know now.

I can't refuse a voice like that. It's not the deepness, not the power in it. It's that it's steeped, dripping, run all through with sadness, though sadness doesn't say enough.

I had thought the woods folk don't feel things the same way we humans do. They get angry, sure, and they get happy and all the rest. But they don't soak in their loneliness until it's in their very breaths, until it spreads through them with each heartbeat. They don't get themselves so bitter, as I used to be, so that the sweetest foods near choke them to death.

Turns out, though, I was wrong. I've never heard an emptiness, a rawness like the one in the dragon's voice.

It takes all I have, everything I am, not to obey at once. "I will," I say, with a voice that shakes, but I don't even care, can't care about a little thing like that just now. "I'll go away, and maybe I won't ever come back, but first, listen."

We're staring at each other, and I can't feel anything but the space between our eyes. I gather all my will and stay there, an inch from the tip of his nose.

"If you change your mind," I say, clear and slow, "and decide you want me back after all, you're not to send your woods again. Not ever again. My land, every bit of it, will be protected. Not only by the king's army or by the farmers and the villagers with their axes. By *me*. I know you. I know your woods, and I'm not feared of anything they hold. I'll come running from wherever I am, and I'll pick up an axe of my own, and I'll cut down your trees myself. And what I cut down, dragon, will stay down.

"For every foot you take from us, I'll take one from you. For as long as I live, I swear, I will be on the watch. I'll teach my children, and they'll teach theirs, of the mysteries of your woods. There will always be someone unafraid, someone unwilling to be swayed by your voices, by your dreams. Someone with a mind of her own."

Then I stop and I wait. A minute goes by, or a year.

The dragon drops his head, only a fraction, but I sense the rest of him too, his shoulders lowering, his haunches relaxing, and I know it for acceptance.

Then, because I'll never get the chance again, and because some part of me is breaking, despite everything, to be leaving this beautiful beast, I reach out slowly one more time to touch his neck, to feel the heat of his scales, the wild pounding of his heart. He holds quite still, as still as I am.

As I'm pulling back, he says, *"You are wrong, though. I did love her, dragon's daughter."*

I stop, half turned away. "Not enough," I whisper, only the faintest echo of a sound. Then I keep going, away from him and out of his great dark cave.

*　　*　　*

The queen starts to speak as I reach her, but when she sees my eyes, she stops and hands me the reins to my horse.

The griffins and the phoenixes are spread out over the slope as before, still watching us, still strangely silent.

We lead our mares back down through their ranks. At the edge of the trees, we mount up. The sun has nearly set over the western woods.

"*Tulip*," the lady says as we start off.

I stop; she's standing at my horse's shoulder, looking up at me. "My girl," she says, and again, "my Tulip."

I lean down and hand her mine. She cups it in her hands until it glows with a pale pink light. "So you won't either of you forget," I tell her.

She shakes her head, eyes burning. "Never."

Never. The word pours right through me, and before she can say another one, I move my horse along and leave her behind.

We're not bothered this time. The woods folk, the lady, the griffins, and the phoenixes—all of them let us alone, and we're free to work our slow way down the mountain, over the foothills, and through the lowlands until we reach the house again, where my mother hid me all those months. The moon is rising to the south, over the king's land.

It isn't a clearing anymore. The trees are gone, all the way back, so that the path running down from the front step leads clear into meadows and fields and, a few hills away, a village. In the afternoon and evening it took to climb to the dragon's cave and back, our world has returned to the way it was.

We pause at the front of the house. I'm near to asking the queen if we hadn't better stay the night here, rubble or no. I've slept on rougher ground than this, and I reckon the queen came prepared for sleeping in the woods. And while I'm ready to ride straight on till morning, most likely she's all worn out by this point.

But before I can speak, she's grasped my arm, her eyes white in the dark. "Here they come," she murmurs. "I wasn't sure they'd actually follow me."

I look where she is looking, down the path, across the hills. I hear them, and then I see them galloping north: two strong mares and two dark-haired men — the king and Lord Edgar of Ontrei — heading straight toward us.

Faster than I can think of what to do, they've reached the clearing and have us cornered; the ruins of the house are at our back, and their horses angle at our flanks, ready to run us down. We stare all about at one another — or they do. I look only at the king. He's glowering, as usual, to see me, but he makes no move to grab my arm or otherwise do me harm. None of us knows what to do with this meeting, it seems. The queen is hanging back a bit. I can't see her face, but I reckon this is a moment I'll have to decide on myself. For a single crazy heartbeat I near turn my horse around and run back to the woods.

Then I take a breath and lift my chin. "Well, Uncle," I say. "Are you going to kill me now that I've come back home?"

He considers me. "Only if I must."

The queen makes a strangled sound behind me. *"Roddy—"* she begins, but I cut her off.

"Luckily," I say, "there's no need for such drastic measures. As you'll see, the trees have taken themselves away."

"So they have." He looks about at the open land. The moon is shining full now, so that it's almost bright as day.

"You might say I've struck a bargain. They should be done with moving in from now on." I nudge my horse up closer to the king's.

He shifts, nervous, as if a girl like me could hold her own against a grown man.

Well, and I could. But that's not what I have in mind.

"I've no wish to take your throne from you," I tell him. He's looking at me with my own eyes, and I feel a jolt at the way his hair curls about his ears. We stayed away from each other so fully in the castle, we hadn't the chance to remember how similar we are to each other, to my mother, to Gramps. "We're not the best of friends, Uncle"—he half snorts at this, as if he can't help himself —"but I reckon we're going to have to get along, or at least live with each other." I eye him up. "As long as we can manage, anyway."

When he opens his mouth to speak, I see that missing tooth. "You might not believe me, Marni, but I'd rather not kill you if there's no need. I don't rejoice in spilling my family's blood." He looks around again at where we are. Maybe it's the moonlight, the way it makes the clearing seem like another world, silver and sparkling. Maybe he's had time to think since I went to the woods. Whatever it is, something eases in his face, and he says, softly, "I would have—I would rather have never had a need to kill *her.*"

His words hang in the air. There's no fit reply to them. Nothing but a scream or a knife in his heart. It isn't only the king who is going to find it difficult to live in peace.

When he looks back at me, he must see the rage on my face. He blinks and turns away, uneasy.

This time, the Lord of Ontrei breaks the silence. "May we offer you a ride home, lady?"

I see the king glare at him. I keep my own gaze on my mare's back as I say, "Thank you, but no. The queen is tired, and I'm wishing to be getting on."

"I'm well," the queen says at once.

I twist to smile at her. "I promise I'll not go back to the woods again. I'm only wanting to see my Gramps." I reach out a hand, and she lifts her own to take it. She is bone weary; I can see it in her eyes. But I can see, too, the relief she feels at having me back, the honest joy in that bright smile. I squeeze her hand. "Thank you," I say, and I hope she knows I mean not just for coming to get me, but for missing me at all, and for giving me that key, and for her friendship those weeks in the castle.

She nods.

I turn then, and I finally look at the pretty roan to the king's right and the grinning man on her back. Oh, that grin.

"Lady." He gives me a bow from the saddle.

"My Lord of Ontrei," I say, quite cool, or as cool as I can anyway, but I feel his gaze right through me, and it heats up my cheeks.

And then I can't help it anymore. I let myself smile, a great big smile that I'm sure sets my eyes to sparkling all brilliantly. I know I'll regret this smile in days to come—he's getting that look again, just as if he knew he could have me for the asking, just as if he felt himself almost crowned a king.

That trouble's still away in the future, though, and I let him think what he will for now. The king's face is twisting as he looks past me, toward the empty doorway of his sister's last house. "Uncle," I say.

A shudder goes through him.

I don't say anything more. It's enough. What he's seeing now, what he's remembering—he'll remember it every time he sees me. Every time I call him "Uncle." He'll never be free of it.

I edge my mare between them—the tortured king and his charming lord—and I kick her into a walk and then to a canter, and soon we're galloping across the hills, into the kingdom and out of the woods for sure.

And as I'm hunched down over my mare's back, hill after hill rolling by, something rushes over me, something I've never felt before. It's in the soft wind blowing past my face. It's in the grasses under our feet and the stars above our heads. It's in the close huffing of my mare's breath, and most of all, it's in the thought of where we're going.

They kept offering it to me, didn't they? The lady, the queen, the dragon. Even Edgar. They kept telling me I'd found my way home. They were wrong, though. I didn't know it full until now, until the open meadows and the pounding hoofbeats lifted up and wrapped me round, whispering, *Home. We're going home to Gramps.*

ELEVEN

E'S SITTING OUT on the porch.

It's the middle of the afternoon two days later; I've slept in meadows, rejoicing in the brush of long grasses against my skin, looking up now and again to track the moon on her travels all across the wide sky. I've ridden as fast as ever I can so the news of my return won't get here first. I didn't stop in the king's city. I took the road around, and soon enough I was riding up to that turnoff you might miss if you weren't paying enough attention, but I was paying attention, and there's no way in the world that I could miss it.

Then I'm coming down the hill, through the bushes, and I see the porch columns first, wrapped round with morning glories as they always used to be. I see a flash of white — his hair, I guess, though it was half black still when last I saw it. And then there he is, sitting with a new cane across his knees, watching me come. Alive.

"Back so soon, Emmy?" he calls out as I'm rounding the last of the bushes. He's hardly changed; he sits as tall as ever, and when he turns to look at me, his eyes are as clear and sharp. There is that white in his hair, though.

He doesn't say another thing. Just looks at me.

I get down off my mare and tie her to the porch railing. Then I stand there at the bottom of the steps, waiting.

"Well, Marni," my Gramps says at last. He takes a breath, as though to go on, but instead lets it slowly out, gripping his cane.

"Well, Gramps," I say, and then, to give him time, I walk up the steps and slide along the wall until I'm leaning in my old place, hands behind my back, feet bare against the porch's wood. Someone must have cleaned this place before he moved back in. The chairs are dry and strong, newly made, I reckon. The leaves that covered the porch have been brushed away. The bushes that threatened to take it over have been pruned back.

It's as it was.

I wait for him to speak again, looking out over our yard to where the path crawls up the hill. I've waited two years. I can wait a minute more.

It's three or four before he says, "Where have you been?"

I smile, not at him. "Why don't you go first?"

I've forgotten what it's like, to stand so separate from the ground, from the bugs that crawl all across you, from the plants that brush against your legs. Even the birdsong, shrill and sweet, sounds far off from up here.

"Please," he says, "won't you sit down?"

It surprises me; I look at him, and then I can't look away again. The shock is gone. He's holding tight to the table and to one arm of his chair, holding himself back, maybe. I know every line on his face; I know the curve of his nose and the shape of his ears. I know how they look when he is sad or mad or happy. I've never seen the thing that's on his face now.

"Please," he says.

I walk around him, around the table to the other chair: my chair, the visitors' chair. I wonder, do the lords and the ladies come again to buy his flowers? Do they bite their tongues to keep from asking after his Tulip?

"She's been taking care of you, then," I say when I've sat down, before he can start in on it.

"Emmy?" he says. "Yes. For you, I think."

Seems everything is surprising me today. "But she hardly knows me."

"Well, maybe not, then. Maybe she's taking pity on an old, lonely man."

I'm like to start crying, I think, and I don't want that. "I went to the woods," I say. "I followed the voices, took the lady's hand, and ran all the way to the dragon in his cave."

He's scarce breathing, he's that still.

"I ran away from myself, Gramps. I didn't think there was nothing left for me."

He says, all soft, "What brought you back again?"

"I'm not going to have a baby, if that's your guess."

"I'm not guessing anything, Marni. I've given up on that."

I haven't heard that name from that voice in a lifetime. It's as if a string's been plucked somewhere inside, and the note sounds through my bones, across my skin, changing me, back into something I remembered once.

"I was wrong," I say. "It wasn't enough for me, running about in the woods. I still cared."

"About—" He wants to ask it, but he cuts himself off before he can. "About what?" he says instead.

"About you, yes," I say. "About words and people and—and horses. About what I was going to grow up into. About finding out the answers to things." I can't say it, not right away, and I stop. He waits. I look him in the eyes; if I'm to ask it, I'm going to ask it right. "Where did you go," I say, "that night I came back and you were gone?"

Now he's the one who looks away, and while he talks, he faces out onto the grasses and the bushes, where the wind sends ripples across the hill and the sun strikes dazzles along the path's rocky dirt. "You were growing up," he says. "They were all after you: the village lads, the lords, and . . . the others. You didn't want any of them. You wanted to stay with me here, growing flowers until you died. But it wasn't going to be like that, Marni. Not for you. It couldn't be.

"You were — what, sixteen? I'd seen it before. I saw it with your friend, Annel. She wasn't ready for whatever was coming her way. She didn't want it, so she ran, just as your mother had run. And they, both of them, had a thousand more reasons to stay than you did — and neither of them had the very trees folding in around them, coming in closer every day. You didn't realize, maybe, but I knew. I knew one afternoon you wouldn't come back from the woods.

"Oh, yes, I knew," he says with the twitch of a smile, turning back toward me. "You thought you were so clever, my girl. But you had so little happiness, and so much to weigh on you, and I didn't want to take away the bit of freedom you had. You weren't yet the age for the fairies to be whisking you away.

"Until one day, you were.

"And I couldn't stand it." His voice has dropped from his storytelling lilt to the murmur of a confession. "I couldn't stay here to see you disappear too, wait to see whether or not you'd ever come back, with a baby or without one. I couldn't lose you, Marni."

"What did you do?" I say. His every word is sounding in me now, shifting everything I thought I knew. "What did you do to stop me?"

"I made a deal," he says. "I knew that as long as I was around, there'd be no place for you at court, and that was the farthest I could get you away from all this." He sweeps a hand around the porch, the yard, through the door toward the back.

"Not just the woods, but the loneliness, the exile. He promised to find you a place in the king's castle, to watch you, to keep you from the woods if he could manage it."

"You made a deal with the king?" I say. I scarce can credit such a thing.

But he is laughing quietly, shaking his head. "No, Marni," he says. "The king knew nothing about it."

"Who, then?" I say.

He pauses, his face all serious. "I'm not sure I should tell you. You had a vengeful streak, even as a child. There was a village boy once, a year or two older than you, who went stomping around in the daffodils when his mother wasn't looking. Do you remember this?"

I shake my head.

"Oh, you screamed when you saw it. You vowed destruction upon the poor lad, who went crying to his mother. You thought it was the worst of crimes to ruin the flowers. You wanted to tear out his eyes and roll him in mud and shred his little boots until the offending soles were strips of leather." He's chuckling. I don't think he's ever told me this before. "You would have punished that rascal to within an inch of his life if he hadn't looked up at his mother, all teary-eyed and scared to death, and begged her not to let the witch get him."

"The *witch?*" I say.

He shrugs. "Well, there were stories then about what you might grow up to be. The boy must have heard his parents talking. The mother apologized to me, of course, and I would have been a great deal angrier about it, except it gave you a harmless method for getting your revenge."

"I cast a spell on him," I say.

"You cast a spell on him. You gathered up your roots and your fly wings or whatever it was you thought would be magical enough, and you chanted your little heart out and sent him a plague, or nightmares or something similar."

"I hope I didn't really," I say.

He looks at me. "Could you have?"

I don't answer that. In truth, I don't know. "Did anything bad happen to him?"

"He grew up a happy and healthy young lad," my Gramps says, "and with no hard memories, or anyway nothing that kept him from coming by to court you twelve years later."

"Jack?" I say.

"Henry."

I nod, as though I remember one from the other anymore. I say, as if it's a joke, "I promise I won't cast a spell on whoever made you a deal."

"Ah." He doesn't say anything more for a moment. Then, "The Lord of Ontrei," he says. "The one who walked down from the castle to ask for your hand."

"I remember." I wonder what he knows of my months in the city, of how I could never forget that day now.

"The things he said—I knew he was right. Roderick had left us alone for so many years, I didn't want to think it would change. But the woods were moving, and Roderick had always believed your mother's death had sent them back the last time they were coming in. He's not a bloodthirsty man, Marni, but when he thinks a thing must be done to keep his kingdom safe, he does not hesitate to do it. And Lord Edgar's words — they showed me how your uncle's mind was turning yet again, this time against you."

"And?" I say, a whisper. "What did you do?"

"You made it clear that you would go nowhere if I was still around. And in any case, I thought Roderick would be more likely to take you in if I wasn't here. No king feels completely safe while his predecessor's living just next door.

"So the next day, when I woke and you'd disappeared again into the woods, I sent a message with a farmer's boy to the Lord of Ontrei at the castle. He came down to the hut, and we made a deal. I would disappear, make it seem as though I had died. When you came back home — if you came back home — the Lord of Ontrei would be there to offer you a place, to bring you back to the castle with him, to give you a new life."

"You meant me to marry him."

My Gramps smiles, but it's tentative. "I never told him that you would. But he agreed the castle was the safest place for you to be, both from the woods and from the king. With all the lords and ladies there to watch, we thought he'd hesitate before doing you any violence. And I think Lord Edgar had some idea that he could win you after a time."

Oh, didn't he just. "Where did you go?" I say.

"Lord Edgar sent me away with some of his men. They put me on a horse and took me with them, all the way to the Ontrei estate on the northern meadows."

"You didn't even take your cane."

"Authenticity," he says. "We thought of everything."

"I see." And I do — how they'd been anticipating my every move. How they'd figured it all out — that I'd go straight to the castle, that I'd begin to fall for Edgar. Only it hadn't turned out quite as they'd planned. "You were wrong, though, weren't you? It didn't matter to the king in the end whether I was there or here, not with the woods still moving in like they were. He was bent on taking my head no matter what you did."

"Yes," says my Gramps. "Both of us got that part wrong. We misjudged — him, the woods . . ." He's looking as if he wants to say more, but he pauses.

I dash a hand across my cheeks, angrylike, and blink my eyes back into focus.

"Marni, if I'd known—"

I don't let him finish. "What did they do with you, then, when the trees came in? I reckon Lord Edgar's place was well buried by them."

"It was a funny thing," he says. "On three sides of us were the trees, going farther and farther south, but his house and his yard and his stables — they were spared. It was like an island in a sea of green. I'd never seen a thing like that."

I stare at him. "Yes, you have," I say, slow.

"You mean this hut? I heard it was left alone as well, but I never saw it. I never came back until the woods were nearly gone."

"No," I say. "I mean when you went with the army up north, those seventeen years ago. I mean when they killed my mother."

Now it's his turn to stare. He doesn't ask how I would know such a thing. Maybe he figures I've seen people and gone places he'd not be able to imagine since we last spoke. Well, and I have.

"It's still there," I go on. "Still untouched by the woods, that house and their garden and their stones. I reckon—I reckon the same thing that kept back the dragon's woods there kept them back from you, too. You both were willing to stand up to him, weren't you, to keep him from what he wanted? You—and her."

"You've been there." It's a breath, no question in it.

I nod.

It seems the world must have turned itself over and inside out since we started talking, or at least that the sun would have gone clear across the sky or the birds would have changed their songs. But no. When we stop long enough to hear it all, to see it all again, it's just as it was. It's a perfect day, really. Breezy, sunny, blue and green, not a drop of rain or an ominous cloud. This is how I remember every summer day of my childhood. I reckon children don't feel cold and heat as much as older folks. I reckon if the sun is shining and they're able to run through a meadow, pick flowers, sing themselves a song, any day seems like this one.

My Gramps was drawing something before I came riding down to the hut. I see the charcoal and the bit of paper on the table, one part covered by his hand, the other showing half a face — a woman's face that looks to be smiling.

I reach out to the pull the sketch toward me; he lifts his hand.

Her eyes are crinkled up as she laughs; her head turns slightly, as though listening for something, as though ready at any moment to run off on another adventure. She's like me, I can tell, but she's all her own, too. There won't be another just like her, as there won't be another Gramps or another just like me.

"Marni," my Gramps says into the silence, and his voice is rough and raw, so that for an instant I think myself back in the dragon's cave, peering into the dragon's bottomless eyes. "What is that on your hand?"

The ring has started to stick on my finger already; it doesn't want to slide, but I work at it until it's slipping down into my palm, gleaming golden in the porch's shade.

I hand it to him. "It was hers."

He lifts it up and twists it around, reading the inscription. "I gave her this," he says. "I suppose she left it behind when she ran from us. You'll have found it in the castle?"

"No," I say. "She brought it with her. I found it *there*, where the woods never dared move in."

He looks up at me, scare able to believe it. "She kept it all that time?"

"It's true," I say. "It's yours. She'd want you to have it."

"No." He holds it out to me; he puts it back in my hand.

"I had a lifetime with her. I don't need a ring to remember that."
Then, quieter, "I don't deserve a ring to remember that."

"Gramps—"

"Tell me, Marni," he says, now looking me full in the face.
"I realize I maybe don't deserve this, either, but tell me what
you're planning on doing now."

For a moment I don't say a thing. There's a part of me, still,
the part I fed for sixteen years with bitterness, that wants to walk
away from this man and never come back—to run all the way
over the mountains maybe, to the queen's land, with its sorcerers
and its wide, shining sea. It's the way he was ready to use me, as
much as Edgar ever did, to make all my choices for me. It's the
way he left me alone, without a word to give me hope that he
lived. He was ready never to see me again. There's nothing he has
the right to claim from me now.

It's not often, though, is it, that you learn what you should
do before it's too late to change a thing. I reckon my Gramps
must have felt that way many a time, thinking on what happened
to his daughter, thinking of the thousand ways he might have
been able to save her. I reckon the dragon might have felt it, even,
when I came up to his cave and told him, straight and clear, what
he'd done to her. Some, like the king, never do figure it out.

I bend across the table, kiss my Gramps's cheek. I smile at
him. I say, "I've never thanked you, Gramps, for saving my life
and all."

"You don't need to, Marni," he says. "It's what a Gramps
is for."

So then, because it's what a granddaughter's for, I reach over and take his hands. I say, "Gramps, there's nowhere I'd rather be than right here. I'm going nowhere, you hear? Not to the woods, not to live with the king in his castle — not every day, at least. I'll go as much as is needed to keep the lords calm. And as for the rest — well, it's what I've always said I wanted, isn't it? You and me, Gramps, and the flowers."

I watch him. He's twisted his head away from me. I know this look, though. I've seen it many times when he thought I couldn't: at night when he thought I was asleep; before the fire when Annel would tell a story somewhat too close to home, and he'd tilt his head so that the firelight burned right into his eyes, so he could blame his tears on that if we ever asked, which we never would have. We wouldn't have done that to him.

He clutches my hands with both of his. I see him shudder, and then, as he's never done, as he's never let himself do since as long as I remember, and I remember many long years, he lets his posture, his dignity go, and he bends forward until his forehead is against our gathered hands.

This man, who was once a king, and he's sobbing over his granddaughter's fingers.

I get up, leaving him one hand, and I go around to put my other arm across his back, my face on his shoulder.

We stay like that. The sun sparkles on the stones of our path. The birds call from their bushes.

It's a while before we move again, and when we do, there's no more need for talking. Gramps dries his eyes, ruffles my hair.

After a moment he picks up the sketch from the table and puts it in his shirt pocket with the charcoal.

I haven't said nothing about that drawing, and I don't reckon I ever will. There's some things words would only ever make more difficult. I came back to him, just as he came for me all those years ago. But that won't ever fix it, not what happened to her, not the way your breath is still like to rush out at the slightest reminder, leaving you all hollow, wishing for impossible things.

It's the way it is, and all you can do is keep on going, keep on choosing the best that you can. So I know she's there, against my Gramps's heart, but I don't say a thing about it. Instead, I go back over to the other chair, and I sit there with him all through the perfect summer afternoon. We talk about little things, things that we forget the next moment, and the day slowly fades away until we're watching the dark move in, seeing the fireflies flitting, smelling the night wind, cool and wonderful.

She's still there. She always will be. Yet there's no need to do anything about it but let her be, just as she is, running all through our hearts.

See, sometimes my Gramps understands things.

And sometimes I do too.

THE WOODS DON'T whisper to me anymore. But they're there, beyond our garden wall, waiting. The lady doesn't call to me anymore, but she's there too, sure and certain. Just beyond the first line of trees, knitting away on her log, singing her dark lullabies.

As the days become weeks and the weeks become months since I came home, Gramps doesn't ask if I ever go back to walking off into the woods.

Could be I don't. Could be I've had enough of such things and I spend the afternoons when I'm at our hut working with the flowers or soaking in the sun with my Gramps.

Or could be some days I do. It would be easy to slip out over the wall when my Gramps is sleeping the day away. Could be sometimes I turn myself into whatever creature I'm yearning to be, and I run and fly and forget the drama of my uncle's court, and what I do or don't think of the Lord of Ontrei, and all the complications of being human for a time.

I wouldn't tell my Gramps if this were so. He's had enough to worry him. It's enough for him that I've come back home, that despite it all, we're together again.

But he knows as well as I do, too, that we'll never fully be rid of the woods. Oh, they come and they go these days, like the wind, like the sun, like the seasons. Folks don't fret about them that way, not fearfully.

But there are still one or two who go, now and again, not every year, but enough that the farmers and the villagers keep a watch on the woods, and a watch on the girls who seem too drawn to them, for fear they'll disappear one bright night. I reckon there's not much they can do to stop them, though. Look what my Gramps did trying to stop me — it doesn't matter, once the woods get into a girl's head.

After all, as our folk will tell you, it's not just the creatures of the woods that require wariness. It's not just the obvious: the lights and the voices and the speaking owls, the faces in the branches.

It's the trees themselves.

There's something there, they'll say, whispering through the leaves, sleeping in the trunks. There's something that seeps through the spongy ground but never shows itself in any way you would recognize. If you walk enough in these woods, you'll start to understand its language. The wind through the trees will murmur secret things to you, and you'll be pulled by them, step by step by step, out of the human realm. You'll be drawn to the shadows, toward the soft flashes of moonlight through the branches, into the hidden holes and tricky marshes.

The villagers won't let their children go into the woods, not even to the very closest edge, not even when the wind is silent and the sun shines full through the trees. It's an insidious thing, they say, the soul of these woods. It will rock you and soothe you until you've nothing left but trust and belief and naivety. It will fold itself into you, and you will never know it's there, not until you're ten nights out and there's not a thing that can bring you back again.

And despite what I said to the dragon, I wouldn't dare try to stop the girls who go. If he sends his trees too far into our land, yes, then I'll fight him back. But the woods are his, and the girls he takes choose it with some deep part of them.

And could be at times, in some deep part of me, I miss it. It's not a thing that leaves you fully, is it? Out here, out where the shadows drift across the wall and the flowers grow more brilliantly the closer they are to the trees — out at our hut, we find the woods harder to forget than most.

Especially when we've got a certain small blue blossom growing all throughout our garden.

You wouldn't notice it, maybe, among the stunning roses, the bright lilies, the elegant irises, but it's everywhere. I don't try to prune it back or tear it up. I doubt it would make any difference; it never did before. It doesn't kill the others, anyway. It creeps up their stalks; it burrows under their thorns. But it doesn't stop them from growing, not as it used to do.

Besides, I've no wish to get rid of it. It makes me think of Annel, of my friend, off screaming her heart out into a wild wind. It makes me think of what she said about there being some things, some parts of you, that won't ever go away unless you reach deep down inside and rip them out.

She wouldn't do it; she wouldn't tear out half her heart, and I guess I won't either. I'll let the flowers stay, and I'll let myself look off north toward the mountains sometimes and think on the ones who run and fly free there, and remember what those days were like — what it's like for them still, the ones who never come back, the ones who give themselves up to the woods.

ACKNOWLEDGMENTS

First, many thanks to Reka Simonsen, for saying yes to this story and for always managing to ask just the right questions. Thanks also to the members of the Semi-Secret Society of Alien Meese; may you sound your varied calls and grow your deciduous leaves most joyfully. And thank you to my family—to Mom and Dad, to Matt, Ben, and Jonathan—for everything.